Mai Tai Malice

Tanya Westlake

Impractical Press

Chapter One

The handsome young pirate fought bravely against his attacker in the warm Florida sun, raising his sword in defense as the marauder charged him again.

"You dare to accost me here, on this day of all days?" he called.

His foe ignored the question and rushed forward again, swinging his silver cutlass angrily.

Dodging gracefully, the young blonde pirate called out again, "The invasion has only just begun, friend. We should be fighting the natives, not amongst ourselves. Will you not heed wisdom?"

Again, his enemy paid no mind, slashing even more aggressively.

"If this is your decision, I shall be happy to engage," he cheered, lifting his own sword and charging the attacker viciously. The grace of his footwork belied his overwhelming height, and the foe was quickly sent running.

Kallie Brooks and her best friend Tess Russo sipped their diet cokes and watched from the sidewalk as the handsome pirate waved his sword after the departing attacker and warned him not to return.

"I love Gasparilla," Kallie sighed.

"I thought it was bizarre when I moved to Tampa, but now thousands of pirates swarming the streets seems perfectly normal," Tess agreed.

"Our seats are only a block away. You still doing okay, Dad?"

Kallie's father, Benny Brooks, grinned happily. "I'm fine, kiddo. I haven't been to the parade in years. It sure has gotten a lot bigger since the last time we went!"

"I thought I had outgrown it, but I'm excited to see it too," Kallie laughed, adjusting her pirate hat, which was tilted rakishly over her long auburn hair. "I'm glad we got seats this time, though."

"Much nicer than having a drunk pirate fall in your lap," Tess agreed.

As the trio slipped through the dense crowd and approached their reserved seats, Kallie pulled out the tickets, and they were quickly ushered to the second row.

"I don't know why I never thought to get us reserved seating before," Benny mentioned as they sat down with a collection of relieved sighs. "This is really nice."

"Even after taking the trolley, that was a lot of walking. I don't know how we did it all those years," Kallie replied.

"We certainly weren't wearing these high-heeled pirate boots, back then," Tess groaned, wiggling her toes. Her long dark hair was in braids under her pirate hat, and a few curls stuck out attractively.

"I think we had a little more sense back then," Kallie agreed. "But we also didn't have any money."

They had all dressed up for the parade, and even Kallie's dad was looking dashing in his long burgundy coat and striped pants. Luckily, it was late January and not too hot.

"Do you think they'll still throw us beads?" Benny asked, making the girls both laugh out loud.

"I'm sure you'll get a ton of beads, Mister B!"

They had all gathered to watch on television earlier in the week as the fearsome scallywags dragged Tampa's mayor out of her office and demanded the key to the city. Bravely, she stood on the downtown waterfront and faced down the pirate leaders — in front of cheering crowds and television cameras — refusing their demands and ordering them to leave her fair city in peace.

Tess had tsk'ed and mumbled, "That's what they all say..."

The pirates had given the mayor a few days to change her mind, but they'd vowed to stage an overwhelming invasion of the city if she didn't relent. And this morning, like clockwork, the pirates had reappeared, sailing an enormous pirate ship, the *Jose*

3

Gaspar, up the river into the Tampa waterfront to invade the city, as promised. Cannons fired noisily from the decks, and a huge flotilla of smaller boats followed in the ship's wake.

And of course, Tess was proven correct. The mayor, like many before her, bowed to history and gave up the key to the city. The celebration began in earnest.

The Gasparilla Parade and Festival had begun in 1904, but the invasion by ship hadn't started until a few years later. A Children's Parade had been added in 1947, adding to the revelry. Since then it had become a tradition in Tampa, with every famous politician, celebrity, and family vying to be the Grand Marshall at least once.

"Oh, they're coming," Kallie said with a smile, leaning forward to look down the street anxiously. "I can hear the marching bands!"

The man sitting next to Benny — who was dressed like a middle-aged marauder, with braids in his beard and a dangerous-looking gash on his cheek – heard Kallie, and whispered to his wife.

The woman leaned forward, displaying a beautifully airbrushed black eye and a long scar across her eyebrow, and pointed with a smile. "I can see the first float," she cheerfully responded to Kallie.

"I love Gasparilla," Kallie repeated to Tess, on her other side.

"Are you sure you don't want to stay with us, Mister B?" Tess asked, when the parade had finished, and they were leaving their enclosed seating section. "I included you in the dinner reservation."

"He and Anna have a date," Kallie replied with a smile.

"It's not really a date; we're just fixing dinner together at her house, but—"

"Sounds romantic," Tess observed, adding to Kallie, "I'd ditch us, too."

"We'll walk you back to the trolley, Dad."

"Thanks for thinking of me, Tess. We'll all have to come back down here for dinner someday when it's not so crazy."

They walked back up the street through the teeming crowd, dodging left and right to avoid pirates of all sizes. Some were singing or dancing, some stumbled, and others seemed tired and bound for home too.

After seeing Kallie's dad safely on the trolley back to their distant parking lot, with hugs and a lot of blown kisses from Tess, they headed back out to their dinner reservation. It was only early evening, and the weather was beautiful, but being January, the sun was already out of sight behind the buildings at five o'clock.

"I'm working tomorrow morning, so let's not

stay too late," Kallie said. "Besides, it's already getting dark."

"You're preaching to the choir, bestie. It'll be a madhouse down here by eight."

"Even *more* of a madhouse," Kallie laughed.

They battled their way against the crowd for another block and then slipped into a popular sushi restaurant that Kallie had been wanting to try.

"I can't believe you were able to get reservations during Gasparilla!"

"That's because I booked them right after you got us the parade seats – back in September," Tess laughed.

The evening air had started to get cool as it grew darker, and they were both slightly chilled, so they ordered a carafe of hot sake to split while they talked and checked out the elegant restaurant.

Their server soon came back and set a tray of hot towels on the table, and handed Kallie and Tess each a small tablet. The electronics were covered in thin, decorative covers, which had obviously just been replaced for cleanliness. She commented on their cute costumes as she left the table.

"That's so smart," Kallie pointed out. "We can't fill out our sushi order with a plain old pencil and paper anymore, right?"

"I don't mind a pencil and paper. It is pretty

clever, though," Tess replied with a laugh. They both checked out the dinner options and used their touch screens to choose their sushi. Tess added, "I'm getting nigiri, but do you want to split a Spider Roll?"

"Yum, absolutely," Kallie agreed.

When their waitress returned, she delivered bowls of soup and explained that they could each touch the 'Order' button at the bottom of the screen, if they were ready. They handed the tablets back, and she slipped them into a pouch tied at her waist – to be cleaned and re-covered later.

"Wow, this soup is amazing," Tess said with a smile. "Look at these tiny mushrooms."

Kallie stirred the clear, golden soup and watched a dozen minuscule mushrooms spin in the broth, as a man knelt by their table.

"I knew that was you," the handsome young man grinned.

"Kenji!" Kallie gasped in surprise. "Oh my gosh, I haven't seen you in ages!"

"I've been tending bar here since we opened last year. For such a trendy place, everyone's really nice," he added with a laugh.

"Wow, that's so—"

"Not as nice as you all at the Lazy Gecko, of course," he grinned.

"Well, that goes without saying," Kallie agreed.

"Tess, this is Kenji. We worked together for a while, a few years ago."

"And you left the Gecko?" Tess asked with a smile. "I thought everyone stayed there forever."

"I wish I could've, but I live here in Tampa," he explained, sincerely. "It was a tough commute. Listen, I have to get back to the bar, but I wanted to say hello."

Kallie and Kenji hugged briefly and he hurried away, back to work.

The waitress soon returned with their gorgeous sushi, and small glasses of plum wine from Kenji, and Kallie and Tess ate happily.

* * * * *

When Kallie and Tess walked out of the restaurant, the street had transformed from a crowded street party into an insane mess. The crowd was louder and rowdier, and there was barely room to move.

"Did we really think this was fun when we were younger?" Kallie asked, incredulous.

"I don't think it was this crazy when we were twenty-one," Tess yelled over the noise. "The parade has gotten a lot more popular in the past few years. People fly in from all over the world."

"Let's get out of here," Kallie shouted in agreement.

"Yes, ma'am. We can't get a rideshare down here. They aren't allowed this far into the crowd. We'll have to either walk out of the parade area or take the trolley." They backed up against a wall and Tess took out her phone, investigating for a minute or two. "It's only about two blocks to the rideshare pickup spot."

"Great," Kallie sighed with relief. "Let's go."

The sound of laughter and cries of "Avast, ye mateys," enveloped them again as they stepped back into the crowd, being pulled along by the masses. They were both more tolerant of the revelers, now that they were headed home, and they both briefly joined in with a group singing "A Pirate's Life For Me."

Suddenly a hand fell on Kallie's shoulder, and she was spun around backward on the sidewalk. She threw up her right arm in a defensive gesture, startled as a young woman her own size stumbled against her heavily. Dressed in a corset and skirt similar to her own, the girl's pirate hat fell askew as her knees seemed to buckle. Kallie grabbed her instinctively, to keep her from falling in the crowd and being trampled.

"Careful," she cried. "Hey, are you okay, lady?"

The girl silently grabbed Kallie's hand, making eye contact, and then stumbled off into the crowd again.

"What was that about?" Tess asked, staring after the woman. "Kallie, are you—"

Kallie saw her best friend's eyes go wide with shock. "I'm fine, Tess. That girl just ran into me, that's all."

"Kallie, your—"

She followed Tess's gaze, looking down to see that her ruffled white pirate blouse was covered in stains. Her forehead crinkled in confusion, and she reached to touch the damaged fabric, only to find that she had something in her left hand.

Dazed and disoriented, she looked back up at her best friend, then down at her hand again.

Tess's lips moved, seeming to form the words in slow motion, "Put... That... Down..." as more hands grabbed Kallie roughly from behind.

"Drop the knife!" a man's voice yelled angrily from her left, as her other arm was bent awkwardly behind her back.

She shook her head, no. "I'm not holding—" As she looked back toward the man, though, she slowly realized what had been in her left hand.

What's happening?!

There *was* a knife in her hand, somehow. She could feel the weight of it. And the man was a police officer. A very large and angry police officer, who seemed to be reaching for something on his utility belt.

Shock finally rattled Kallie back to reality, and she mechanically opened her hand and backed away from the weapon, as it fell to the sidewalk with a clatter. She stumbled back into the officer, wanting to get as far from the strange knife as possible, and looked up at Tess again.

"She didn't do anything," Tess was pleading to the two officers, "I was with her. It's not her knife."

Kallie touched the previously white blouse again, now covered in blood. Her hand, which had been holding the knife, was bloody too.

The crowd closest to them had fallen silent, staring, but the rest of the party still raged around them, oblivious of Kallie's shock and confusion. She stared back at them, hoping to wake up from this bizarre, horrible dream.

Then the police were pulling her away, down the street toward their parked patrol vehicles, and another female officer held Tess to keep her behind. Her friend seemed to be getting smaller as Kallie was dragged away, looking back over her shoulder.

Pulling against the officer's restraining hand, to no avail, Tess yelled, "I'll get your dad, Kallie! And Morrison!"

Chapter Two

Kallie sat on the jail cell bench, too tired to sleep. Too scared to blink. She opened and closed her hand, seeing the bloody knife there again. Appearing like a nightmarish, backward magic trick.

Where's Tess? Where's my dad?

Where's Morrison?

The drunks in the temporary holding cell around the corner were laughing and shouting and swearing like pirates. Occasionally it sounded like someone vomited, and the others cheered or swore louder.

How am I going to get out of this mess?

They'd booked Kallie as soon as she arrived at the police station, and they'd taken her clothes for evidence. She was miserable but admittedly grateful to be out of her bloody costume from the parade. Not so grateful to have a bogus booking photo to her name. On the other hand, she was just about ready to kill someone — for real — in exchange for a hot shower.

Do jails even have hot showers? Even a lukewarm shower would be acceptable right now.

She leaned back against the bars and closed her eyes, trying to sleep a little. It had to be after midnight, and she was pretty sure it was too late for anyone to come get her. Surely visiting hours didn't start until morning, and she needed to rest.

But every time she closed her eyes, she saw the woman falling into her arms – and Kallie's eyes flashed open in shock, wide awake, when she saw the knife again.

Okay, so if I'm not going to sleep, what else can I do?

I can't figure out how to get out of trouble, because I don't know what happened. Did that woman stab someone? Kill someone?

Could it all be some huge mistake? Just another skillful but artificial display, like the swordfighters we saw in the morning?

No, if it was all an act, I wouldn't be in a very real jail cell. And my cool new blouse wouldn't be ruined and crusty with dried blood.

And the officer that booked me said they were charging me with... murder.

Kallie's heart sped up at that thought, and she suddenly found it hard to breathe. She leaned back and tilted her chin up, eyes closed, trying to calm down.

Relax Kalliope. You didn't kill anyone, so this will all be cleared up in the morning.

Wasn't there a guy on the news who was proven innocent after he'd been in jail for forty years?

More deep breaths.

Hey, don't I get a phone call or something? Although, it probably wouldn't matter at this time of night. No one I know would answer the phone at this hour.

Gosh, I hope my dad isn't sitting up, waiting and worried sick about me. Kallie's eyes teared up at the thought.

I don't think he would. We went to the parade every year for most of our lives, and he knows we always stay out late.

Not this late.

Hopefully he already went to bed. Would he call the police if it got too late? Would they tell him I'm in custody? For murder?

And would he think it was all a terrible joke? Or a bad dream?

That makes two of us. I'm still hoping it's a bad dream.

Maybe there was some exotic species of fish in my sushi, and I'm hallucinating?

Or maybe I have the worst luck on the planet, and I'm really being blamed for a murder I didn't commit. And I'm all alone and no one's coming to help me and why does this crazy stuff always happen to

14

me?

Kallie curled up in the fetal position on the uncomfortable metal bench and finally managed to cry herself to sleep.

* * * * *

In her dream, the police grabbed her and pulled her away again. This time, to her horror, as she was dragged away, the stumbling woman slunk back out of the crowd and lifted the knife, stabbing Tess in the back. Her best friend's pirate hat spun away as she fell to the sidewalk—

Noooooooo!

Kallie's dreaming scream woke her up, this time making her yell out loud. The cold sweat sat clammily on her skin, but she was at least glad it was only a dream. She sat up angrily, irate at her own brain for giving her that shock, and vowed to stay awake until she saw her best friend again.

Leaning against the bars, she shook her head roughly to wake up, and then waited.

But an hour later, Kallie still sat quietly in the holding cell, alone. If she waited long enough, someone had to eventually come back and explain what was happening. The remaining smears of blood on her hands had dried into a crust, and the small sink in the corner wasn't working.

Her tears had stopped eventually, too.

She could still hear other drunk and disorderly prisoners in another cell down the hall, but they were apparently just drying out from Gasparilla. Not important or dangerous enough to warrant their own private cells.

How did this happen? Do they really think I stabbed someone?

Dozens of people saw us eating dinner. Why aren't the police talking to them?

Tears of desperation started to slip down Kallie's cheeks again. She'd never felt so alone and helpless before.

Tess, where are you?

With a sudden start, she realized that Tess might've been arrested too. Would they consider her an accomplice?

Kallie walked over to the bars and tried to look down the hallway, but the angle was wrong. "Tess?" she called quietly.

She paused for a minute, and then tried again, a little louder, "Tess?! Are you here?"

The cacophony down the hall quieted a little, so someone must've heard her, but no one responded.

Good. If she's not here, then maybe she's out getting help. And I think they do have to allow me a phone call eventually. Right?

I hope that's not just in old TV shows...

She sat back down on the hard bench and closed her eyes. Trying to relax, and stop her growing anxiety, she took a few deep breaths. But it was no good, she was fighting a panic attack, and it was winning.

The chatter from the other cells had become a constant rumble, making her feel even more isolated and alone, and Kallie tried to keep her hands from shaking.

Get ahold of yourself, Kalliope. This is easier than being chased by angry killers. Heck, this is easier than wrangling Spring Break frat boys at the Lazy Gecko.

You're safe and warm right now. Just wait for your friends to help you. This will all get sorted out in the morning.

That helped a bit. Her breathing slowed, and her shoulders relaxed a little.

Good girl, Kalliope. Deep breaths, and then—

Her eyes shot open as the thump of heavy boots came up the hallway, and she jerked her head toward the sound.

She heard the voices of two men talking, and the *tap-tap-tap* of heels.

"Kallie!" a voice cried out, and then a man's voice, "Stop, young lady."

A few more seconds, and then the Tampa sheriff

17

himself, Grayson McReed, was standing outside her little cell, escorted by a Tampa police officer. She recognized the sheriff from the local news, but he looked much bigger in person. "Miss Brooks, you have two visitors."

She looked around as he waved toward the hallway for his guests to enter the room. "The police can't let you out until after the bond hearing — if the judge grants you bond, of course — but *this guy* speaks highly of you." He jerked his head sideways, and Detective Morrison stepped into view.

"Thank you, Sheriff," her detective friend replied with a nod. "I can vouch for Miss Brooks, but I understand she can't leave."

Tess emerged from the hallway and immediately ran around the two men, hugging Kallie desperately through the jail cell bars. They were both crying again when the sheriff gently pulled them apart.

"I really can't let you do that, Miss Russo," he explained quietly.

"I'll get dried blood all over you, anyway," Kallie joked awkwardly, with a choked laugh.

Tess wiped at her eyes and smiled. "I brought you some clean clothes, but I see you've adopted a new fashion statement," she indicated Kallie's oversized orange jumpsuit, pretending to appraise its glamour. "I can't say it's really your color. I tried to bring in some baby wipes, too, but they made me leave them at the desk."

"My sink doesn't work," she pointed out to the sheriff, who looked abashed at the comment.

"I'll see if I can get the maintenance crew up here to fix that," he replied, taking out his phone and typing a message. "I don't have any actual power over this kind of thing at PD, but I have a few friends here…"

Kallie was surprised but thankful, still hopeful that she'd be gone before it was fixed.

"You're very lucky to have such good friends, Miss Brooks," he added. "Detective Morrison and I have known each other for years, and he's always been a very good judge of character."

"Except that I'm friends with you, Sir," Morrison joked quietly, but Kallie could tell he was touched by the sentiment.

"Yes, well, everyone deserves a mistake or two," the sheriff chuckled.

"So what happened, Sheriff McReed?" Kallie asked, as she sat back down. "Can you tell me that much?" She sat shivering on the hard cell bench, hoping to hear something that could prove her innocence. "They said I've been charged with murder."

"I don't have much information, myself," he replied. "The sheriff's department hasn't been officially involved yet, since it happened in the city limits, but I know Tampa PD is putting the pieces together."

"Well, obviously someone was stabbed," Tess interjected.

She was sitting on the floor outside the cell, as close to Kallie as she could get. Kallie considered telling her she'd be cold and sore later, but her best friend was her only consolation, and she wanted her as near as possible.

"Apparently stabbed by a woman in a pirate costume, since they grabbed *you* by mistake," Tess continued. "Which doesn't narrow down the suspects much, considering it happened in the middle of a sea of pirates."

"Someone was murdered at the parade?" Kallie asked.

The sheriff shook his head but replied genially, "Don't look at me. This is a City of Tampa case, and I haven't been read in yet."

"That must be what happened, since they sent *multiple* officers to restrain a female suspect. One of whom was *itching* to tase you, by the way," Tess answered, sounding defensive. "The amount of blood on your blouse supports that theory too."

"And it must've been pretty public," Kallie mused, "since the police were on the scene so quickly."

They both looked at Morrison, who immediately put his hands up in surrender. "Don't look at me either. This isn't even my *county*. I'm just here to help Kallie."

"Well, we'll hear most of it on the news in the

morning, right?" Tess suggested.

"I'll still be *here* in the morning, Tess," Kallie replied, eyes tearing up again.

"You'll see the judge first thing in the morning," the sheriff said, "and she'll explain everything. The TPD detectives are working the case already, and I think she'll grant you bail when she hears the evidence. I know they've verified that you were eating in the restaurant — and while that doesn't give you an airtight alibi, it's pretty close."

"What? Why not?" Tess asked, surprised.

"It was too crowded. They can't give us an exact time that you left, even with the receipt."

"Don't they have cameras?"

"Yes, Miss Russo, but restaurants almost never own their security systems. TPD will have to subpoena the video from their supplier."

"Won't that take forever?" Kallie asked, looking worried.

"It could take a few days, depending on where they're located. But it would've been tough to get from the restaurant to the attack scene, commit the crime, and return to the restaurant that quickly."

"But not impossible," Tess concluded for him.

"Correct," the sheriff agreed. "Plenty of killers have tried similar tactics, to fake an alibi. But Gasparilla is a social media fever dream, so I'm sure someone —

probably multiple people — will have filmed the attack, whether intentionally or coincidentally. The IT team is already checking the usual social media websites to see if anyone has uploaded it. If they can find that quickly, it might eliminate you as a suspect."

"But the girl with the knife was dressed just like me," Kallie moaned.

"So I've heard from Miss Russo. Which means we'll need a good look at her face too. But with your waitress's statement about the restaurant, and the good detective's vouching for your character, the judge'll probably reduce the charges and grant you bail."

"Probably?" Tess asked.

"I can't promise anything. It depends on what else happens between now and then."

"Can I even afford to pay for bail?" Kallie asked. "Isn't it pretty expensive?"

"You'll have to pay ten percent of whatever amount she sets," the sheriff explained. "That will depend on the exact charges. But you don't pose a serious public threat of violence or flight—"

"You're not going to run off to Switzerland, are you?" Morrison asked with a smile.

"I've always wanted to visit Peru," Kallie answered, smirking through her tear-smeared mascara for the first time.

"She's not going anywhere except work," Tess

interrupted with a serious tone, then looked back at Morrison, "Can you help me find a bail bond office?"

"You bet. There are about fifty of them within five blocks of here."

"Okay, we'll worry about that in the morning," Tess replied with a nod. "What about hiring a lawyer? I can check with Winchester in a few hours and see if he recommends anyone."

Her three visitors discussed the benefits of hired representation as Kallie listened absently. She was exhausted and scared, and shivering with a combination of fear and chill. She couldn't afford a decent lawyer anyway. She was just glad to have her friends nearby and worried about her.

Tess noticed Kallie shivering and took off the oversized sweater that was tied around her waist, reaching up to pass it to Kallie. The sheriff stopped her and gave the sweater a quick physical inspection to make sure there was nothing dangerous in it. After a moment's hesitation, he nodded that she could hand it over.

"I brought this for you to wear. It might be a little short on you, but it's clean—"

Kallie reached out and pulled Tess in for another hug, trying not to start crying again.

"Have you talked to my dad?" Kallie asked, wrapping herself up in the sweater.

"He didn't answer the phone when I called,"

Tess explained, "and I didn't want to leave such a terrible message on his voicemail."

"I'll text him and see if he's still awake," Morrison spoke up. He and Kallie's father had become good friends, and she knew her dad wouldn't be spooked by a text from him. "But it's after midnight."

"I don't want him to worry."

"I think that's out of the question," Tess replied with a smile. "But we'll keep him as calm as possible."

"You two are the best," Kallie replied from her uncomfortable bench.

"No answer," Morrison added a minute later. "He must be asleep. If he was reading or watching TV, he'd still answer."

"He knows you might be willing to talk hockey scores with him. The poor guy's just *surrounded* by women," Kallie joked.

"I'll stop by the house, so he doesn't wake up and find that you've been out all night," Tess added. "And I'll call Marcy, too. But hopefully you'll be out of here before she expects you at work."

"I do need to ask you both to leave," the sheriff finally stated, sounding a bit sorry. "You're the nicest suspect we've had in here for months, but rules are rules."

Tess was allowed one last hug through the bars, and then she was escorted politely out of the jail. She waved back one last time as the little group rounded the corner, and Kallie saw Morrison put his hand on her shoulder comfortingly.

Kallie leaned back again and sighed, trying not to cry. She felt even more alone than she had before they came – but at least now there was hope.

Chapter Three

Kallie's court-appointed attorney came to see her in the jail cell at exactly eight o'clock that morning to discuss her options.

She'd considered Tess's suggestion to hire a lawyer – and her offer to call Winchester, her boss, in Louisiana and ask him to recommend someone — but the sheriff had explained that she'd only be entering a plea today.

Morrison had agreed, adding that there was no reason to waste her time and money on this first visit. The judge would have her notes on the case, and she'd just ask for Kallie's plea. The sheriff wouldn't be in the courtroom, but he said he'd talk to the judge first and explain their findings. Kallie's lawyer would request bond, and they both thought she'd get it. Easy peasy. It'd be over in fifteen minutes at the most, and an expensive lawyer wouldn't do anything different than the court-appointed one.

Now, if things went sideways, Morrison had said, they'd reconsider.

Kallie tried not to think about things going

sideways as she sat cold and alone in her cell with the lawyer, who looked about seventeen.

"I have good news and bad news," her attorney began, after introducing himself as Chris Solomon, Esquire.

"Okay, let's get to the bad news first," Kallie agreed, trying to sound cheerful.

"The stabbing victim died at the hospital—"

Breathe, Kalliope. Breathe!

"They said they were booking me for murder," she whispered, voice cracking. "I hoped it was all a mistake."

"Okay, but here's the good news," he continued, encouragingly. "We'll be pleading not guilty. I've seen the details of the case so far, and several people in the restaurant have already sworn that you were there, including your waitress, the bartender, and the couple sitting next to you. There's no way the judge is going to detain you."

"Are you sure?" she whispered.

"It's impossible to be perfectly certain, but they just downgraded you from murder to manslaughter, which is a good sign. For a murder charge, there's almost never an option for bail in Florida."

Kallie closed her eyes and took a deep breath. *I never thought I'd be relieved to hear the word 'manslaughter.'*

"The amount of media coverage will also be a factor, though," Solomon continued, sounding older and wiser than his apparent years. "This is an unusual case. Happening at a huge event like Gasparilla means the news has already spread across the country."

"Who was the victim?" she asked, bracing for the worst.

"It hasn't been announced yet. They were still calling him a John Doe, when I got here. But sometimes these convoluted cases have a lot of external political pressure. And it's an election year."

"Oh," Kallie replied, starting to get worried again, then her forehead wrinkled in confusion. "Wait, what do you mean by 'convoluted case?'"

"The police are holding half a dozen videos already, posted to social media or sent directly to them by the public, but none of them show exactly what happened," her attorney explained. "Security video from a jewelry store shows a commotion in front of the restaurant, where you appear to be just standing there, and then the police grabbing you thirty seconds later—"

"Yes!" Kallie exclaimed, starting to feel a glimmer of hope. "That's what we were saying. Tess and I were just standing there."

"—but it's filmed from half a block away, so it's not very clear," he continued. "And another video, which is close and *very* clear, shows you covered in the

28

victim's blood and holding a knife. So you can understand that it's caused quite a bit of public outcry."

"Really?" Kallie asked, sounding worried.

"There are people demanding that you be released, and another group is insisting that you're obviously guilty. This kind of disparity can cause problems if you get a judge who's sensitive about 'the court of public opinion' trying to force his hand."

"Oh," she groaned, slumping against the bars.

This is like a roller coaster. Let's just get it over with! she thought to herself.

"Do you know which judge will be there? Is it a nice judge?" she asked.

"It should be Judge Williams, who's very good. Very fair," her lawyer replied, nodding.

Kallie smiled, nodding back. "Great."

"But she was out sick with the flu on Friday. I'm not sure if she'll be back."

Kallie tried not to groan. "And the replacement judge?"

"Judge Anderson. He can be a little more complicated. He's not unfair, but he can push back if he feels like he's being railroaded."

"I'm not trying to railroad any judges," Kallie assured the young attorney, pleadingly. "I just want to go home."

"If it's Judge Anderson, we'll stick to the details

and emphasize the sheriff's opinion. He respects the sheriff. I'll make sure there's no mention of the demonstrators demanding your release."

"The *who,* doing *what*?" Kallie choked out.

"It's just a few. You know how public police sentiment has been lately."

"I have *demonstrators*?" She wasn't sure whether to be flattered or horrified, so she went with being confused. "That's crazy. The cops didn't beat me up or anything. They were perfectly nice, considering—"

"It's just a few women out front with signs. Maybe a dozen. I saw them when I got here," Solomon tried to reassure her. "Although one of the officers did say it was getting bigger."

"Great," Kallie moaned.

"Don't worry," her lawyer smiled. "The judges don't enter the building from the street, so they probably won't see them. And if it's Judge Williams, it won't affect her decision one way or the other." He looked at the old-fashioned watch on his wrist — an analog watch with visible gears on the face, not a smart watch, Kallie noticed — and announced that they needed to leave for the courtroom.

"Is the guard going to handcuff me?" she asked, eyes tearing up unexpectedly.

Haven't I cried enough for one night? Toughen up, Kalliope.

"I don't think so, but we'll see. That's usually reserved for belligerent inmates."

The guard must've been standing just out of sight, because he returned to the cell just as he was mentioned.

"Do you need to cuff her?" Solomon asked.

The guard silently shook his head no, and unlocked the cell to let them out.

Another guard stepped in behind them, and the four of them walked toward a door at the end of the hall. The young lawyer stayed supportively at Kallie's side, which she appreciated more than she could've expressed.

The previously loud drunks in the next room had fallen silent, either released or just sleeping off their night of pirate-themed revelry, and the sound of Kallie's jail-issued slippers echoed noisily down the hallway. The guards led her into a private elevator, and she silently watched the floor numbers slowly blink on and off, with a sense of rising dread growing in her stomach.

The ambient noise ratcheted up as the elevator doors opened and they entered the judicial area of the building. Serious-sounding voices travelled down the hallway, as the guards led her toward the active courtroom. When they entered the austere room, a few of the waiting defendants glanced back at her, but none seemed interested. Just bored and curious.

31

Is that what I am now, too? A defendant? A criminal?

She looked around to see if the sheriff was in the room, but she saw only orange jumpsuits and a few well-armed police officers. She glanced at her lawyer, but he only gestured for her to sit down.

She chose the end chair of the third row, and her attorney turned to leave, touching her shoulder silently before making his way to the back of the room. Apparently this section was only for the accused.

After about twenty minutes in the warm courtroom, though, Kallie was fighting to keep her eyelids open. Following a long and stressful night with only a few minutes of exhausted rest, the waiting was putting her to sleep. Suddenly a booming voice charged, "All rise!"

She jumped to alertness and stumbled to her feet, as a middle-aged blonde man with sharp, dark eyes entered the room in severe black robes, and took a seat in the judge's chair.

Kallie tried not to groan out loud. She'd been hoping for the easy judge. She glanced around again hopefully, but she didn't see the sheriff. Her heart started beating faster.

She turned in her seat, and her eyes darted to her lawyer again, but Solomon was reviewing his notes studiously and didn't look at her.

I need someone to help me. She blinked away

the start of tears and bit the inside of her lip. *Be brave, Kalliope.*

The next fifteen minutes passed in a blur as the judge addressed some of the other defendants and asked how they wished to plead. Most of their lawyers pled not guilty and asked for an extension, which he granted.

Will they all just stay in jail until their next court date? she wondered. *That could be weeks or even months.* Her eyes teared up again as she thought of staying in that cold cell, without seeing Sherman or her dad, for so long.

Finally the bailiff called Kallie's name, and Solomon touched her arm gently, back by her side. She stood up and he led her to the podium.

The judge opened the case file and looked up at Kallie over the tops of his glasses. "Miss Brooks."

Kallie thought the judge would say something else, or ask her a question, but he just nodded and looked back at the folder. "Christopher, how is she pleading?" he asked the attorney.

"Not guilty, your honor," the young lawyer answered. "We're requesting bail."

"I've never seen so many sticky notes in one eight-hour-old case file," the judge noted, shaking his head. "You know I don't bow to public pressure, Christopher."

"No, sir," Solomon answered quietly.

"I'm not impressed with that group of protesters who seem to think their opinions are more important than facts and legal precedents."

"No, sir," the lawyer repeated, as Kallie suppressed a whimper.

So much for the judge not seeing the crowd outside.

"But I've seen the preliminary video from the jewelry store." He turned his attention toward Kallie. "You've been accused in the death of an, as yet unidentified, stabbing victim in Downtown Tampa last night, Miss Brooks. I'm sure your attorney has informed you that your initial charges have been reduced from murder to manslaughter. Do you understand the charges?"

Kallie nodded silently, but her lawyer touched her arm and nodded toward the judge. "Yes, sir. Your Honor," she added, out loud.

"Your client has no prior criminal record, and doesn't appear to be a threat or flight risk," the judge added to Solomon, after checking the file folder again. "I'm granting bail. Fifty thousand dollars."

What?! Fifty what?!

"Thank you, your honor," the lawyer replied, and Kallie thought she heard relief in his voice.

"But that's so much—" Kallie whispered, but he squeezed her hand to shut her up.

The next defendant was called as her attorney led her back up the aisle, and her mind raced at the huge bond amount. No one she knew had that kind of money.

"Fifty thousand dollars is *really* low for a felony manslaughter case, Miss Brooks," her lawyer whispered. "And he could've set your bond for a million if the charges hadn't been downgraded. Or denied it completely."

Kallie whimpered at that thought and kept walking, her feet and hands growing numb.

Murder?! Manslaughter? A million dollars? What in the world have you gotten yourself into, Kalliope? You've been in the wrong place at the wrong time before, but this is a whole 'nother level.

"Now shush until we get back outside, please. We don't need to add a Contempt of Court charge to your current problems."

* * * * *

"Okay, don't panic," Tess stated calmly on the phone.

"Are you insane?" Kallie tried not to scream. "My bail is *fifty thousand dollars*, Tess. I haven't made that much money in… ever!"

She heard her best friend sigh loudly, and tried to shut up.

"If you were going to be locked up for the next six months, I wouldn't have told you not to panic," Tess continued. She paused to make sure Kallie wasn't going to start yelling again. "I talked to Morrison, and he explained how this bail stuff works."

"It's so much money," Kallie whined quietly.

"So we can go to a bail bond company, which we talked about at the jail. You pay ten percent of the bail amount, and they spring you—"

"That's still five thousand dollars, Tess," Kallie interrupted, sounding horrified.

"Hang on, I'm not done yet. That's when you were still booked on a murder charge. Morrison was being nice, because he didn't want to scare you to death, but he didn't think bail would even be on the table. It's almost impossible to get bail for murder in Florida."

Kallie groaned. "Remind me to thank him. I really would have dropped dead right there in that ugly jail cell."

"If you get the money from a bail bondsman, you pay ten percent, but that's their fee for the service. I somehow *missed* that part in my legal dealings with Winchester," Tess sighed audibly, annoyed at herself for missing anything, ever. "As long as you show up for court, you don't owe the rest of it, but you don't get that ten percent fee back. And neither of us has five grand laying around."

Kallie whined softly.

"Wait, it's okay, though," Tess added quickly, sensing more tears on the immediate horizon. "They take collateral!"

"What? Tess, I don't have any collateral. You know how much money I make. All I have is my beat-up old car, and they wouldn't give me ten dollars for that."

"Honey," Tess snorted a laugh, and Kallie could almost hear her best friend rolling her eyes.

"What?" Kallie asked, knowing from experience that she was going to feel very foolish in about thirty seconds.

"You own a house in Owhiro, Florida. Outright. No mortgage."

Kallie sat silently, trying to avoid saying anything dumb. She'd taken over the payments for the house when her parents got divorced, not wanting to move. It was a darling little place on a charming lake in a seaside community, and—

"Oh," she finally replied.

"Do you even know how much your house is worth?"

"No," Kallie whispered, as her cheeks burned in embarrassment.

"Of course you don't," Tess laughed. "I'll show you the estimate when we get you home. But for right now, don't worry about your bail. You've got it covered."

"As long as I show up for my court date," Kallie added, still feeling a little shocked.

"Your dad and I will drag you to court, if you get scared. We still have some paperwork to finish, but we'll be there to get you this afternoon."

Kallie was so relieved, she almost started crying again.

Chapter Four

Tess, Kallie, and her dad sat on the couch with bagels on Monday morning, watching the news. Tess and Sherman were cuddled abnormally close to Kallie on both sides.

She'd been gone for less than thirty-six hours, less than a trip to Disneyworld, but Sherman instinctively knew something was wrong, and he hadn't left her side since she'd been home. He followed her to the kitchen to put bagels in the toaster, and then back to the couch, where she gave him a bite of bagel with cream cheese.

"Doesn't this seem familiar?" Tess mumbled jokingly. "I feel like we've done this before."

"We're the queens of the press conference, my dear," Kallie replied, hugging Sherm as he rested his chin on her lap. She was still happy to be home.

"We definitely watch a lot of press conferences, but they never seem to reward our loyalty by starting on time," Benny sighed, looking at the clock across the room. "They said it was going to start at nine o'clock, and it's already ten minutes past. Are you girls going to be late for work?"

"Marcy told me to take the morning off and see how I feel," Kallie answered. "And I don't think Winchester is even in town."

"He's in New Orleans researching a case, and he doesn't need me until noon, eastern time," Tess verified. Her boss was nominally retired from practicing law, but he still took the occasional case if it interested him. He couldn't stand to be bored in his sprawling mansion.

"Okay, then I guess we'll just wait," Benny shrugged. "Can I get either of you more coffee?"

They both handed their empty cups over, and he carried them to the kitchen for refills.

"Oh, I think this reporter is on the scene now. Maybe the press conference is starting," Kallie leaned forward to see what was going on in the background, but the reporter was just covering the story.

"It was on this corner in downtown Tampa, where a yet-unknown male victim was stabbed to death on Saturday evening, as the partygoers of Gasparilla frolicked around him," the reporter announced seriously, gesturing to the locale around her. Kallie recognized her as Elizabeth Kwan, one of the top reporters for Tampa News Twelve.

"She's my favorite," Kallie noted with relief. "She's won a bunch of Emmy awards for her investigative reporting. I'm glad she's on the story."

Kwan's cameraman took a wide view, showing the charming, expensive neighborhood still decorated with pirate flags and other lovely but sinister-looking decorations for the month-long celebration.

"Police are expected to make a statement this morning about their investigation, and our sources say that the victim may finally be identified, as the next of kin are believed to have been found and notified," the reporter continued.

"They still haven't identified the victim?" Kallie asked, confused.

"No, a few famous names have been mentioned, but no one seems to know for sure. There are rumors that it's a conspiracy, or some kind of cover-up," Tess replied, shaking her head. "Like the police have something to hide and have been trying to suppress the story. But the sheriff said they just had trouble reaching the family."

"Oh, did you talk to the sheriff?" Kallie asked, surprised.

Tess laughed. "No honey, *you're* the one with the clever and likeable detective boyfriend with great connections. The rest of us watch the sheriff on television, like normal people."

"He's not my boyfriend," Kallie whispered, mostly to herself.

As they waited, and the reporter continued speaking to fill the delay, the news station aired footage from the night of the murder. Pirates filled the streets again, captured on cell phone video and security cameras. In one clip, some of the partygoers looked shocked, many were crying — and incongruously, others passed who were cheerfully oblivious in the background.

Kallie, who hadn't seen any of this footage yet, leaned toward the screen, eyes wide. Grainy black-and-white security video showed a sea of people, and Kallie gasped sharply when she realized what she was seeing. She drew back, unprepared, as the jewelry store clip from outside the restaurant flashed on the screen.

Tess reached for her hand, and they watched themselves on the television, silently chatting and laughing as the presumed killer stumbled into Kallie. The young woman staggered, transferred the knife casually but strategically, and moved out of the camera's view.

She did it on purpose. She framed me.

"I'm sorry, I should've warned you that would be in the rotation," Tess apologized.

"No, it's okay," Kallie replied numbly, her eyes still glued to the screen in a daze. "So that's how she did it? It happened so fast—"

And my lawyer was right, the camera's too far away. You can't really see anything at all.

"I can change the channel—" Tess began to say, but the station switched back to the reporter abruptly.

"We've been showing you the video collected from the night of the murder," the reporter started speaking again. Her hand was on her earpiece, where someone had apparently just let her know what was on the screen. "Interestingly, no video of the actual attack has surfaced yet, but the police aren't giving up."

"That *is* odd," Kallie mumbled. "I mean, we live in a world that's constantly being filmed."

"The police are requesting that anyone who was downtown around eight o'clock on Saturday night check your camera," Kwan added. "Someone may have caught the incident without realizing it. Even if it's in the background, it could help."

"Yeah, it's almost certainly just a matter of time," Tess replied.

"In the meantime," the reporter continued, "we have a sketch of a person of interest in the case. If you recognize her, you're asked to call the tip line in order to receive the reward."

She paused and the station cut away from her, switching to air a black and white police sketch of a young woman dressed in a ruffled blouse and corset, with a rakishly tilted pirate hat.

Kallie's dad whistled. "Wow, you weren't kidding, kiddo. She really does look like you."

"It's just the costume," Tess insisted, sounding a little annoyed and defensive. "I only saw her for a second, but they really didn't look that much alike. The

43

witnesses must've confused the two of them, when they were describing the suspect."

"She's trying to make me feel better," Kallie explained to her dad, with a choked laugh. "Even I didn't get a good look at her, except the top of her hat, so that sketch is probably a wild guess. Luckily, I have a pretty good alibi. As we just saw."

Two years ago, she would've been in a full panic attack after all this madness. Now, it was just par for the course.

The station cut back to the reporter, who was walking down the street, gesturing to important locations. "The attack took place in this immediate area, and the police are asking for any information that the public might have. If you saw something, please say something. There's currently a $2500 reward for information that leads to—"

Kwan put her hand to her ear for a moment, and then frowned and nodded. "We've just been informed that the press conference has been postponed until noon. There's some additional information that they need to address." She paused and nodded again. "We'll show the sketch again, and then go back to the studio. Charles?"

The sketch was displayed on the screen, and then the channel cut back to the anchor desk. Benny muted the television. "Well, that was a letdown," he added.

"That's okay, I'm just glad to be sitting here with you three," Kallie sighed with relief, and scratched Sherman's ears again. "Can I get anyone more coffee?"

Chapter Five

"Well, you're looking better today," Morrison said over a cheeseburger and potato salad, later that day – they were having an uncommon lunch at their favorite outdoor breakfast café.

"I should. I washed my hair for about an hour and a half," Kallie replied, smiling shyly. She wasn't sure what to say to him. As much as she'd always liked Morrison, this was the first time he'd been a knight in shining armor, and she wasn't sure if their relationship had changed.

Tess probably dragged him down to the jail, she was so worried about you, her mind interjected. *Don't worry, Kalliope. Nothing's changed.*

"At least you weren't in the main holding cell with the drunk and disorderlies. You'd have to shave your head," he quipped with a smile.

"Thank you so much for rescuing me, Morrison," she answered with unusual sincerity, unsure of why she felt so emotional about a single visit in a stinky jail cell.

"Kalliope Brooks, you don't ever need to thank

me," he replied quietly. He looked at her face for another moment, staring into her eyes, and then shook it off. "That's what friends are for, right?"

See? Right as rain.

"Sure," she answered with a smile. She looked back at him for another moment, then stabbed a French fry with her fork and added with a grin, "I don't have many friends who would call the sheriff for me, though."

"I'm sure you do, Kallie. I'm just the only one who could get the sheriff to *answer*."

Kallie laughed out loud. "That's a very good point. How did Tess even find you?"

"She had my cell number. I think she got it from your dad, actually."

"Really?" Kallie answered. "My dad said she didn't wake him."

"Maybe I gave it to her during the Clemons case," he answered with a shrug. "I'm glad she had it. I don't usually answer an unknown number on my personal phone, especially on a crazy night like Gasparilla — I guess it was just a gut instinct. But I'm sure she would've called the station if I didn't answer. She's a smart lady."

"She really is," Kallie replied, wishing she could tell Morrison the details — that her best friend was a certified genius with a ton of awards and commendations. But Tess would kill her if she spilled that secret.

"She was nearly hysterical. I barely even recognized her voice." He paused, reflecting on the call that night and looking concerned in hindsight. "That's when I knew it must be about you."

"She's actually really level-headed," Kallie replied quickly, protectively.

"That's exactly what I mean. I've *never* seen her panic. Not once. And she's been through some serious trauma with you in the past few years." He gestured with a potato chunk on his fork and added, "You might want to relax on the murder thing, by the way. For her sake, if not your own."

"Thanks, I'll get right on that," Kallie replied with a laugh.

"Great, that'll free up a bunch of *my* time too."

"Note to self, no more murders," Kallie added.

"That oughta do it," Morrison added with a chuckle, clearly unconvinced.

They paused while their usual waitress, Justine, refilled their water glasses and asked if they needed anything else. Kallie ordered a glass of lemonade, and the waitress walked back inside the café.

"So have you heard anything else from the sheriff?" Kallie asked when they were alone again.

"No, but I'm not in his jurisdiction. If he told me anything, it would just be out of courtesy."

Kallie nodded, unsurprised.

"Would there be any point in asking you not to get involved?" Morrison asked.

Involved? No way. Not this time.

"We're not planning to get involved," Kallie answered, sounding confused.

"Well, I didn't think there was going to be *planning*, exactly."

"The police seem to have it covered. There were at least a million cameras filming where the guy was killed. They don't need our help—"

"Oh, thank you," Morrison chuckled. "You think a bunch of trained police officers can manage a murder case without assistance from a bartender and her bestie?"

Kallie tilted her head to the side and pondered for a moment, then nodded sagely. "Probably."

* * * * *

Kallie tapped on the half-open door of Studio Alvarez as she entered the small, pretty space. From the doorway, she could see that the sunlight from the large windows lit her friend's drawings beautifully, making them seem to come alive.

"Come on in, Kallie," Isabel called from the couch in the corner, where she was watching her husband draw on a huge canvas.

"Hey, Kal!" Carlos yelled without looking away from his latest work of art.

Kallie walked across the room toward the couch, admiring the new drawings on the walls and easels, and handed a bottle of wine to Isabel as she sat down.

"Aunt Kallie!" their daughter shrieked happily, as she toddled across the room. Kallie was again shocked at how quickly Lily was growing. It seemed like just yesterday that Isabel was stuck on seemingly-eternal bedrest during the pregnancy. Kallie bent down and the toddler threw her arms around her neck and gave her a strawberry-scented kiss.

"Someone's been eating berries," she said with a smile.

"It's me!" chirped the child, agreeably. Then she looked around the room. "Did you bring Sherman?"

"I didn't bring him this time, sweetie. He's at home with my dad." Sherman loved Lily too, and would probably give Kallie the cold shoulder when she came home smelling like her.

"She loves seeing *you*, too, Kallie," Isabel whispered with an apologetic laugh.

"That's okay, I've accepted that Sherman's more interesting than me," Kallie chuckled. The child clumsily climbed up on the couch with them and cuddled into Kallie's side.

"What's daddy drawing?" Kallie asked her, gesturing toward the easel.

"It's a bubbly bee," she answered very seriously.

"It's a honey bee," Carlos amended. "I don't think we have bumble bees here in Florida. I haven't seen one in years."

His latest huge black and white drawing was taking shape on the canvas in front of him, and Kallie could see the shape of the bee beginning to form. She loved watching Carlos draw, using only charcoal and occasionally white chalk, to create amazingly realistic animal pictures that took up half a wall. The delicate fuzz of the bee's body was already visible in the edges of the form.

Isabel's mother appeared in the doorway and waved to Kallie, then asked Isabel quietly, "Do you want me to take Liliana?"

"Not yet, she wants to sit with her Auntie for a minute," Isabel answered her mother. "But it's almost your bedtime, little miss," she added to her daughter.

The child snuggled in harder against Kallie's side and argued, "I'm not sleepy yet."

Kallie ruffled her curly dark hair and waved back at Izzy's mom. "How are you doing, Mrs. Rivera? It seems like forever since I've seen you." Carlos's family were Owhiro locals, but Isabel's parents lived in Miami, so Kallie didn't see them as often.

"I'm doing very well, Kallie. Glad these two

finally gave me a granddaughter to spoil."

"And she's a pro at the spoiling already," Carlos added from his easel, with a grin. "Heisman Trophy level spoiling."

The doting grandmother smiled and nodded, accepting the truth. "Are you doing okay, Kallie? I saw you on the news."

"That was just a terrible mix-up," Kallie replied, trying to smile and ignoring the tense knot in her stomach that had formed at the subject. "It's all been pretty much resolved."

I wish it was really that simple, but there's no need to worry anyone else. I've got enough stress for all of us.

"Well, good. I'm glad to hear it, dear." She turned to her granddaughter and added, "Come along, *mi amorcita*. Let's get you ready for bed. Your Aunt Kallie can kiss you goodnight, and maybe she'll tell you a funny story about Sherman."

The child pouted and stalled, but she finally slipped off the couch and followed her grandmother. If Sherman was with her, Kallie knew it would've taken five times as long. And Sherm would've pouted just as much.

When she'd left, Carlos turned and asked Kallie, "Are you really okay?"

"I'm better than I was," she replied simply.

"Well, that's a start. I saw the video on the news from someone's phone, and you were covered in blood," he added, turning fully away from his artwork for the first time. "Izzy just about freaked out."

"*Me?*" his wife scoffed. "Don't listen to him, Kallie. He was practically in tears, he was so worried about you."

"You two are so sweet," Kallie answered, touched and a little surprised at their concern. "Like I told your mom, it was all just a mix-up." She paused, not wanting to alarm her friends, but not wishing to be dishonest either. "But it was pretty scary," she added.

"Covered in blood and being dragged away by the police? I can only imagine!" Isabel agreed, clutching her hands toward her heart.

"Who was the guy that was stabbed? Have you heard?" Carlos asked.

"Tess said they're keeping it quiet. Or they hadn't found his next of kin yet. I haven't heard his name."

"Someone at work said he was at the parade with an entourage. I wonder if he was famous," Isabel mused. She owned her own popular yoga studio and had some pretty rich clientele herself. "There are a lot of sports figures and celebrities in town for Gasparilla."

"I think the police would've announced it by now, if it was someone famous," Kallie replied, considering the rumor. "Or it would've come out in the gossip media."

"Well, he must've made someone pretty mad, if that girl stabbed him right there in plain sight, surrounded by thousands of partiers.

"If he was with a big group, maybe it was a gang fight," Carlos suggested.

"Oh, don't say that," Izzy groaned. "There's so much gang violence lately. I hate to think of it so close to our hometown."

"I doubt a gang would be dressed up for Gasparilla, though," Kallie added, growing more interested in the speculation, against her will. "The girl who ran into me was dressed in full pirate gear, so she probably wasn't part of a rival gang."

"That's a good point. I hope you're right," Izzy replied.

"I guess we'll have to wait and see," Kallie shrugged. "The police will have a press release by tomorrow morning. They always do."

"I have to teach a hot yoga class tomorrow morning. Let me know what happens, okay?"

"Sure, Izzy. Tess and I were watching earlier, but the press conference was postponed."

"Did Marcy give you the day off today?" Carlos asked. "She knows about this fiasco, right?"

"Yeah, Tess called her yesterday while they were dealing with the bail money, and she told Marcy what happened. But I'm sure she would've heard about it anyway. It's all over the news. Tess said her mom even saw it on the news in Georgia."

"After the past couple of years, you seem to be collecting dead bodies in your wake," Carlos joked, inspiring Isabel to punch him in the arm. Teaching those fitness classes made her tough, and he winced and rubbed his bicep.

"Don't remind me," Kallie replied, rolling her eyes, glad for a chance to laugh. *But if anyone other than my friends said it, I would've cried.* "Marcy said the same thing."

"If you need another day, I'm sure we can find someone to cover for you." He'd been reassigned as the day shift manager at the Lazy Gecko, after Lily was born, and Kallie was glad to have his support. "I'll bet Marcy's worried sick. After Alexandra—"

Isabel glared at her husband and shook her head warningly.

"Anyway, I'm sure the police will want to speak with you again before it's resolved," Carlos changed the subject, obviously hoping to avoid another punch. "If you need more time, I'll talk to her."

"The police don't think I'm the killer anymore, but the court stuff is more complicated," Kallie answered with a sigh. "That's going to take more time. There's paperwork to finish, and I have to meet with my case manager. And they'll probably want me to tell the story to another ten people."

"What a mess," Izzy commiserated.

"I already gave all the details to *four* officers," Kallie added with a frown. "But when they get the security footage back from the restaurant, showing the exact time we left, that should be the end of it."

"They haven't dropped the charges?"

"Officially? Not yet. There's too much conflicting information," she added, shaking her head. "I guess the State Prosecutor still thinks I could be a co-conspirator or something. And I think I need to see the judge again before he can drop it, anyway."

Carlos nodded, still looking a little concerned about all she'd gone through. She knew he didn't want to suggest anything simple and obvious like rest, or therapy – or anything that might get him punched again.

"Anyway, when does the new Lazy Gecko menu come out?" Kallie asked, quickly changing the subject again. She'd had enough talk about the latest drama for one night, and the spring menu for the restaurant was almost finished. "I heard they're doing scallops this year."

"Marcy said it's been finalized and they're just finishing up at the printers," Carlos answered. "She's always so secretive about it, every year."

"I love scallops," Isabel added. "I hope that's right."

"The food critics love scallops too, especially if they're locally sourced," Carlos agreed. "She's sure to win us more awards this year."

"Cha-ching," Kallie replied with a laugh. "More food critic awards means more tips at the bar, ladies and gentlemen."

They continued gossiping about work, and Izzy opened the bottle of wine while Carlos returned to his drawing. The stress fell off of Kallie as everything returned to normalcy for a little while. She knew clearing the legal mess would get worse before it got better, but she was glad to sit with her friends and relax while she could.

Chapter Six

When Kallie got home, her dad was sitting on the couch, and he called her over. "They're finally having the press conference. You got here just in time."

Kallie sat down on the couch and quickly texted Tess as the local 24-hour news station anchor nodded at someone offscreen and said, "They're ready to start; let's cut to the press conference."

The television switched to an outdoor podium, lit by floodlights, where the Tampa sheriff's office public relations spokeswoman was already speaking into the microphone. She gave a few names, and then spelled them for the assembled reporters, finally introducing the sheriff.

"We've all heard several rumors about the victim of Saturday night's attack after the Gasparilla Parade, and we wanted to get out here to clarify." A plain-spoken man, Sheriff McReed sounded a little annoyed, adding, "The first part Is incorrect. There is no cover-up or embarrassment involved; we just had a hard time finding the victim's mother, who doesn't live in Florida. The other part of the rumor is true. As the tabloid websites have suggested, Saturday night's victim was Marcus Allbright."

The sheriff paused while the reporters responded, talking amongst themselves and texting their offices. A quick series of dings could be heard as a dozen phones in the audience received messages all at once. Then the reporters settled back down to allow the sheriff to continue.

Kallie looked up as Tess opened the front door, then waved her over to sit down. She didn't bother explaining the sheriff's announcement, since he was still talking.

"A little background," he added, "Allbright was a player for the Tampa Bay Buccaneers until three years ago, when he transferred to the Philadelphia Eagles, but he still frequented the Tampa area. In his time as a Wide Receiver, he played on two teams that won their Division titles. He also had some run-ins with the law, both here and in Pennsylvania, but we haven't determined whether his murder was related to any of those cases specifically."

Kallie didn't follow sports gossip, but Allbright's legal woes were big enough to make the nightly news. He'd been in several very public fights, including brandishing a pistol in public. More recently, he'd been accused of beating up his pregnant girlfriend after his new team didn't make the playoffs. The Eagles suspended him for a few games but didn't drop him since he was never convicted.

Benny Brooks frowned but opted not to comment. Kallie knew that her dad had a personal dislike of men who abused women, but he wasn't one to speak ill of the dead.

"His coaching staff says he just arrived in Tampa on Thursday, so it's probably not a new local conflict. But it might be related to another open case in Philadelphia. We'll be communicating with their law enforcement to review our findings," the sheriff concluded. "I'll take a few questions."

Several reporters moved forward, and the sheriff, of course, knew them all. He pointed to a popular local reporter who'd been on the beat for ten years. "Sharon?"

"Is there any threat to the public at this time?" she asked. "Or do you believe it was a personal vendetta?"

"At this point, we think the murder was targeted," the sheriff replied with a nod. "However, if any of your viewers have information on the attack, we advise them to contact the police or the tip line directly, and don't approach the suspect. They should be presumed armed and dangerous." The reporters were waiting politely, so he pointed to the next. "Karl?"

"Marcus Allbright was in a bar fight in Philadelphia two weeks ago and has an upcoming trial date for hitting his girlfriend. Could this be related? An angry father or brother?" the reporter paused and then added with a smirk, "Or a disgruntled fan who thinks he missed too many easy passes from the QB?"

"I've heard of angry soccer fans committing crimes like this, actually," the sheriff answered with a frown. "We're looking into these possibilities, of course, but we don't have any evidence that his girlfriend or her family are involved. She dropped the charges last week, and they appear to have reconciled."

"Are any of the other Gasparilla events being postponed or cancelled?" another reporter called out.

"Not at this time," the sheriff answered. "Most of the other events are much smaller, as you know, but we're already planning to have added security for the races. If we need to postpone the Knight Parade, we'll make that decision next week."

The Knights of Sant' Yago parade was similar to the two earlier parades, centered around pirates and revelry, but it was held at night in the Ybor City district of Tampa. It was a bit on the wilder side, and Kallie hadn't been to one in years. Still, she was glad to hear that the celebrants, hopefully, wouldn't be disappointed.

Surely they'll solve this murder before the Knight Parade. It sounds like Allbright had some known criminal activities, so that should be easy to track down and make an arrest.

"One more question, and then we'll turn it back over to our public relations officer. Yes, Kevin?"

"Was the girl in the video the killer? The girl they're calling 'The Killer Wench?' Have you been able to identify her and get her name?"

"We haven't been able to identify the young woman in the video, because the jewelry store was too far away, and the quality is too grainy — but we're waiting for other surveillance video. We have established that she wasn't the victim's girlfriend. Miss Jackson has been sequestered on a reality show in Philadelphia," the sheriff stated with finality but also a sense of disappointment. "And although we've received a lot of helpful video footage from the public, and from our local businesses, we don't have a good, identifiable image. We have interviewed several people who saw that woman, and we've generated a sketch, which you've no doubt seen. It hasn't led to an identification yet."

The public relations officer returned to the podium and spoke to McReed for a moment, then the sheriff turned back to the microphone and added, "Thanks for your questions. That's all for now. We'll keep you updated." He walked offscreen and the station cut away as the public relations officer began speaking to the reporters again.

"A football player," Kallie said out loud. "I hope it wasn't just an angry fan. That'd be awful."

"It sounds like Allbright has plenty of enemies," Tess mused. "I'd heard about his problems with the law, but I didn't realize it'd gotten to this point. A few of the local crime bloggers picked up on his recent arrests, and they were all talking about CTE."

"It sounds likely, but it still stinks," Kallie agreed with a sigh. She'd heard about chronic traumatic encephalopathy, or CTE, after a former, much-loved Buccaneers player's family had recently donated his brain to science after death. The degenerative brain disease could be caused by head trauma and was increasingly common among long-time professional football players. It could sometimes cause violent behavior and chronic depression. "I hate to think of guys playing a sport for fun, for our entertainment, and getting life-changing brain damage from it."

"Since they can't find it on an MRI or CAT scan while people are alive, hopefully they'll be able to determine if Allbright had it now," her father replied. "I think an autopsy is required in murder cases, anyway."

"Well, the CTE didn't stab him," Kallie observed. "So even if he had it, there's still a killer out there walking the streets. That lady had the knife, so I hope the police can find her quickly. Whoever she is."

"In that crowd, she couldn't have gone far," her father agreed, encouragingly.

* * * * *

"Hey Dad, have you seen my denim jacket?" Kallie called across the house to her father as she

63

hurried through the living room the next morning, running late.

"Do you still own a jacket?" he laughed. "It's probably in the very back of your closet."

"I checked my closet," Kallie sighed, "and I checked the hall closet too. I don't think I gave it to charity."

"Maybe it's in your car. But let me go check my closet, just in case."

"Okay, but hurry. Tess and I have to get to the soup kitchen, and it's really chilly outside this morning. When I was out with Sherman, I was freezing my butt off."

While her dad went to check his closet, Kallie walked out to her own car. She was almost positive it wasn't in the trunk, because that was really hard to open. One of the many quirks of her old beat-up but beloved jalopy. But it might be in the back seat. She opened the driver's side back door to check, brushing away thoughts of the previous trauma. It had taken a year, but she'd finally come to terms with the murder at the Lazy Gecko, and she'd even decided not to sell her car.

"Nothing here," she mumbled to herself, starting to shiver, then bent down to check under the seat. Nothing there either.

"Where was the last place I wore it?" she asked herself as she walked back to the house. It was late

January, so she must've already worn it this winter.

If you can call this winter, she thought to herself. *Compared to Dad's hometown in New York, this is like a spring thaw. But it sure feels cold to me.*

She ran up the steps back into the warm house, her teeth now chattering.

"It's not in my closet either," her dad announced from the kitchen. "Not that your jacket would fit me, but I thought I might've picked it up accidentally, thinking it was mine."

"Thanks for checking. It's the only warm jacket I still own, and it's not cold enough outside for the wool overcoat that I take up north."

"Why don't you wear mine for today, kiddo? I'm not going anywhere this morning, so I won't need it. I'm going to see if this old camera still works." He held up an old analog camera that looked like it'd been new in 1980.

"That'd be great, if you don't mind. We should be back by one o'clock."

Her dad walked back into the bedroom and quickly returned with a faded denim jacket in his hand. Kallie and Benny were both tall, so the jacket wouldn't be huge on her. He handed it over just as headlights flashed across the living room walls in the dim morning light.

"There's Tess now. We're already running late, so I'm sure she won't come to the door." She took his jacket and wrapped up in it cozily, thanking him again.

"Give her my love," Benny replied, walking toward the door with Kallie, "and you two be careful driving in the dark."

Kallie slipped out the front door, trying not to let too much cold air inside, and then waved at her father again through the large front window. When she turned back toward the driveway, Tess was waving at him too.

"Sorry I'm late," Tess apologized, as Kallie climbed into the warm car. "I couldn't find my jacket."

"I couldn't find mine either," Kallie replied with a grin as they pulled out of the driveway. "This is my dad's."

"I think yours might be at my house, actually," Tess replied. "I found a jacket that I didn't recognize in my closet."

"That figures," Kallie laughed. "I was looking for it all morning. I even looked in the car."

"We can swing by my house after volunteering to see if it's yours. It definitely doesn't fit me." Tess was petite and curvaceous, so Kallie's jacket would probably hang down to her knees.

"I like my dad's jacket better anyway. It's warmer than mine, and the denim is softer."

Tess pulled into the parking lot at the huge community shelter in downtown Clearwater. They could see that the place was already lit up and bustling inside. Many lights were on in the live-in wing for the charity's patrons, and the dining building was already filling up with people. Local professional chefs were heating their food on the oversized skillets as volunteers set up the tables and chairs, stacking the first sets of serving trays.

"Oh, it looks warm in there," Kallie sighed as the cold wind hit her face, opening the car door.

"It does," Tess agreed with a shiver. "Let's hurry."

They ran laughing across the parking lot and into the warm building. They were both glad that the charity's owners were also native Floridians who turned on the heat as soon as it got below sixty degrees. The sun was just breaking over the horizon as they greeted and hugged their fellow volunteer friends.

"Want to try today's soup?" the chef called to Kallie with a smile.

"Yes please!" she called back. The charming local chef and his wife were both famous and had been featured on national cooking shows, but they still came to the shelter every weekend.

"It's chicken tortilla soup today," Richard added. "Come eat, so you can take off your coats, at least."

"It will warm your bones," his wife, Andrea, called from the skillet where breakfast sandwiches were being constructed. Frying eggs and bacon bubbled on the surface behind her as she waved to them.

Kallie and Tess slipped behind the counter and accepted two bowls of soup, gladly.

"It's going to be even more crowded than normal because of the cold weather," the chef added. "We're making tons of food. I don't think we've ever brought this many eggs before."

"And tonight's supposed to be even colder," his wife added with obvious annoyance. "Somebody needs to tell Minnesota to come get their weather."

It was nothing like Minnesota, of course. It wasn't even quite down to freezing, but you couldn't convince a Floridian of that. Kallie couldn't even convince herself.

"Hey Madeline," Andrea called out, looking over Kallie's shoulder. "Is that the Cuban bread?"

Madeline, the shelter's meal coordinator, walked into the kitchen area holding a cardboard box. She was still shivering a little so they knew she'd been outside, but she was carrying the box carefully and looking at the contents with a concerned frown.

"This isn't the Cuban bread, but the delivery just got here. Would you mind going out back to get it, Richard?" she asked.

"Awesome! Sure, we'll get it," he answered. "What's in the box?"

"I just found these guys outside, when I went to meet the truck," Madeline replied, as they all gathered around the ratty cardboard box.

Tess suddenly squealed, and Kallie looked to see what had happened. The old box contained a litter of tiny kittens, two black-and-white and two calicos.

Kallie let out an involuntary "*Awwwww*," and they both immediately grabbed for one, snuggling them joyfully. "It's so cold outside! Who would leave these poor babies outside in this weather?"

"You poor thing," Tess cooed to the tiny calico kitten in her hands, "Yes, you poor sweet, cuddly, cold baby."

"I'm going to drive them over to the Humane Society when they open at ten, but I thought you ladies might like to see them first." She set the box gently on the floor, and Kallie and Tess crowded up next to it.

"They aren't even old enough to be weaned," Tess complained to Madeline.

"The shelter will have a way to feed them. They always have kitten formula, but hopefully they'll have a nursing mama cat instead," Madeline explained. Her tone changed when she added, "And then I'm taking the security video to the cops."

"Good," Kallie replied, petting the kitten she was holding, as another one tumbled out of the box onto her lap. "I hope they can identify the creep."

"Yes, the mean old monster who dumped you

here in the cold is going to jail, isn't he, you poor baby?" Tess continued to coo.

"Francesca Maria," Mack called, sashaying across the floor toward them gracefully, clearly hearing salsa music in his mind. "Did you find Miss Lola? She's been gone for so long."

"Good morning, Mack," Kallie called to him happily. "Did you have a cat once?"

The elderly gentleman couldn't remember much about his past, but he adored Kallie — who apparently looked very much like his late wife — so she was always interested to learn tidbits about his past.

"Miss Lola ran away a long time ago. I remember how sad you were, my dear," he sat next to her and reached out a grizzled but gentle hand to pet the kitten.

"We were waiting on a big delivery from one of the local bakeries this morning, which is why I was out back," Madeline explained. "Poor things were crying their lungs out."

The chef came back, carrying the boxes of Cuban bread inside, and Kallie sniffed deeply. "That was nice of the bakery. It's not leftovers from yesterday, either. I can smell that it's fresh-baked, from here."

"We couldn't make it without help from the community," Madeline replied with a nod. "I can't believe you and the others showed up when it's this cold! And we just took on a new volunteer who's great at fundraising. He really knows how to wrangle businesses into helping us, in exchange for advertising in our brochures and on the website. "

Tess laughed. "That's definitely a full-time wrangling job."

"He got us those cases of cocoa too," she added, pointing toward the kitchen. "The genuine article, not the cheap watery stuff. We're going to fix it up during the church service, so everyone has something warm to take with them."

"That's great. It might be a little warmer outside by then, when the sun's up – but not by much. This will definitely help."

"Well, it's eight o'clock and it smells like breakfast's ready," Kallie sighed, gently placing her now-sleepy kitten back in the box. "We'd better wash up and get ready to serve."

Tess grudgingly handed back her fuzzy calico kitten after one more snuggle, and Kallie suspected they might be making a trip to the Humane Society in a few weeks, when that fluffball was old enough to be adopted.

As Madeline carried the box of kittens back to her office for safekeeping until the shelter opened, Kallie and Tess walked back to the volunteers' restroom and scrubbed up, savoring the heat blowing in the small space. Kallie knew they'd warm up once they were in the serving line and people started moving around – but she rubbed her arms quickly, to cut a little of the chill.

As soon as they left the restroom, though, they heard people talking about Allbright, and Kallie was abruptly pulled back into her recent ordeal. It had been years since he played for the local team, but everyone seemed to know his name. Many were shocked that he'd been murdered right on the street in a big crowd. Others weren't shocked at all, considering his reputation. A few insisted that they'd known it was him all along.

There are no televisions in the dining room, but there must be some upstairs. They seem to already know as much as we do.

Kallie and Tess split up at the serving line – Kallie went to help the chefs ladle the soup into bowls and package up the sandwiches, while Tess worked the front line. True to her nature, she chatted with everyone – asking about those she already knew and introducing herself to the new clients. Without even looking, Kallie could hear their voices change from melancholy to cheerfulness as this charming woman made it clear that she genuinely cared.

Add a hot meal to that, and this place could change someone's life, Kallie thought. *I'm so glad we volunteer here.*

When their serving duties were finished, and most of the attendees went to join the small church service, Kallie and Tess helped the chefs package the rest of the food.

As usual, the folks who ran the shelter didn't pry into her life, but they all gently insisted that Kallie should call them if she needed anything. They couldn't help with the legal issues, but they could be a shoulder or sounding board – whatever she needed. She hugged each of them with thanks and forced back emotional tears.

"My brother's a lawyer," Richard added quietly. "I mean, Andrea and I can be a shoulder to cry on too, but in case you need something a little more concrete..." He handed her a business card.

"I have a lawyer—" Kallie started to answer.

"She has a *public defender*," Tess interrupted, taking the business card. "Thank you."

"My pleasure," he answered. "You two are out here doing good work all the time. Someone needs to watch over you, too."

"Hopefully I won't need it, but thanks," Kallie agreed. She hugged the chef, and then his wife, who was just walking over to join them. She looked confused but hugged Kallie back with a smile.

By the time they finished cleaning up and talking, the little church service had finished, and Kallie and Tess began handing out the last batches of hot cocoa. Madeline was right, it was really good.

The folks who lived at the campus drifted back to their rooms upstairs, but the employees encouraged the others to stay for a while. At least until it warmed up a little outside. Some left anyway, impatient or over-socialized, but most stayed. It was still abnormally cold out there. One of the volunteers found a few dominoes sets, playing card decks, and two checker boards, then passed them around. The place was soon quiet as game play started, punctuated by occasional laughter and banter.

"Have you heard anything else from the police about the murder?" Tess asked when their duties were finished.

"Not a peep. It doesn't seem like anyone managed to get a good shot of the actual murder, but I can't imagine how that could happen in such a huge crowd. I mean, even *we* were recorded. But I doubt there are very many cameras left to check after this much time has passed."

"I was sure it was caught on someone's camera. Either a building security video or someone's phone. Especially during Gasparilla." Tess shook her head. "They might still find it."

"I hope so. I'm technically still out on bail, so a crystal-clear video exonerating me would be a lovely gift. I'll have to go back and see the judge, if they don't solve it soon."

I can't believe I tried to help that girl, and she turned out to be a murderer. And she ran off and left me looking like the guilty one!

I don't want to get us involved in another murder case, but if it isn't solved soon, am I going to be out on bail forever? What's taking so long?

"I almost forgot," Tess replied with a smirk. "You're still a criminal mastermind."

"If I was a criminal mastermind, I wouldn't dress like a pirate and go around stabbing random guys." Kallie tried to shove her nervousness away, adding with a smile, "Plus, I'd have a vacation home in Paris."

"And a better car," Tess joked.

"Hey, I like my car!" Kallie retorted. "Broken parts and all."

"When do you have to go back to court? Can the sheriff get you out of it?"

"He probably could, but I don't want to ask him for any more special privileges," Kallie answered with a sigh. "I have to go back next Wednesday, just to check in."

"What a nightmare."

"But maybe I can get some more gossip on the murder while I'm there."

"I should've known that was your plan," Tess replied, rolling her eyes. "You think they're just going to tell you all about the case? When you're currently the *only* suspect?

"It could happen," Kallie answered with a shrug

and a laugh.

It's worth a try, anyway. I've got to clear my name somehow, and it can't hurt, right?

"They can't talk about open cases, remember? Morrison's crazy about you, and even he didn't tell you anything about his case."

"Morrison is not crazy about me, Tess. We're just friends."

"Mmm-hmmm," Tess added, twisting her lips into a snarky bow.

"And I don't need anyone to tell me the details, I'll just listen carefully. I'm good at that."

"Yes, you're the queen of subtlety, Kal," Tess laughed. "Winchester said he's going to be driving across Louisiana for most of Wednesday. Maybe I'll come with you."

"That'd be great!" Kallie replied happily. "That place makes me nervous."

"I bet! I'll try to make sure they don't lock you back up for snooping. Besides, maybe I can help you eavesdrop. Four ears are better than two."

After everyone was settled into their games in the warm dining room, Kallie went to find her friend Mack again. She located him watching a game of dominoes.

"These are my dragonfly socks," Mack said, when he saw her, pulling up his pant legs to show off his teal and black socks.

Wait, did he remember that I liked his striped socks, before? Could he be doing better?

"Those are great socks! Do you know any dragonfly dances?" Kallie asked, jokingly.

"Somewhere between a sock hop and the jitterbug," he answered with a smile, which made Kallie laugh out loud.

Mack didn't live at the shelter, and he had fairly pronounced Alzheimer's — or some other form of dementia — but you'd never know it when he spoke to Kallie. He might mistake her for his late wife, but his spriteliness and sense of humor were still a ray of sunshine. She reminded herself to find some new dance videos online to practice.

I bet he'd be really impressed if I learned the Foxtrot.

She was glad Mack was in here, staying safe and warm. The Tampa Bay area almost never got cold enough to be dangerous to those living outdoors, but a morning like this wouldn't be comfortable. Especially at his age.

He saw some of his friends at one of the other tables, and pointed them out as they encouraged him to join them. Kallie wasn't surprised that the other homeless people liked him too, but he seemed to have known some of them for a long time.

"That's Howard," Mack indicated a man sitting

near the front windows. "He worked in a travelling carnival, running the Ferris wheel and introducing the side show performers."

Kallie was never sure how true Mack's stories were. Was he really remembering the histories of his fellow homeless people? Was he mixing them up with people he met fifty years ago? A combination of both? Or was he just making them up wholesale, for fun?

"Do you remember when we went to the carnival in Daytona Beach on your birthday, Francesca Maria?" he asked Kallie gently.

"When was that, Mack?" she replied.

She never said no when he asked about her memories of Francesca's life. Without any training in handling advanced memory loss, she simply thought her denial would make him sad, and she would never want that.

Mack smiled, as if she was simply encouraging him to re-tell their romantic story. "It would've been around 1976, because they were celebrating the bicentennial, and you were wearing all red, white, and blue, my darling. You looked beautiful, as always."

Tess leaned against Kallie's shoulder; she loved Mack's stories too. They both found it a little melancholy to hear how much he adored his late wife.

"We rode the carousel, and you chose the giraffe instead of the horses. It was always your favorite. Later, I tried to convince you to drive one of the bumper cars, but you always wanted to ride with me instead."

"I never liked bumper cars either," Kallie mumbled quietly to Tess.

"And you were afraid to see the sideshow performers, my dear. They called it a 'freak show' back then, which always seemed so unkind to you. I convinced you to see the snake lady, who had the body of a serpent and the head of a woman. You held my hand so tightly, but you were so brave," he added with a serene smile. "And you told her that she had lovely hair."

Kallie laughed out loud. "That sounds more like Tess than me, Mack."

"Your friend Tess is more like you than you admit, Francesca Maria," Mack replied, looking at Tess for a moment.

Kallie couldn't remember him ever speaking to Tess before, or even acknowledging their friendship. She wondered if Francesca also had a close female friend like Tess. She hoped so.

"What else happened at the carnival, Mack?" Tess asked softly, encouraging him to continue with his story.

"You always loved the Ferris wheel, my darling," he went on speaking to Kallie. "I've never liked heights myself, but I would go with you because it made you so happy. You said we could see across the ocean to Spain from the top of the ride."

Tess sighed, leaning against Kallie's shoulder again. So romantic, but somehow so heartbreaking.

"I never did take you to Spain, my darling," he added sadly.

"Maybe it's not too late, Mack," Kallie whispered. She imagined Mack as a young man, dancing elegantly in Barcelona with his beloved red-haired bride.

"Sorry to interrupt, ladies, but we're closing up." Madeline touched Kallie's shoulder, and when she looked back, she was shocked to see that everyone else had already gone.

Chapter Seven

"What do you think we're even going to find out here?" Tess asked, sounding confused as she peered up and down the sidewalk. "It rained yesterday, and the police already picked up everything important."

Kallie had convinced her best friend to check out Allbright's murder scene on her day off, but the excursion was turning out to be less helpful than she'd hoped.

"I'm not sure. I just wanted to see where it happened. Get a feel for the surroundings."

There were a few mementos left on the sidewalk, probably by the victim's family and fans. Two small bouquets of flowers, like you'd find in a grocery store, and a pillar candle. A photo of the football player, someone's idol, leaned against a signpost in a cheap frame. They had all been damaged in the rain. Tess squatted down to see the ruined photo, looking sympathetic, without picking it up.

"Is this blood?" Kallie called, pointing to a sheltered area in the corner.

Tess walked over to join her, and wrinkled her

nose. "From the smell, I think it's raspberry yogurt. Which has been sitting out in the weather for at least a week. Can we please not *smell* things out here?"

Kallie tilted her head, unsure. "It might be important."

"Or it might have been peed on by drunk people."

Kallie laughed, embarrassed. "I guess that's more likely. I'm sorry for dragging you down here for nothing. Do you want to get an early lunch?"

"Sure, I've been wanting to try the new Cajun place," Tess agreed. "It's just on the next block."

Kallie took some photos of the scene with her phone and noticed that there were still a few local reporters in the area. So she wasn't the only one who thought there might be someone or something interesting to find down here.

But the police were notably absent, so maybe the reporters were all just dreaming of winning prestigious awards.

Or maybe they want to catch the killer, or just figure out the mystery, like me.

Kallie and Tess started toward their chosen lunch spot, Chez Rémi. She noticed that Tess was taking pictures too. When they arrived, the restaurant was still mostly empty, and they were lucky enough to be seated at a great spot by the windows. Since it was just after eleven on a weekday, they'd beaten the rush to the trendy new eatery.

"Have you asked Hannah about it?" Tess asked, after they'd been seated and checked over the menu.

"Sorry?" Kallie replied, distracted by the smells coming from the kitchen.

"Your friend Hannah. The crime blogger?" Tess hinted. "I'm sure she'll have information on the murder."

"That's a great idea!" Kallie responded. "I didn't even think of that."

Tess was the real true-crime fan, who followed all of the local news and online gossip. Kallie was only interested in crime as a side effect of finding herself up to her eyeballs in it for the past few years. Hannah had been a favorite blogger of Tess's until they actually needed her help with a previous murder.

"She doesn't have much on the blog about it yet," Tess added. "I checked last night. But I'll bet she's been contacting all of her sources. Maybe she's planning to write another book."

"I'll email her when I get home," Kallie responded, but then her face fell. "Oh, but I don't have any information to give her this time. I hope—"

"Kallie, she's your friend. You don't have to *trade* with her," Tess laughed. "Besides, you wrote some blog entries for her."

"And if she's writing a book, she'll want to

mention my arrest," Kallie continued hopefully. "Maybe I can tell her about that."

Tess sighed, shaking her head.

When their waiter arrived, Kallie and Tess both ordered gumbo and tried to decide between jambalaya and crawfish étouffée. In the end, they ordered both, with plans to share. The restaurant had great reviews, and neither of them could believe they'd managed to get a prime seat so easily.

"It's still early, so we have to stay for the peach cobbler," Tess added.

"Twist my arm," Kallie joked.

Through the front window, they could see another reporter looking for someone to interview, but everyone pushed past him, hurrying to get to work or to lunch.

* * * * *

After lunch, they were walking back to the car, both thinking about the excellent gumbo and still pondering the murder. An older man with a heavy backpack and sad but hopeful eyes called out quietly to them as he passed, wishing them a blessed day. He was dressed for a physical job – maybe in a warehouse or on a construction site, Kallie thought – but his shoes were ragged.

Tess stopped in her tracks and silently looked at

Kallie for a second. She glanced back toward the man, who was continuing up the street, then she looked back at Kallie again. Kallie knew her best friend was weighing her options about something, but she wasn't sure what.

She's still thinking about Mack and the way he finally recognized her. I don't think she needed to be real for him until it happened.

Tess tilted her head and graced her friend with a crooked smile. "A man with eyes like that would've seen a lot in his life, wouldn't he?"

"What?" Kallie asked, confused. "Who?"

Before Kallie could stop her, Tess pulled a couple dollars from her pocket and turned around, hurrying back toward the man. Kallie ran after her best friend, and caught up with them just as Tess was offering her thanks for his kind wish.

Tess gave to charity, and volunteered at the shelter, but this kind of giving was unlike her. Concerned, Kallie walked closer and called quietly to her friend that they should go, but Tess was already talking with the man. She grabbed Kallie's hand and pulled her closer.

"Are you okay?" Tess asked, sincerely, softly. "We work with a shelter in Pinellas County. We could find someone to help you."

He smiled and shook his head. "I'm alright. This is my home." He gestured around widely at the empty sidewalks in the trendy neighborhood.

"Here?" Tess asked, encouraging him to continue.

"This neighborhood used to be very different," the old man answered Tess. His voice was gentle, and hoarse from the dry and chilly winter air, but clear. "Before the hockey stadium was built, this area wasn't so expensive."

Kallie tightened her grip on Tess's hand, but she was becoming hypnotized by his story too. She slipped an arm around Tess's waist in case she needed to pull her friend away, but the man's sad voice was strangely calming.

"My apartment building was torn down a few years ago, but it was nice. Old-fashioned. I lived here for a long time. Until one day I was living in my car."

"That's terrible," Tess responded sympathetically. From anyone else it would've sounded flippant, but Kallie knew she meant it. A moment later, Tess slipped away and sat down on the sidewalk, making Kallie cringe inwardly, and the old man sat down near her.

"Well, it's my own fault. When my landlord raised the rent for the second time in a year, I knew I couldn't afford it. I told myself a dozen times, 'Elijah, this isn't the place for you anymore.'" He shook his head sadly. "I should've moved out right away, gone out to the suburbs. It was dirt cheap to live out by the airport back then. I might even have been able to buy a little house. But I convinced myself that I could make it work."

Kallie started to reply, but the old man only had eyes for Tess. It was as if he'd known the beautiful brunette his whole life. Like she was a long-lost sister to him, encouraging him to pour his heart out.

She had that effect on people.

"But it had been my home," he continued quietly. "Before my wife died, we lived here for years, talked about raising kids here. I didn't want to leave those memories behind."

Kallie approached them slowly and sat down next to Tess, close enough that their knees touched, but neither of them looked at her.

As her nerves subsided, Kallie saw that the old man — who probably wasn't really any older than sixty, judging from his story – was wearing second-hand clothes, and she could see the squared outline of some small electronic device in his backpack – probably an old transistor radio or one half of a walkie-talkie set.

Why would he be carrying anything like that to work? Why lug the extra weight around, like he had to protect an old radio?

Oh my gosh, are those his only possessions?

As if confirming her thoughts, he continued, "I have a good job now. Not like my old job, but enough that I can save. I won't make the same mistake again, when I can afford a place in the suburbs." He smiled, slightly forlorn but assured. "I'll stay there, this time."

It was broad daylight, so neither of them was particularly uncomfortable sitting on the sidewalk, in the open. But it would be more dangerous at night. Kallie hated to think of this gentle old man being stuck in that life. Even for a little while.

Even worse, she tried not to think of Mack, her elderly dancing partner, living like this. She knew he didn't live at the shelter; did he live out in the open like this? Did places like this exist in Owhiro?

"Is this neighborhood safe? The police told us that there was a murder here during Gasparilla?" Tess mentioned gently.

"They don't even see us during Gasparilla," the old man said with a sigh. "I was parked right there, trying to sleep because I had to work the next day. I saw it happen, in the alleyway."

"The *alleyway*?" Kallie whispered.

"We heard the murder happened on the sidewalk," Tess added.

"The man was stabbed on the sidewalk, alright," the old man nodded. "The lady who gives me sandwiches told me so, and I know she wouldn't lie. But the girl was stabbed in the alleyway."

Tess looked at Kallie quickly, then back at the man. "A *girl*? *What* girl? Was she stabbed by the same person?" Tess asked, clearly surprised by this whole

88

turn of events.

"I didn't see the first one." He nodded and added, "But I think he wanted the girl all along. Yup, yup."

Kallie and Tess looked at each other again, and Kallie mouthed the word, "He?!"

Is he making this up? Did he imagine it? But Kallie could take one look at this stoic, hopeful man and see that he wasn't crazy or desperate. His eyes were sharp and bright, his voice convinced.

Did he really see it? Maybe. But he definitely believes he did.

But the police think Allbright was killed by that woman with the knife. The Killer Wench. Is this murder totally unrelated?

Or is it imaginary?

"The police need to hear this. Are you sure you won't talk to them?" Kallie asked.

"Nope. No, no, no. No police," the man seemed to be on the edge of panic and slid backward awkwardly, suddenly ready to run. "I'm telling *you*. That's all I can do."

"Okay. Okay, that's fine." Tess leaned out and touched his hand to calm him down. "No police."

He settled down and came back to his place on the ground with them, returned to Tess's warmth. A few office workers nearby looked at them strangely, and

Kallie saw one person cross the street, but no one interrupted them.

"Could we record your story?" Tess held out her phone, showing it to him cautiously without turning it on. Kallie knew she had a dictation recording application on there that she used for work.

This time his eyes grew wide, and he backed away, stumbling to his feet.

"Whoa, whoa, whoa," Kallie said quietly. She made way for him to escape, afraid to grab him.

Don't go. Please don't go. We need to hear this...

Tess slipped the phone back into the thigh pocket of her cool but elegant linen cargo pants as if it had never been there. She couldn't record him without his consent, Kallie knew. On the off-chance that his story helped find the killer, it would be inadmissible in court.

And Tess simply wouldn't do something that callous, anyway. This guy has enough problems, without us making it worse.

Without standing up, Tess opened both hands to show that they were empty. Then she held out one hand and waited for him to take it. After a very long minute or two, he accepted her hand and sat back down.

As skittish as a deer smelling a hunter in the woods. Tess could probably hand-feed a wild fawn too, Kallie thought with a smile.

"You were telling us about the girl in the alley," Tess prompted him.

"Yes, the pretty pirate girl..." he began.

* * * * *

> Hey Hannah. Just wondering if you wanted to talk about the Gasparilla thing?

Kallie hit send on the text and set her phone down next to the oven. Peeking in through the glass, the homemade pizza looked ready, melty in the middle and brownish on the edges.

She was just opening the oven door to take it out when the phone rang.

Wow, is that Hannah already?

"Hello?" she answered with a smile.

"Hi Kallie. I got your text about the Gasparilla murder. And since I *know* you and your crazy ways..." Hannah added with a laugh.

"Are you writing another book?" Kallie asked.

Might as well cut to the chase.

"Not yet, but you know I'm considering it. Just waiting to find out if it's juicy. Famous victim, party scene, gory crime — looks like another book in the making."

Kallie had initially been put off by her friend

Hannah's fascination with true crime and desire to write about it. She had seemed mercenary at best and exploitative at worst. But after getting to know her, and later reading her book about the local murder of Alexandra Clemons, her mind was completely changed. Hannah's interest might seem shallow from a distance, but her treatment of the victims was caring and genuine. Lex's murder had touched Kallie's life personally and indelibly, and Hannah's book about it had brought Kallie to tears.

"Tess and I were just downtown—"

"I knew it!" Hannah laughed out loud. "I knew you wouldn't be able to stay away."

"Well, we were just—"

"Oh, I know. I'm not criticizing you, sugar. You were dragged into this mess, literally – and in handcuffs, no less — through no fault of your own. I'd be down there too, if they tossed me in jail for someone else's crimes."

"Thanks Hannah," Kallie answered, suddenly feeling fully understood.

"But most people aren't like you and me. They'd still be hiding under their beds," Hannah added with a laugh, "So it's still total Kallie-For-The-Win, as far as I'm concerned. What did you find out?"

"Does that mean you'll help us? Quid pro quo again?"

"Girl, you're my *friend*. This isn't like two years

ago, when I was bargaining for your information. I'll tell you everything I have, if you want it."

Kallie thought back on Tess telling her this would happen and felt a glow of happiness at her amazing, trusting, and brilliant girlfriends.

"You're the best, Hannah," she answered with tears in her eyes. "But I think we found something that's going to convince you to write that book."

"You're kidding. You found something new? What is it?"

"This might sound crazy, but hear me out. It looks like there was another murder," Kallie announced, hoping Hannah hadn't already discovered it. Still wanting to impress her clever friend.

"Wait, what?" Kallie could hear that Hannah was confused. "Someone other than the football player was killed at Gasparilla?"

"That's what we heard."

"From the *police*?" Hannah asked.

"No," Kallie sighed. "The police aren't telling us anything. We talked to a guy who was sleeping in his car."

"Oh," Hannah groaned. "You mean *permanently* sleeping in his car, don't you? Not just sleeping off too many beers? I can't use a homeless guy as a source, Kallie."

Kallie was disappointed, even though Hannah's

answer made sense. But she wasn't giving up that easily. "He wouldn't agree to be a source, anyway," she answered with a shrug. "He's way too scared. But I believe him. *We* believe him. Tess too."

There was silence for a few long seconds, and Kallie held her breath.

"Okay, I know you're a good judge of character. If you want to tell me what he said, I'll see what I can dig up."

"I can't tell you his name. I mean, it might not even be his real name. But he saw the murder. He said he feels like a ghost sometimes, and that he was totally invisible to all those rich partiers. Including the killer."

Silence again, but this time she thought she heard Hannah start typing on her laptop.

"He said he thought the football player might have been a distraction. Or just collateral damage."

"Really? How so?" Hannah finally asked.

"He said he thought the killer was after *some girl* the whole time. That she was the intended victim."

"A girl? That doesn't make any sense, Kallie," Hannah sighed. "The football player is filthy rich, and he has a nasty reputation for running his mouth and antagonizing people. Even his fans."

"I've heard."

"An easy target with no shortage of enemies," Hannah added. "Plus, need I remind you? There was no woman's body found."

"He said it was in an alley."

"Okay, I know that neighborhood, Kallie." Her friend sounded like she was regretting this conversation. "There are no alleys there. Most of the construction is new, and every spare inch of space is reserved for parking."

Hannah lived in downtown Tampa, so she knew the area much better than Kallie and Tess – who lived almost thirty miles away. Kallie was sure her friend could picture that block easily in her mind.

"I don't think it was at the exact same murder scene. It sounded like she tried to run, and he followed her."

Kallie could hear Hannah's pen tapping absently on the desk now.

A sure sign that she's thinking. Considering. Becoming intrigued.

"No way. It was Gasparilla," Hannah finally said. "If there was another dead body, even in an alley, someone would've stumbled over it. If not that night, then certainly by now." Then a moment later, she added, "Oh, you have a theory about that, too, don't you?"

Kallie could sense her face heating up, feeling a little foolish about her idea — and about telling it to someone who knew so much about crime. "You don't think I'm crazy?"

"No, not crazy. No way." Hannah answered seriously. "I'm not saying you're right, yet. But it's not out of the realm of possibility."

"I wish we could've recorded his story, but he was so scared—"

"Let me put some feelers out, and see if anyone's on this. I think you're the only one talking about it," Hannah answered, then added, "If it's even true."

"Okay."

"You don't have any idea where this mysterious alley might be?" she added.

"No, but we thought it must be between Allbright's murder scene and the restaurant where I was arrested."

"Maybe..."

"If you find anything out?" Kallie hinted, adding with a smile, "Or hear about anyone else finding a giant pool of dried blood?"

"You'll be the first to know, I promise," Hannah answered with a chuckle. "Are you going back down there?"

"You already said you know how crazy we are," Kallie answered, blushing.

"Not just obsessed but *predictably* obsessed. And that's a dangerous combination if the killer finds out. Be careful, okay? And let me know if I can help with anything."

"You're already helping us a ton, Hannah."

"I'll let you know what I hear. And I won't give up your source. As far as I'm concerned, it's purely hearsay."

"Thanks, Hannah. Thanks a lot."

Chapter Eight

Kallie hurried into work the next morning, running late after a fitful night's sleep. In every dream, strangers popped up with knives, chasing her into pitch-dark alleyways. She poured a cold diet coke at her station and guzzled it, hoping the circles under her eyes weren't too bad.

Only Barry was in her section, and he looked up from his writing to give her a wave. He'd found a cup of coffee, so Kallie grabbed a pot and refilled it for him. "Can I get you anything from the kitchen?" she asked. "I hear the new sourdough French Toast is great." Barry didn't often order breakfast, so she sometimes made a suggestion so he didn't get hungry before lunch.

He gets so engrossed in writing that novel. Besides, if I'm in it, I want my character to be nice. So no harm in a little bribery.

"That sounds good. I didn't know I was hungry until you mentioned it," he answered with a chuckle, his studious, greying goatee turning up as he smiled. "Could I get some fruit on the side?"

"Of course. They always have a fresh fruit

option," she replied with a smile. "And I'm pretty sure citrus and melon have been scientifically proven to cancel out all that fat and sugar."

"Naturally."

Kallie placed his breakfast order on the computer and finished rearranging her station to her liking. The night bartender always moved things around – she suspected he was left-handed. Then she took out a few lemons and limes from the tiny refrigerator under the counter and started rolling them on the wooden bar surface.

Cutting the fruit for garnish had been a cathartic exercise for Kallie for years, but it had especially helped her focus when she was engrossed in the Owhiro Murder, as the press called it. She took out a cutting board and started chopping the first lime.

Hannah's right, this all sounds completely insane.

But she's checking into it, so she must not think we're completely nuts.

I'm going to be so embarrassed if this was all a figment of Elijah's imagination, and Hannah wastes her time – and resources – on a daydream.

On the other hand, if he's right, her book will have the scoop!

Either way, I'm so glad she trusts us.

The first lunch patrons began filtering in,

distracting Kallie from her thoughts. She quickly boxed up the fruit she'd cut, surprised to see that during her reverie, she'd finished chopping six limes, eight lemons, and a grapefruit.

Yikes. I guess everybody's getting extra fruit garnish today. No scurvy here, mateys!

Snapping the last Tupperware container shut, she added to herself, *Really, a grapefruit? I hope a lot of people are in the mood for a Salty Dog.*

Kallie took drink orders, from her tables as well as the computerized ordering system, and served a variety of cocktails and beer as the room filled up with lunch guests. The Lazy Gecko was as popular at lunch, with its award-winning menu, as it was at night. On weekdays, even more so.

When one o'clock rolled around and the last lunchtime stragglers headed back to their offices, leaving only the day-drinking regulars, Kallie settled in to clean up. Listening to the background music, now audible without the noisy crowd, she collected the last glasses and plates for the kitchen staff, took the bottles to recycle, and scrubbed the staging area below the bar.

Humming along with the music, she was a little startled when a stranger sat down on the nearest barstool.

"Oh, hi," she greeted him. "Welcome to the Lazy Gecko. What can I get you?"

"Do you know how to make a Mai Tai?" he asked

with an odd smirk.

"Sure," Kallie answered. "Lots of rum, lots of sugar," she added facetiously with a squint, unsure of his strange smile.

"My father went to Trader Vic's after he came back from the war," the man explained. "In the mid-1940s. And he had the original Mai Tai, made by the guy who invented it."

"Oh wow," Kallie replied, leaning forward with her elbows on the bar.

"I've been reading through his old papers and letters to my mom, lately, looking for information about our family, and he mentioned it in a notebook full of war stories. He said no one else ever made it *quite* right, not like the original."

"And now you want to find the real thing," Kallie finished his sentence. "The bona fide article."

"It sounds crazy," he laughed.

"What? No, it doesn't sound crazy at all," Kallie answered, more emphatically than she intended. "It was your dad, of course you want to experience it." She added, with a shrug and a smile, "Maybe I'm biased. But if it was a photograph, you'd try to find the exact place where he took it, right? This is no different."

"So you have the original recipe?" he asked, sounding a little excited.

"I don't," she sighed, trying not to watch the

disappointment on his face. "But I'll find it. My best friend is amazing at research. If the original recipe still exists in the world, she'll be able to find it."

"Excellent," he replied with a nod, handing her a business card. "Give me a call if you and your friend figure it out. I'll throw in a five-hundred-dollar tip and free advertising."

* * * * *

Kallie knocked on Tess's door later, surprised that her friend wasn't outside waiting when she drove up. They were going to see Carlos and Isabel, and Tess had been excited for the dinner all week. Kallie heard a shout telling her to come in, and opened the door.

"Are you ready to go?" she asked. "We're running late."

"I'm sorry, I fell down a rabbit hole, Kallie. Come over here and look."

Tess was hunched over her laptop, and she explained, "I uploaded the photos. The ones that I took on my phone at the crime scene."

Kallie went from impatient to fascinated in the blink of an eye, and she sat down at the dining room table next to Tess. "What did you find?"

"I'm not sure yet. Maybe nothing, and maybe exactly what we need." She turned the laptop toward Kallie and opened the folder. "Look through them while

I get dressed. I know we're late, and I'm *starving*."

Kallie waved her away to the bedroom to change clothes for dinner and started looking through the photographs. She opened each one and zoomed in on the most interesting parts with Tess's photo viewer.

Wow, I really need to get a better phone, she thought to herself after looking at a few of them, comparing them to the pictures she'd taken at the same location. *I can't believe the quality of these photos. They're really good, even blown up.*

Tess had taken more pictures than Kallie had realized. There were a whole bunch from the actual crime scene and the surrounding shops and restaurants – Kallie had seen her take those, and had taken several herself as well. But Tess had continued taking shots on their way to the restaurant. It didn't seem to all be related to the murder – there were some from lunch, and even a few shots of Kallie mixed in.

"Have you gotten to the last set yet?" Tess called out from the bedroom. "I saved a few of them for you."

"No, I'm still on the first ones," Kallie replied. "Were you taking pictures the whole time?"

Tess walked out from the bedroom, finishing up with earrings and a few bangles, but she was blushing uncharacteristically. "Oh, yeah," she mumbled. "Everyone around here is so artistic, and I can't draw a stick figure. I'm trying to make up for it with my photography."

"These are great, Tess," Kallie replied, looking at her friend when she sat back down.

"Well, most of them are just wannabe crime scene photos. But I love this picture of you." She pointed at a photo from the restaurant, where Kallie was in profile, looking out the front window – presumably watching the dejected reporter search for witnesses. The mix of shadows from the dark restaurant and sunlight through the glass made Kallie look like a 1940s film star.

"I wish I looked that good in real life," she muttered, squinting at the photograph of herself.

For a moment, Tess looked like she was going to argue, but then she grinned wickedly and asked, "Should we send it to Detective Morrison and see what *he* thinks?"

"Don't you dare!" Kallie whined. "Fine, I surrender. Thank you for the lovely picture, and can we *please* talk about the crime scene now?"

Tess smiled in mock victory and opened four photos that she had saved together, showing them all at once. "Do you see what I see?"

Kallie looked at them again and replied, "I'm pretty sure this is the place, right?"

Tess took out her phone and pulled up someone's cell phone video, showing the attack aftermath. A moment later, she paused it and pointed at one section of the image. "You can see *that* doorway and framed menu in this video. And when he pans around..." She turned and pointed at the laptop. "There's the neon sign, in that bar window."

Kallie looked at the video as it restarted automatically and nodded. "This is exactly where the first murder happened, and your pictures capture the whole block. Which means the alley must be here somewhere too."

Tess put her phone down and gestured back to the photos on her laptop. "Do you see an alley?"

Kallie looked at her and scowled.

"I'm not giving you any clues, Kal," Tess replied, shaking her head. "I'm not sure myself, and I don't want to influence you. What do you see?"

Kallie flipped through the series of photos taken before their Cajun lunch again, twice, and finally shook her head. "I don't see an alley."

"Elijah sounded pretty sure," Tess replied, leaning back in her chair.

"He was really sweet; I just want us to remember that homeless people don't always make the best eyewitnesses."

"Okay, understood," Tess agreed. "Take one more look, and we'll go. We can check them again later."

"I didn't see anything in the video that looked like an alley, and I don't see it in these pictures either," Kallie answered with a sigh. "But the girl's attack doesn't need to be right here, in this exact same spot."

"Yeah, he didn't say it was close to Allbright's murder. But it couldn't have been too far away, or someone would've seen the killer walking around with the bloody knife."

"But *everyone* had at least one knife," Kallie clarified. "I had a sword."

"Hmm, good point." Tess reconsidered, "So we'll call it two blocks in any direction."

They opened a map website and checked the immediate area but found nothing that could really be considered an alley. Downtown Tampa wasn't like New York or Chicago — many of the streets weren't lined up in perfectly square city blocks. Some were, but others swerved and turned, seemingly at random, to avoid the various intersecting rivers and channels, as well as parks and green spaces.

Much of that specific area had been either industrial or dilapidated, and was torn down, as Hannah had pointed out earlier, and alleyways in the rebuilt section were uncommon. There were driveways and parking lots, but nothing secluded enough to hide a murder. Kallie tried to keep an open mind about what they might be looking for.

Zooming in to the map and comparing it against Tess's photos, they started covering the nearby streets, searching for any kind of passageway, tenant entrance, outdoor hallway — even a long portico or canopy.

"I don't see anything secluded, but big enough to fit two people," Kallie sighed. "Especially when one of those people was stabbing the other. There had to be some amount of privacy."

"What about the walkway to the back entrance of this nightclub?" Tess asked, pointing at one of the photos.

"That club was packed with partiers that night – it's really popular. It looks a little like an alleyway, but there would have been a hundred people jammed in there, hoping to get into the club. Or maybe to just see a celebrity."

"Yeah, you're right," Tess sighed.

Kallie closed her eyes and thought for a minute, then reconsidered, "Hmmm."

"That sounds like an idea forming," Tess responded with a grin.

"Maybe we're making this too complicated. I'll bet there wasn't a single square inch of Downtown Tampa that wasn't occupied on Gasparilla night," Kallie mused. "Could he have stabbed her *right there* in the crowd?"

"No way," Tess answered, shaking her head. "In that crowd? Someone would've seen it."

Kallie stayed silent this time, letting her best friend think.

"Okay, *maybe*," Tess continued, doubtfully.

"Maybe if she was *really* drunk. But too drunk to scream? Is that even possible?"

"In my experience, people scream *more* when they're drunk," Kallie added, rolling her eyes.

"But if she *was* that drunk, and everyone had seen it, then if she collapsed after she was stabbed, he could just act like he was helping her walk it off." Tess frowned, and added, "He could've dumped her body fifty miles from here."

"It's possible. That's not a bad idea, but I'm not sure—" Kallie considered.

"Yeah, we're totally grasping at straws, now," Tess answered with an annoyed sigh. "This is ridiculous."

Kallie suddenly reached out and snapped the laptop shut. "Let's go. We can look at this stuff later, and I'm starving."

"Me too," Tess answered with obvious relief.

"Hannah said she'd check with her contacts, so I'll tell her our idea," Kallie added, pulling on a cardigan and moving toward the door. "Right now, Isabel's arroz con pollo is calling my name!"

"I want to stop at the store and pick up a bottle of wine," Tess added. "I hate to show up empty-handed."

"They won't care, honestly, but I'm fine with that. As long as we don't take too long."

"Sure, I'll just stop at the grocery store on the corner," Tess agreed, grabbing her car keys. "They have decent wine."

They pulled into the grocery's parking lot a few minutes later and rushed to the wine section.

"What wine goes with arroz con pollo?" Tess asked.

"You're asking me? Most of the wine I serve comes in a jug."

Tess smiled and pulled out her phone. "Okay, the internet votes for a medium-bodied red. Merlot?"

"Sure, that sounds—"

"Hey Susan," a voice whispered loudly, close behind them. "Isn't that the woman who killed that football player?"

Tess froze with a fierce expression on her face and set the bottle back on the shelf.

"She should be in prison," another woman's voice hissed, not trying to be subtle. "This country's falling apart, letting criminals walk the—"

Tess spun around and stepped toward the women. "Excuse me, but neither of you have any idea what you're talking about."

An unattractive woman with stringy hair and small eyes – but Kallie might be biased – replied, "I know *she's* the woman they caught at the scene, holding a knife and covered in blood." She glared at Kallie in anger and visible disgust.

"The police cleared her because she has an *alibi*," Tess retorted, trying to stay calm. Kallie could see it wasn't working. "Maybe you've heard of an alibi? Or is that too complicated for you?"

"They didn't say she was *cleared*. We watch the news, lady," the other woman answered with a self-righteous sniff. "They said she's out on bail."

Tess started to answer again, but Kallie took her arm. "C'mon Tess. We're going to be late." She grabbed the wine and pulled her best friend toward the self-checkout lane, feeling equally grateful for her friend and guilty for getting them into this situation.

They checked out quickly and walked back to the car, but Kallie could tell that Tess wasn't recovered from the argument.

"Don't worry, Tess. We'll figure this out. And those stupid women don't mean anything."

"It's going to be more than just those two women, Kal." Tess sighed. "We need to help the police get this sorted out before it gets worse."

* * * * *

"Auntie Tess!" Lily shrieked as she ran to hug her friend, before they were even fully through the door of Studio Alvarez. "Mom, Grandma! Auntie Tess is here!"

"And suddenly I'm chopped liver," Kallie joked, watching them hug.

Tess didn't visit very often, but she was a house favorite, especially for their daughter. She immediately sat down on the floor to see Lily's latest crayon creation, and then they watched Carlos draw at his easel for a few minutes while the toddler gave the play-by-play on each step.

"What, child?" her grandmother called from the courtyard, where she was deadheading the flower garden. "*Who's* here?" She stuck her head into the studio, and cried, "Tess Russo! You're a sight for sore eyes, young lady!"

"Hi, Mrs. Alvarez!" Tess called from the floor where she was sitting with the toddler.

Carlos's mom carefully wiped her hands on her garden apron and took off her shoes before stepping inside to hug Tess too. "Did you come over to see the new artwork?"

"Isabel invited us over for dinner, but the new drawings are amazing," Tess gushed. "This sea turtle is spectacular. It looks like he could swim right out of the canvas."

The older woman glowed at the compliment like she had created the drawing herself, perhaps even more so. She was very proud of her son, and loved his recently-discovered talent. "A gallery in St Pete paid thousands of dollars for his work, just for two drawings."

They could see the back of Carlos's neck turn red, as he blushed at the uncomfortable compliments from everyone.

"I should have snatched one up before they got so expensive," Tess replied with a laugh. "We're both so proud of him."

Mrs. Alvarez went back to the garden, and Kallie sat down to talk with Carlos. "A guy came in and offered me a big reward if I can find the original Trader Vic's recipe for a Mai Tai," she told him. "From the 1940s. My recipe is great, but it's improvised."

"Did he say what was different about the original?" her friend asked, without looking away from his drawing.

"No, he never tried it, himself. It was his dad."

"You tried googling it already?" Carlos asked.

"Yeah, I checked on my phone after he left, but there are too many variations. A lot of them have pineapple juice or orange juice, and I know those are wrong."

"I know there's no fruit juice except lime, but I don't have the original recipe," Carlos concluded.

"I'll see if I can find it when I get home," Tess called from across the room, where she was studiously admiring Lily's collection of toy unicorns.

"Thanks, Tess! He offered me a giant tip, plus

advertising for the bar," Kallie answered with a smile.

"Well it's got to be out there somewhere. I'll find it, even if I have to call a library in Hawaii," Tess added with a laugh.

Isabel came walking out from the house, where she'd clearly been cooking, and hugged Tess too. "Why don't you two come inside and grab some dinner? I made my mom's arroz con pollo recipe."

Kallie replied, "You don't have to tell me twice. I've been dreaming about your cooking all day!"

Isabel waved for them to follow her, then added with a laugh, "You too, husband. Put down the charcoal and pick up a fork."

* * * * *

Kallie, Tess, Lily, and Mrs. Alvarez were all huddled around the table, chatting and laughing with Isabel while she took a spinach salad out of the refrigerator. Tess passed the bottle of wine across the table.

"I worked a double shift at the studio today, because one of my instructors is out sick. Hot yoga and high-intensity aerobics back-to-back." Isabel slumped against the kitchen counter. "That was all before noon, and I'm still so exhausted, I feel like I'm going to fall over."

"I hope you're not getting sick," Kallie replied,

looking concerned. "You used to do that every day, right?"

"Yes, and more!" Izzy replied. "But I'm an *administrator* now." She sighed and rolled her eyes. "I have to do the advertising and payroll and purchasing for the classes now. All the boring stuff."

"Oh, what a pain," Kallie commiserated.

"I didn't think I was so out of shape—" she continued.

"You are definitely *not* out of shape," Tess insisted. "You look amazing."

"I just mean comparatively. I could have done five classes in a day when I was running the place by myself. Now I feel like I got hit by a truck after just two," she laughed.

"Well come over here and sit down, lady," Tess replied. "You relax, and we'll get dinner on the table. It smells fantastic."

"If you're sure, that would be great. Thank you." Isabel took the advice and sat down at the table while Tess and Kallie got the dishes ready. "It's comfort food for me. It never comes out quite as good as when my mom makes it, but I needed a great dinner after this morning."

"What happened this morning?" Carlos asked, finally coming into the kitchen with clean, charcoal-free hands.

"Oh, I was just saying that I was exhausted after teaching two classes," Izzy explained. "I'm so tired, I feel almost like I've been drugged."

What? Wait, what did Izzy just say?

"I'll get you a bottle of ice water out of the garage fridge," Carlos replied. "The water in here isn't super-cold lately. Can I get you two anything while I'm out there?" he added to Kallie and Tess.

But they were oblivious, staring at each other with wide eyes.

"That's it," Kallie whispered.

"It must be. It makes perfect sense," Tess agreed, nodding.

"I'll call Morrison." Kallie pulled her phone out of her back pocket and started to dial — but then realized that everyone was staring at them. She caught Isabel's eye and quickly put the phone down on the kitchen counter. "Sorry," she laughed, embarrassed, opening the silverware drawer and taking out a handful of knives and forks.

"It can wait," Tess added. She grabbed a few potholders and a serving spoon, and carried them over to the table.

"Well *tell* us," Isabel yelped with a laugh. "You know we live vicariously through your insane crime-solving adventures, you crazy girls."

"Yeah, what did you just figure out?" Carlos

added.

"We both saw your faces light up, like you had some kind of shared epiphany. If we helped you solve a m-u-r-d-e-r," Isabel said, spelling the word so Lily wouldn't repeat it, "then you have to tell us *how*!"

"Oh, you just said you felt like you'd been drugged," Kallie started to answer as she poured a glass of milk for the toddler. "That explains how—"

"We need to start from the beginning," Tess interrupted. "And I'm about to faint from smelling this amazing dinner. Let us get the food on the table, and we'll explain it all later."

Their gracious hosts agreed, being equally hungry and also not wanting to discuss the details in front of young, sensitive ears. Tess and Kallie finished setting the table and delivering the food, and they spent half an hour eating and discussing normal, non-murder related subjects.

After the table was cleared, though, Isabel was ready to continue the conversation.

"So you were *saying*," she hinted, "about your revelation?"

"Don't you *dare* start without me," Carlos's mom insisted. "Let me get this little one to bed, since she's already up past her bedtime. But I want to hear it too."

Kallie and Tess laughed, and Isabel agreed to the conditions – so Kallie loaded the dishwasher while

Tess and Isabel talked about the aerobics studio.

"Okay, I read her a story, and I think she's asleep." Carlos's mom announced, returning to the kitchen.

"Unless she's faking it and *eavesdropping*," Carlos replied with a chuckle, looking toward the stairs, but Lily appeared to actually be asleep. It was well past her usual bedtime.

"Come into the living room and relax. What did you find?" Isabel asked.

They all sat close together, so they didn't need to talk loudly and risk waking the baby. Tess started the explanation with an apologetic tone, "We're not completely sure yet, but we met someone who said maybe—"

"Okay, we *get* it," Lily's abuela exclaimed. "You have a good hunch and some clues. Now *get to the nitty-gritty!*"

Kallie grinned at her moxie and replied, "It looks like there was a second victim."

The answer had its expected effect. Carlos, Isabel, and Mrs. Alvarez all looked completely and appropriately shocked.

"We found a witness who told us that he saw a *woman* being stabbed at Gasparilla too."

Their audience still sat in stunned silence.

"But we can't figure out how or *where* someone

could've been attacked in that huge crowd without anyone seeing it," Kallie added.

"Then Isabel said she felt like she'd been drugged," Mrs. Alvarez added quietly, nodding in understanding.

"And we thought that *might* be—"

"—How the killer caught the girl," Isabel finished her sentence. "That does make perfect sense."

Tess added, "He could've put something in her drink, since they were all outside, but—"

"Maybe he chloroformed her with a handkerchief, like in the old movies," Carlos chimed in.

"Oh man, we're *really* rubbing off on you guys," Tess laughed.

"Except we stay home, safe and sound, while you two are charging into danger. Have we mentioned that you need to be more careful?" Isabel sighed.

"Yes, and we're trying."

A voice from the stairs called, "Be more careful," and they all whipped their heads around in surprise. The toddler stood at the top of the steps, wagging a warning finger. "Careful."

"Liliana Sofia, *what* are you doing out of bed?" her grandmother asked, and then whispered, "I'll be right back."

"We're really being more sensible this time," Tess added. "We promise. Even though it doesn't seem like it right now."

"Less charging into danger and more poking danger with a long stick," Kallie added.

"Oh, that's much better," Carlos chuckled.

"Yes, and if you'd start telling that *handsome* detective about the clues you find, instead of running out to confront the killer yourselves, we'd approve much more," Isabel added.

"I told you he was handsome," Tess whispered.

"*She* knows he's handsome," Izzy added, looking quizzical. "And she's seen the way he looks at her too."

"Huh? *What* way?" Kallie asked.

"She really hasn't," Tess sighed. "But I'm working on it."

"Honestly, girl," Izzy shook her head in disbelief and dismay.

Chapter Nine

Kallie and Tess rarely went out for dinner, since they were both great cooks, but it was a beautiful evening and they were both in the mood for local seafood. They walked to a small restaurant near the beach and sat outside on the patio, grateful for the unusually warm early-February weather. After watching the sun set, they ordered dinner, laughing about two dogs chasing each other around the tables. Dog-friendly outdoor restaurants were common in the area – one of the local highlights – but Kallie and Tess were clearly both still consumed by the murder.

"So, I was thinking," Tess began as she picked at the last of her fries, dipping them in cocktail sauce, "if the killer was using the football player's murder as a distraction to get to our mystery victim – and this is still a huge 'if' – then he and Allbright must've known each other."

Kallie thought about this for a moment, but she didn't get the connection. "Why? Elijah didn't say he saw the girl *with* Allbright."

"I really don't know anything about Marcus

Allbright. I mean, I follow the Bucs but not every player, and he was here a *while* ago." Tess shrugged apologetically. "I knew his name and his criminal history, but not much else. So, I was researching him online. Kallie, he *always* travels with an entourage. In the pictures and videos I found, he had bodyguards and groupies all around him."

"Okay, sure," Kallie nodded in agreement, not yet understanding her best friend's point.

"If the killer didn't know Allbright personally, he never would've gotten within twenty feet of him."

Kallie's hand, holding a forkful of linguini with clam sauce, paused midair. "That's a good point. But if those groupies and bodyguards like him so much, why didn't anyone report him missing?" Kallie asked.

"I didn't say they *liked* him," Tess answered. She sounded flippant, but Kallie could see that the idea troubled her. "I think most of them were paid to hang around and make him look rich and popular. The bodyguards, especially."

"I'll bet those bodyguards won't be getting any new big-name clientele anytime soon," Kallie replied with a whistle. "When your client gets very publicly stabbed to death on your watch, it's probably bad for business."

"No wonder they didn't tell the police," Tess agreed. "I'll bet they were busy trying to cover their butts and salvage whatever existing business they could."

"No kidding," Kallie answered.

Missed the day in class when they explained the 'guard' part of 'bodyguard.'

"I collected all of the photos I could find online of Allbright, both here and any recent pictures from Philadelphia, and I tried to narrow it down to people who were with him more than once.

"Wow," Kallie replied. "That sounds like a lot of work. What did you find?"

"Well, it's not perfect, obviously. But we have to presume that no guy would be able to get close enough if they'd only met once."

"Right, a pretty girl might manage that, but not a guy," Kallie agreed, musing. "Unless he was a friend of Allbright's teammates, or his manager, or something. But aren't we thinking that the girl with the knife is the killer?"

"That's how I started, actually," Tess explained. "I was looking for *her* in any recent videos. I didn't get a good look at her, but she's your height and build. And string beans like you stand out in a crowd—"

"*Hey!*"

"It's good to be unique," Tess added with a grin. "But that's really not Allbright's type. There was no one fitting your description that I saw, except for the occasional fan asking for an autograph. No one who hung around enough to be a danger."

Kallie nodded, considering these new facts.

"So I started looking at the guys around him. Thinking maybe one of them hired her, or blackmailed her into it, or something. I was just following my gut. You know how that is."

Kallie nodded again. *I definitely know how that is.*

Tess pulled up a series of photos on her phone, and Kallie moved to the other side of the table to look, grabbing a fry in the meantime. Tess pointed out a few of them. "This blonde guy is there for four nights – two in Philly and two in Tampa." She swiped over and continued, "And this guy is there for three nights in Philly."

"That guy's hot," Kallie replied. Tess turned and gave her a scathing look, but Kallie held her ground. "What? Objectively. He's hot. Look at those green eyes."

Tess sighed and continued, "There are a few others, but these two seem like the most likely hangers-on who aren't involved with either of the football teams. I eliminated anyone that I could identify from the Buccaneers or Eagles websites."

"I don't recognize either of them, but that's hardly a shock," Kallie answered, squinting at the tiny pictures on Tess's phone. "I don't even know all of the current Bucs players, much less the former players or their groupies."

"Yeah, I didn't recognize them either."

"Maybe my dad could help. He and Morrison talk about football all the time."

"I don't think either of these guys is a professional football player," Tess mused. "I didn't check any other teams' websites, but they just don't have that... I don't know... swagger?"

"Well then, we just have to figure out who they are. Is there any facial recognition software online?"

"Jeez, I hope not," Tess answered with an alarmed tone. She searched quickly and sighed with relief. "Nothing publicly available. It would help us right now, but it's a scary thought."

"Maybe we could send it to the sheriff?"

Tess chuckled, "*Some* of us don't have the sheriff's personal email address, Kal."

Kallie blushed and added, "I'll talk to Morrison about it. Maybe he can check them out."

"He's going to think we're crazy."

"Oh, I'm sure he's already well past *thinking* we're crazy, Tess," Kallie laughed. "Email me those pictures and I'll ask him."

* * * * *

"Why, Kalliope Brooks," Morrison answered the phone. "This is a pleasant surprise. You almost never call me at work."

"Um," Kallie began haltingly. She'd just gotten home from the restaurant, and couldn't resist discussing Tess's idea with her detective friend. But now she wasn't sure where to start.

"Which almost surely means you've either antagonized a serial killer," Morrison continued, "or some innocent homeowner just chased you down the street with an axe to make you leave him alone."

Kallie felt vaguely persecuted but couldn't help laughing. "What, I'm not allowed to stalk the occasional murderer?"

Morrison's chair squeaked, and she heard a door close. The background noise disappeared. "As long as you're stalking them *online*, Kallie. And not trying to get yourself killed," he answered, sounding serious.

Kallie hadn't mentioned their homeless ally or the possible second victim to Morrison yet. She knew they were stretching his patience, and she didn't want to worry him.

Or make him think we're completely bonkers.

"Well, you know how Tess loves her true crime stories—"

"Oh, we're making this Tess's fault now?" Morrison stifled a laugh.

"Well, she's pretty smart," Kallie replied. She quickly stopped herself from giving up exactly *how* smart her best friend really was – a certified genius, which she didn't like others to know.

"I've noticed that," Morrison answered sincerely, but Kallie could hear the smile in his voice. "But she's also not usually the one getting into trouble."

Kallie sat down on the arm of the couch, considering exactly what to say. "We were talking about the football player that was killed."

"Kallie—"

"I mean, we were there, Morrison. I was personally involved—"

He sighed deeply. "Okay, go on."

"We were talking about the football player, and Tess looked online and saw how he's always in a big crowd of players and security and fans and stuff. And she thought that the killer might have slipped into that crowd—"

"Grayson told me his forensics team has been following that same idea, actually," he replied. "To make Allbright relaxed and get close enough for the attack."

Of course they already thought of this. They have a whole forensics team. What were we thinking?

"Oh, well, she narrowed it down to a couple of guys. I thought you might be able to identify them?"

"Their forensics department is backed up with other cases, just like ours. And this is just an abstract theory, so it'll take them another week to get back to us with their own analysis. Who did Tess find?"

"Oh, I thought because he's famous, they would—"

"We don't backburner other cases just because he's famous," Morrison replied with an exhausted sigh. He sounded like he'd already had this conversation a dozen times in the past week.

Kallie's heart relaxed a little, and she was suddenly so proud of her friend for remembering the little guy who was in line before the celebrity. "Oh. Well, you know we're glad to help. I can send you pictures of the two guys who seem most likely." She lowered her phone and quickly texted half a dozen of Tess's photos to him. "It might be nothing, but—"

"But it might not," his voice dropped a little as he held the phone away to look at her photos. "These guys both look familiar to me. They don't play for the Bucs, but I've seen them somewhere." Kallie heard him tapping on a keyboard. "This won't take a long time to check. I can have a deputy run their faces without waiting for forensics."

"Oh, okay."

"I'll let you know what we find. Are we still on for breakfast?"

"Of course! I'll see you then."

"One of the guys at work went scuba diving at Rainbow River last weekend, and he said it's great," Morrison told Kallie, when they met at their usual café. "It's spring-fed, so it's always warm, even in the winter."

"That sounds perfect," Kallie answered. "Are there manatees?"

"Lots of manatees," her friend answered, reaching for the orange marmalade. "He said it was a little crowded on the weekend, but it might be better on a weekday."

After their usual waitress, Justine, delivered their coffee and orange juice, Kallie asked what she'd been wondering all morning. "So did your deputy find anything from those pictures?"

Morrison lifted his arm theatrically to look at his watch, tapping it gently. "Seventeen minutes and forty-eight seconds."

Kallie felt her face heat up as she blushed to the roots of her auburn hair.

"No offense taken. I didn't think you'd make it that long," he added with a grin. He pushed out his chair and stood up, pulling a tablet from a messenger bag under the table, then walked over to Kallie's side. He sat down in the chair next to her, and the smell of his shampoo and aftershave engulfed her for a moment, clean and slightly wild.

What in the heck is wrong with you, Kalliope? Are you fifteen?

She bit her lower lip and tried to clear her head, as Morrison leaned over the arm of his chair so she could see the tablet screen. Their first suspect was visible, and her friend pointed at him. "This guy is Ronan Williams. You and Tess were correct in observing that he was following Allbright. He's shady and greedy – but he's a recruiter for the Green Bay Packers."

"Oh," Kallie sighed.

"He's poaching out of season, which is why he looks so guilty in this picture. That's not technically illegal, but he could get his team in trouble," Morrison explained. "There's a *very* short 'legal tampering' window when teams can try to hire a player on another team – under specific rules – but we're not in it."

"But he's football shady, not murder shady," Kallie concluded.

"I don't currently have enough information to verify that, but it appears to be the case."

Kallie nodded in disappointed agreement.

"This guy, on the other hand," Morrison continued, switching photos and pointing at the nominally hot suspect that Kallie and Tess had discussed, "has a nasty history."

"You were able to identify him?" she asked.

"Max Brockaway," Morrison replied. He swiped to a few other pictures. "Completely unrelated to sports, but the FBI has their eye on him for interstate fraud."

"Oh. Fraud?" Kallie asked, disappointed but trying not to sound like it.

"He's been loosely connected to identity theft, medical fraud, extortion, burglary, and grand theft."

"But not murder?" Kallie tried not to whine.

"Not murder. And he usually keeps enough distance from the actual crime that he can shake off every accusation. He's never been *convicted* of anything. Not even once. He's very clever." Morrison sounded annoyed about that.

"Slippery."

"Mmm," Morrison replied. "But even Al Capone went to jail for tax evasion. Sometimes you have to catch criminals where they get lazy."

"Okay," Kallie nodded. "Not ideal, but I see your point. So if he always keeps his hands clean, then maybe he hired the girl? The Killer Wench?"

Morrison shrugged noncommittally.

"His name's Max Brockaway?"

Morrison nodded, still silent but looking curious about where she was going with this.

Kallie tapped on her phone without looking up. "Tess is amazing at this kind of thing," she added, clicking send.

She turned her phone face-down on the table and smiled. "Now tell me all about these manatees."

* * * * *

When Kallie got off work that evening, the response from Tess was already waiting.

> ➤ Found some info on Brockaway. Come by when you get off work and I'll show you.

Kallie took the turn toward Tess's house and pulled into her driveway a few minutes later. Her friend had cooked a white pizza, and it was almost ready, so the house smelled amazing. Kallie sat on the couch, and Tess handed her the laptop so she could read the research details.

"This guy's a real piece of work," Tess called from the kitchen as she took the pizza out of the oven. "He's handsome and charming, and as devious as a snake. It seems like he's been exonerated from every crime *except* murder."

"You don't think he did it?"

"Well, he might be escalating, or he might've snapped. It's hard to say," Tess replied, thoughtfully. "And he definitely would've hired someone, not done it himself. But if he had some kind of personal vendetta against Allbright, I didn't find anything about it."

"Sounds like he's the *only* person who didn't have a fight with him."

"Exactly. But I didn't see any indication that they'd been lifelong friends either. So it's weird that they're so up close and personal in the photos from Philly. And this connection seems to be recent, so he was motivated by something to infiltrate the group. Money, fame, resentment, revenge—"

"Or he didn't care about Allbright at all, and he was just after the female victim?"

"If there even *was* a female victim," Tess grumbled.

"Are you starting to lose faith in that?" Kallie asked, curiously.

"It's just so strange that they haven't found her by now," Tess answered. "And no one matching her description has even been reported missing. I'm starting to think our witness might have been wrong about the whole thing. Or maybe just crazy."

"He didn't *seem* crazy..." Kallie noted.

"No, he didn't, did he?" Tess recalled, seeming to shake off her frustration a little. "Well, either way, we need to figure this out and clear your name, so let's focus on Allbright's killer for now."

"Sure. What else did you find out about this Brockaway guy?"

"He has a penchant for blondes, and the tabloids

say he has... uh, let's just say he has *fetishes*."

"Oh," Kallie answered, frowning.

"And not one, but two, of his recent blonde girlfriends have disappeared in the past two years, shortly after dating him."

"You're kidding," Kallie replied. "And no one looked for them?"

"The police looked for them, but didn't find anything. And they're grown women, so with no evidence of foul play, they had to let it go."

"Grown women are allowed to disappear, I guess," Kallie answered with a shrug. "I'd probably want to disappear if I dated a guy like that too."

"And neither of them turned up dead. So either Brockaway's innocent—"

"Or he's really good at being guilty," Kallie completed the thought. "What else did you find in his background?"

"Nothing that screams homicide, to be honest. Wait... he *did* make a bunch of money in pharmaceuticals," Tess answered.

"So that could be where he got the drugs to knock her out." Kallie nodded encouragingly.

"It's possible," Tess agreed, but with a frown. "But being a big stockholder doesn't mean you have access to a pharmacy. Not everyone who invests in Virgin Galactic has a rocket in their backyard."

"Okay, true," Kallie conceded.

"Anyway, I called his office from my desk phone, so it would show up as a law firm on their caller ID, and asked if he was still in Philadelphia."

"Oh, is he?" Kallie asked.

"Nope, his assistant said he's back here in Tampa, and she'd ask him to call me."

"The plot thickens."

"Tens of thousands of people flew into Tampa for Gasparilla, and he does have a house here – so that doesn't really prove anything. But he definitely doesn't look innocent," Tess continued, tapping one perfect fingernail on the laptop keyboard. "I'm not sure if it's just his thoroughly nasty background, but this guy bugs me. The fact that he apparently appeared from nowhere a few weeks before Allbright's murder and weaseled his way into the entourage..."

"Weaseled?" Kallie questioned with a smile.

Tess leaned back to think about her assessment. "I mean, he's rich – albeit illegally. And handsome – albeit..." she paused, looking for the right word. "Douchy. So he *could* just be doing the wealthy fanboy thing. Buying his way into the popular clique, to look cool and feel important..."

Kallie nodded, waiting while her best friend considered.

Tess leaned forward and stared at the photos,

and Kallie could tell her brilliant mind was processing all of the details. "Nah. He bugs me," Tess concluded with a frown. "Something isn't right here."

Kallie leaned over to look at the screen. "Your notes say that he likes expensive sports cars and expensive wine."

"And expensive women," Tess added with a smirk. "He loves tall, elegant blondes."

"Well, I guess we're not setting a honey trap for him, then," Kallie replied with a laugh, since she was a redhead and Tess was a brunette.

"A honey trap," Tess repeated softly, musing. Kallie could see that some clever wheels were turning in her mind. She suddenly smiled wolfishly. "We know a tall blonde who might think this is right up her alley. So to speak."

Chapter Ten

"What's he doing now?" Tess asked as blithely as possible, while she took a sip from her diet coke. The elegant restaurant's dim lighting wasn't helping their stakeout, plus her seat was facing in the wrong direction.

"He's still looking at the menu," Kallie mumbled back, fiddling with her napkin.

"I don't know why they couldn't put us in a booth, so we could both see him..."

"Nothing's ever that easy," Kallie whispered. "Oh, he just put the menu down. They're talking. I think they're going to order."

"What's Hannah doing?"

"I think she's flirting, actually."

"*What?*" Tess whispered, harshly. "No. What's she *thinking*?"

"She put down her menu, and she's... She just flipped her hair."

"Seriously? That's definitely flirting." Tess let out a barely audible whine.

"Oh my gosh, she just touched his hand," Kallie whispered in alarm.

"You're kidding," Tess replied with a grimace. "Kallie, please tell me you're kidding."

Kallie shook her head. "Nope."

"But she knows—"

"We don't really *know* anything yet. But yeah, she knows." Kallie paused for a moment, squinting, trying to stare without *staring*. "I think it's just an act."

"Are you sure?"

"No, of course I'm not sure," Kallie snapped, and then forced herself to lower her voice. "I hope it's an act."

"She's really smart. It must be an act."

Kallie nodded but didn't say anything else. To any other dinner patron, their subjects looked like a cute couple on a very lucky first date. Hannah looked lovely — Kallie had never seen her dressed up before, or even wearing makeup — and of course their suspected killer was shockingly handsome, as always.

Hannah had jumped at the chance to take part in one of their amateur investigations, and she had no hesitation about meeting Brockaway at a local wine shop – where she'd 'accidentally' bumped into him while shopping, and then casually introduced herself. When she told Kallie that he'd invited her to Rustico, the newest trendy Italian restaurant for dinner, she looked like she'd just won the Grand Slam. She wasn't worried at all, but Kallie's nerves were starting to jangle, and it seemed like Tess was feeling the same way.

With those striking good looks he could get away with murder.

Maybe literally.

Hannah laughed girlishly, and Tess gritted her teeth, visibly forcing herself not to turn around in her seat and look.

"They're both sipping their wine," Kallie continued her color commentary while looking at the menu for the twenty-fifth time. "He's not going to stab her in the restaurant, you know."

"*Probably,*" Tess scowled. "But I don't want her to lead him on. It's not safe."

"She's not going to get anything useful out of him, if she doesn't flirt a little."

Tess nodded grudgingly.

"He needs to think she's really into him. That's what he's used to — all of the girls falling for those big green eyes. He is really charming. And I *think* she's faking the flirtation, but it's pretty believable."

Their waitress came to the table and asked them if they were ready to order, putting a brief halt to their spying.

"I'd like the chicken piccata with mushrooms, please," Kallie responded with a smile. "Extra mushrooms."

"I'll try the manicotti," Tess added. "And another diet coke, please."

"Oh, another diet coke for me too, please."

I'll need to take an extra shift to pay for this, Kallie thought to herself. The restaurant was nice, but the prices made her head spin. *Eight bucks for a diet coke?*

But it'll be worth it if we catch a killer.

When the waitress turned away, Kallie's eyes immediately zipped back to the other table.

"Okay, I don't think anything has changed. Their food hasn't arrived and they're still chatting," she resumed, taking a deep breath. "She's actually batting her eyelashes at him now."

"Stop it, you're going to give me an ulcer," Tess groaned.

"Are those fake eyelashes?" Kallie pondered. Then she whispered, "Oh no—"

"What? *What?!*" Tess squeaked.

"She just picked up her purse. She must be going to the restroom."

Tess looked like she was carved out of stone, she was trying so hard not to turn around. "She can't do that. What if he drugs her wine or something?"

"And they're far enough in the shadows that he might get away with it."

Hannah, don't get up. Stay at the table.

But her friend stood up anyway, despite Kallie's effort to mentally shove her back into the chair. Kallie and Tess watched her walk away from the table like she was going on a one-way trip to Mars, leaning out to keep her in sight until she turned the corner. A moment later, Hannah was gone.

"What's Brockaway doing now?" Tess whispered.

"Nothing yet. He's taking out his phone."

Tess let out her breath. "Oh good. Maybe he'll be so distracted that he doesn't have time to touch her drink before she gets back."

"I think he's texting someone."

The seconds ticked away as they both grew more tense. "Go over there and knock her drink off the table," Tess hissed.

"*What?* I can't do that!"

"Why not?"

"First of all, it would cause a huge scene, and probably get us kicked out. And besides, he'd recognize me!"

"Shhh, people are staring at us. Maybe we should go to the restroom and talk to her."

"I'm staying right here to keep an eye on her drink," Kallie insisted. "If he slips her a roofie, she's in big trouble."

"Okay, I'm going to the restroom, then," Tess replied, biting her lower lip. "I can at least ask her if she's really flirting."

"He can't really see us over here. But if we interfere, we might spook him."

"Well, he's only seen pictures of us in our pirate costumes, right?" Tess asked.

"As far as we know. But if he suspects he's being watched, he might be watching us too."

"That's a comforting thought," Tess sighed.

"Maybe it's not even him. We really don't know anything yet, except that he likes blondes and has weird... *proclivities*."

"Is that what we're calling it?"

"For now."

"*Why* is she taking so long? I'm going to find her." Tess stood up, straightened her dress, picked up her purse, turned toward the couple's table, took one step – and then immediately backed up and plopped back down into her own seat.

"Subtle."

"She just came back," Tess whispered.

"Good," Kallie answered with a sigh.

"Nothing in her drink, right?"

"Nope. He was on his phone the whole time," Kallie answered, feeling relieved.

"So we don't have to worry about her being drugged, at least right now," Tess remarked. "But now I'm worried that he's texting an accomplice for help in abducting her."

"Great, thanks," Kallie moaned, growing worried again.

Hannah had fixed her hair, which was looking uncharacteristically glamorous. Kallie thought she'd added lipstick too. Their pretty blonde friend slipped gracefully back into her seat and said something softly to her date. He laughed and nodded, looking at her admiringly.

Like he's surveying a dessert tray. Or watching a particularly graceful deer through a rifle scope.

Hannah took a sip from her wine glass as a server arrived with their entrees. She and Brockaway both smiled graciously and thanked him as they admired their lovely plates.

"Wow, she got the calamari," Kallie whispered. "Holy cow, I hope *he's* buying."

"Shhh," Tess replied with a quiet laugh.

Brockaway put away his phone and took a bite of his dinner, and then gestured toward her plate. She nodded happily and smiled. All obvious, simple body language, discussing their food. Kallie wondered again if they had the right guy — *he seems completely normal, maybe even boring* – and then reminded herself that he wasn't going to attack his victim in the middle of the most expensive restaurant in town.

Hannah's flirting seemed to be working, though. He was getting more affectionate, touching her wrist and staring into her eyes when they spoke.

Kallie was convinced that the trap was set. Hannah was an expert at crime, and she had him hooked. If he was the killer, he'd definitely pick her for his next assault.

"We'll need to get back outside before they leave," Tess whispered, sounding tense. "I'm afraid he'll grab her in the parking lot."

"Good point. How are we going to do this? We need to keep an eye on them in here, but run interference somehow, if he tries to get her into his car."

"When they ask for their check, we'll need to split up."

"Our dinner hasn't even—" Just as Kallie spoke, the waitress arrived with their dishes.

For an expensive restaurant, the entrees weren't too stingy. And it looked delicious. Tess's manicotti was brimming over the dish, and Kallie's own chicken piccata was luscious, including a metric ton of side pasta and veggies, and they hadn't skimped on the extra mushrooms.

"I'm too on edge to be hungry," Tess complained.

"Then can I have yours?" Kallie answered with a

grin. "It smells fantastic."

Tess ate a bite and nodded with raised eyebrows. "It's good. Not as good as my Nanna's manicotti, I mean, but really good."

"Well, *obviously* not as good as Nanna's," Kallie agreed with a laugh. She'd had Tess's grandmother's cooking, and agreed that it was probably true. Her laugh cut off sharply, "Oh no, they're leaving already?"

"*What?!* They just got their dinner!" Tess hissed.

"If he's trying to get her out of here that fast, he must be shady."

"I don't care if he's a killer or just a slimeball," Tess growled softly. "Let a girl finish her dinner, dude."

"Excuse me," Kallie called gently to their waitress, who was walking past. "We have an emergency at home. Could we get these to go?"

The waitress nodded agreeably and took both plates to box them up, and Kallie felt her stomach twist with worry. Hannah was their top priority, and she whispered, "I'm going outside now, to get ahead of them."

Tess nodded, turning around to watch them, no longer pretending to be disinterested. "I need to pay for this, but I'll catch up as soon as I can."

"Okay, but get our doggie bags," Kallie added with a final look at the retreating waitress, as she dropped her napkin on the table and dashed toward the door.

* * * * *

Walk slower, Hannah, Kallie thought to herself in annoyance, as she darted awkwardly behind the next car – yet another Mercedes – while following the couple. *I'm trying to protect you, here. Slow down.*

Hannah and her creepy but very handsome date made their way across the parking lot toward her car – Kallie took a moment to be thankful that Hannah had driven by herself and met him at the restaurant. They arrived at Hannah's Jeep, cool enough to not stand out in the field of luxury cars.

Kallie couldn't hear them, but they seemed very cozy, and her stomach lurched again with worry. *Don't you dare kiss him, Hannah!*

She stifled a groan as Hannah leaned in for an unnecessarily romantic kiss. *You're killing me, girl. Get in the Jeep.*

Brockaway reached behind his back as the lovely, seemingly-enamored couple chatted in the dimming evening light, and Kallie tensed, preparing to spring. *Hannah, run! Go, he has a gun! He has a knife. He has a—*

Laughing, Kallie's criminal quarry looked at the phone in his hand, and Hannah laughed too. Some

145

quiet joke between lovebirds. A song or a previous text. Her friend smiled up into the suspect's eyes and Kallie gritted her teeth.

Hannah reached into her very expensive purse – an embarrassing gift from Kallie's ostentatious mother, which Hannah had borrowed for the mission — and took out her keys. Kallie took a breath, for the first time in what felt like an hour.

She watched as they kissed again, and then Hannah pushed him away coyly, with a smile. Tess suddenly, finally, ran up and crouched next to Kallie, receipt still in hand.

"What did I miss?"

"She's leaving," Kallie breathed, grabbing Tess's hand without looking away. "I think she's leaving."

Hannah kissed him one more time, and then climbed into her Jeep and closed the door.

"Now we just need to make sure he doesn't follow her home," Tess whispered, as they heard the Jeep's engine start. She took a deep breath and suddenly leapt to her feet, taking off at a full run across the parking lot as Kallie was left in shock. "Please, help me!" Tess yelled, desperately.

Brockaway was knocked back a step as Tess ran into him, but he caught her deftly. His face registered concern, Kallie noticed. "Sure, what is it?" He stepped forward protectively and looked around, apparently expecting someone to be following her.

"Someone tried to rob me when I came out of the restaurant," Tess gasped, by all appearances terrified and out of breath. "I kicked him and ran away, but he started chasing me."

Kallie watched with relief as Hannah's Jeep made the turn out of the parking lot and into traffic.

"I don't see anyone," Brockaway replied to Tess. Then he added with a smile, "You must've scared him off."

"I think it was *you* who scared him off," Tess laughed tearfully. "Thank goodness you were here. You're a lot more intimidating than I am."

Kallie knew Tess could easily hold her own in a butt-kicking contest, and briefly considered nominating her best friend for an Academy Award.

"Let me walk you to your car and make sure no one's following you," he added. Kallie's nerves stood on end, but his demeanor was completely different with Tess.

This guy must seriously love tall blondes. I've never seen anyone so immune to Tess's feminine wiles. And I've never been so glad.

He walked Tess to her car and looked around cautiously as she unlocked it. "You should file a police report," he added. "I'm sure they have security cameras – maybe they can catch the guy."

Don't we know it? Kallie thought to herself with an exhausted sigh. *A million cameras everywhere, and it might just be your downfall, creep.*

Tess thanked him again and got into her car and locked the doors. When he turned back to his own car, she made eye contact with Kallie and pointed toward the opposite corner of the parking lot.

Kallie watched as she pulled out into traffic, giving Brockaway another grateful wave as she drove past him. When he got into his car, she finally stood up and walked in the opposite direction. She only stood on the sidewalk at the corner for a few minutes before Tess pulled up to retrieve her.

"Did Hannah get away?" she immediately asked when Kallie sat down in the passenger seat.

"Yep. Clean escape."

Tess exhaled thankfully and slumped back in the driver's seat.

"I can't wait to tell her how you ran interference for her," Kallie chuckled. "She'll love it. I'm sure she'll *say* you were overreacting, but I bet she'll recruit you as a writer for her blog. And buy you a pony."

"She can keep the writing gig. I don't have time, and she's better at it than I would be." Tess answered with a smile. "But I've always wanted a pony."

Kallie laughed and then added, "Make a left here, and let's go back to Rustico. I'm starving and I want my chicken piccata."

* * * * *

The smell of leftovers in the microwave wafted across Tess's kitchen, as Kallie re-read her notes on the case the next morning. "Is that your manicotti from the restaurant? It smells amazing."

The waitress had packaged up their dinners beautifully and had them ready when Kallie ran back inside.

"Doesn't it? Yours is in the fridge."

"I'm not sure how it will reheat," Kallie noted as she pulled open the refrigerator door, "But thanks for trying. It still smells good." She sniffed the cold, very expensive chicken piccata that had eluded her the night before.

"Don't microwave it, or it will get rubbery. You need to bake it," Tess insisted, pushing a few buttons to turn on the oven. Then she leaned back against the counter and crossed her arms with an exasperated sigh. "What did we miss, Kal? I was *sure* he was going to grab Hannah. Or at least try."

"I thought so too," Kallie answered, looking at her notes and shaking her head. "Maybe the restaurant was just too public? Maybe he was setting her up for a second date somewhere private? Or maybe you really did stop him from following her home?"

"Maybe. Did you talk to Hannah?" Tess asked. "Did he ask her out for another date? Maybe he'll invite her over to his house."

"I texted her, but she hasn't responded." Kallie added quickly, "But she posted on her blog this morning, so she's not dead or anything."

Tess snorted a laugh. "I think you can auto-post a blog entry that you've pre-written, but we'll take that as proof-of-life for now."

"She takes even better notes than I do, so she's probably working on the book while it's all still fresh in her mind," Kallie explained.

"If this works out, she'll probably get a Pulitzer Prize."

"As long as he doesn't kill her first. I know she thinks it's worth the risk, but I still wish she wasn't flirting quite so hard with him last night."

"She's luring him into her web, my dear," Tess replied with a sinister grin.

"She's not that cocky. Looking back on it today, I think she was just encouraging him to talk, not planning to spring a trap."

"Still, she did great."

"She really did," Kallie agreed. "He was totally intrigued by her. I'm so used to her no-nonsense crime side – ponytail and glasses – I would never have imagined that glamorous, sexy woman was hiding in there. She deserves an Oscar, if she doesn't get the Pulitzer."

"No kidding. But that's enough sleuthing for now. I have to leave for work soon, and so do you," Tess reminded her. "I'm taking a shower. Finish cooking your chicken and text me if Hannah contacts you."

"Okay," Kallie answered, checking on her chicken. "And I'll call her, if she doesn't text me back before I get to work. I don't want to be worried all day."

And I don't want to track all over town to make sure she wasn't murdered. Come on, girlfriend. Just a quick text.

"I'm sure they have another date," Kallie added out loud. "I just hope she doesn't go to his house."

"She's not stupid," Tess replied, sounding reassuring.

"No, but she's very, very driven. And I know she wants that story. I just hope she doesn't put herself in danger to get it."

"Well, she already has, technically. And she knows his type – she'll be careful."

"If he's the killer, he might have a torture room somewhere," Kallie mumbled, starting to worry again. "Probably in his house."

"That's a cheerful thought," Tess replied, with an arched eyebrow. "But she knows that too. Psycho killers are *literally* her business."

"True. That actually makes me feel better, for some reason."

"Good. I'm showering before I'm late. Winchester needs me to be on New Orleans time with him, for the rest of his trip, so I'll be working earlier hours," Tess explained. "He's interviewing a retired police officer this afternoon, and I need to be on the call."

"Go, I'm fine. My chicken's done, and I'll be gone and locked up by the time you're dressed. I'll text you later."

"Give your dad a hug from me, and tell him we're taking him to dinner in Ybor next weekend," Tess added.

"He'll love that."

Tess turned and disappeared back into the hallway for her shower, and Kallie opened the drawer for silverware. The chicken piccata was as delicious as it smelled.

It should be, for that price.

The pasta, potatoes, and vegetables on the side were also surprisingly good.

No wonder it's expensive, if they can even make cooked carrots taste good.

Wishing they could stay home and keep investigating this guy all day, Kallie finished her late breakfast and put her plate in the dishwasher with a sigh.

As she was making the short drive to the Lazy

Gecko for her shift, her phone finally dinged, showing Hannah's number.

Kallie read the text when she pulled into the parking lot, and immediately called her friend back. "You had us scared to death, girl. What happened?"

"Oh, Kallie," Hannah gushed. "He was *dreamy!*"

Kallie held the phone away from her ear and stared at it like it'd turned into a cobra. "Hannah, tell me you're kidding."

Her friend laughed. "Of course I'm kidding. Now the calamari, on the other hand? That really *was* dreamy." She sighed and added, "I wish I could go back there, without taking out a second mortgage."

"What happened?" Kallie asked. "I'm relieved that you're still alive, but what did you manage to get out of him?"

"Well, he's a total narcissist, but that's probably not a shock. I didn't even need to grill him for an alibi, he talked about his latest three-week trip to Sweden for most of the night."

"We knew he liked blondes," Kallie laughed, jadedly. "Of course he would go to the source. I presume he just got back?"

"Yep, and he showed me a dozen photos. He wasn't even in the country during the parade. Looks like a solid alibi," Hannah replied. "Sorry, Kallie."

"I can't believe you kissed him. I just about had a heart attack."

"Well, he *is* hot, sugar," Hannah answered. "I pretended I was seducing a dangerous spy." She made kissy noises into the phone, and Kallie laughed out loud. "Hey, I wanted to talk to you about something else. Have you seen these posts about you on social media?"

"About me?" Kallie asked, surprised.

"Yeah, it has me a little worried. I mean, social media is cruel, even at the best of times, but there's a group out there who really think you killed that girl."

Kallie groaned. "We met a couple of them in person. What's *wrong* with people?"

"I have to go, but I'll send some screenshots to you and Tess. Maybe you can get your cop friend to do some damage control."

"I'm not sure I want to see it, but thanks for letting me know. And I'm glad you're safe." Kallie hung up and immediately texted Tess with all the details.

"Back to the drawing board," she mumbled, as she walked into the Lazy Gecko to start her shift.

Chapter Eleven

"We're running out of ideas," Tess sighed. It was Saturday, and she didn't have to work, so she made breakfast for them. After a feast of homemade breakfast burritos, though, they'd returned to their frustrating search.

Kallie grunted in annoyance, flipping to the next page of her notes.

"I was sure it was Brockaway," Tess grumbled.

Kallie nodded. "Me too. Believe me, I was ready to crack him over the head with a brick when he was in the parking lot with Hannah."

"But it's not. He's just a run-of-the-mill slimeball," Tess added. "Unless... do you think he could've hired the Killer Wench from Sweden?"

"I doubt it," Kallie answered. "The sheriff said Allbright just got here that Thursday, and it sounds like it was a last-minute decision."

"I don't have any other suspects."

"Me neither," Kallie replied sulkily. "Allbright's girlfriend was in Philly, and she isn't seeing anyone else.

The guy from the earlier fistfight was already in jail."

"Maybe it was someone who didn't even know Allbright—"

"It's starting to look that way," Kallie groaned, feeling dejected.

"Which only leaves us with half a million people," Tess continued, "We need to narrow that down a little before we can even speculate about a motive." She sighed and went back to reading from her laptop, but looked up a few minutes later and added, "Hey, I was thinking..."

Kallie lowered her notes, suspicious but hopeful.

Tess pursed her lips in hesitation. "What do you think about hiring a private investigator?"

Kallie laughed out loud. "A *private investigator*? Tess, I'm still making monthly payments on that chicken piccata!"

Tess laughed too but stayed on the subject. "I don't think they're that expensive, are they? Winchester told me he had to hire one for the case he's working on in New Orleans, and it got me thinking."

"Well, sure. He's got an expense account, and he'll get paid by his client in the end. Nobody's going to pay us."

Tess looked crestfallen. "That's true. I guess it was a silly idea. I just don't want anyone to still be thinking you were involved in this murder, Kal. I hate the way those ladies looked at you, when they recognized you from the news."

Kallie watched Tess, looking so defeated, and she gave in. "Fine. I'm sure we can't afford it, but I'll see what I can find. Maybe Morrison will know someone who works cheap."

"Really?" Tess asked with a half-smile.

"I'm pretty sure they charge hundreds of dollars an hour. But maybe we'll find someone who's building his resume," Kallie agreed with a smirk. "Is there a private investigator school? Maybe we can find a dropout."

"He doesn't even need to *find* the killer," Tess sighed. "As long as he finds us any new lead. Or just a clue. At this point, I'd take a fingerprint."

"Okay, I'll see what I can dig up," Kallie answered, thinking. "Maybe I can find someone in the classified section of the newspaper or something. Thank you for being worried about my reputation," she added with a small smile.

"Well, you know, it'd look bad for me to be hanging out with a psycho killer," Tess added, teasingly.

"Of course. We can't have *that*."

"And who would eat chocolate-covered beef jerky with me? And blue dinosaur ice cream, and watermelon with Tajín?" Tess asked, faking dismay at the thought.

"Now you're making me hungry," Kallie replied with a smile. "Do they sell fresh watermelon in February?"

"I'm pretty sure I saw some in Publix last week, pre-chopped."

"Awesome, and I've got a bottle of Tajín at home. Let's go."

* * * * *

Barry sat in his usual corner of the Lazy Gecko, writing in his trusty notebook and occasionally taking a bite of his chicken nachos or a sip of his beer.

At least one thing never changed. Kallie smiled in his direction, but he never looked up from his writing. She wondered if he was still writing his book about all of the Lazy Gecko inhabitants, and figured he must be. *Surely he would've told us, if it was done.*

She delivered a pitcher of beer and a round of drinks to two tables in her section, and stopped by his table — his office, as she'd come to think of it — to check on him.

"Can I get you anything, Barry? Another beer?"

"What?" he looked up, not exactly startled, but definitely distracted. "Oh, hi Miss Kallie. Sure, I'd love another beer. Thanks for thinking of me."

She checked on another table — everyone was

very relaxed for a Tuesday afternoon, and no one seemed to be in a hurry to get their check and run back to work.

Her favorite kind of Tuesday.

Kallie poured a draft beer for Barry and carried it back to his table. This time he looked up. "Thanks, Kallie." She almost asked about his book, but decided she didn't want to know how she looked in his world, so she returned to the bar.

There were still a lot of tourists in town for Gasparilla season, she noticed. Even though the largest parade was over, there were still a lot of events planned in the next month – dozens of parties and huge charity events, plus a fifteen-kilometer race and a music festival. Add to that the State Fair, the huge Strawberry Festival in Plant City, and football and ice hockey – plus the beautiful weather, and this was the busiest tourist season of the year in the Tampa Bay area.

They weren't all staying in Owhiro, of course. Her hometown was still a quiet little seaside retreat, missed by most of the tourists, but some of them came to Owhiro just for that very atmosphere.

As if on cue, a couple of obvious tourists entered Kallie's section of the Lazy Gecko and sat down at the bar. She gave them a few minutes to look around and check out the drink menu.

"Hi folks, what can I get you?" she asked cheerfully.

"I'll just have a beer, please," the husband answered. "But my wife wants to try one of these pirate drinks."

Kallie smiled. She'd been tending bar for years, and this was a common request during Gasparilla, even from some locals. "The historians say most pirates drank rum mixed with citrus, to keep from getting scurvy—"

"*Arrr, scurvy,*" the husband responded with a growl, earning an elbow jab from his wife.

"Go on, dear," the wife added to Kallie, rolling her eyes at her husband's silliness.

"Straight rum and lime juice isn't a big seller," Kallie continued with a smile, "but it's thought to be the origin of the modern-day daiquiri. A Mai Tai and a Rum Runner are also mostly rum, but they're a little stronger than a daiquiri. Those are both very popular around the festival, but they're not historically pirate drinks."

"What's the traditional drink for this festival?" she asked. "What do the locals drink?"

"There's a drink called Milk Punch, which is popular with the parade Krewes, and it's served at most of the parties around the parade."

"Milk Punch?" the husband asked, raising an eyebrow. "That sounds repulsive."

Kallie laughed. "It's better than it sounds. It's not fruit punch with milk poured in it, I promise. It's made with brandy and milk, and ours has vanilla and fresh nutmeg, and just a touch of cinnamon, so it's a little like a Brandy Alexander."

"That sounds really good," the wife replied, sounding surprised.

"You definitely wouldn't want to drink it in July," Kallie added with a smile. "But it's perfect for our mild winters."

"I'll take one of those," the wife answered, nodding.

"You actually almost sold *me* on it," the husband added. "I'll stick with my beer, but I'll try a sip of hers."

"If I let you," she smiled.

Most of the local Gasparilla events had Milk Punch in giant vats, which reminded Kallie of a college party's notorious 'Hunch Punch' garbage cans, to serve hundreds of people quickly, but the Lazy Gecko didn't need to work in huge volumes. Kallie served the husband's beer, and then returned to make the wife's drink.

The unusual drinks were her favorites – the cool, retro Harvey Wallbangers and Blue Hawaiis and Old Fashioneds, delicately layered shots that relied on specific gravities – the ones that made Kallie feel like a mad scientist brewing over a beaker that might explode. She served a lot of beer and wine, and simple two-part cocktails like scotch and soda, rum and coke, gin and tonic – and they had their merits. But she liked a drink with personality.

Not when they were *busy*, of course. If someone ordered a Long Island Iced Tea at eleven o'clock on a Saturday night, she'd be cursing them for hours. But on a boring Tuesday afternoon?

Give me a challenge!

Milk Punch certainly wasn't as perfectly balanced as a great martini, or as temperamental as a B-52, but as a Tampa Bay native, Kallie loved Gasparilla and was happy to acclimate a tourist to their customs – especially one this delicious. She pulled out the brandy and whole milk, the cinnamon-flavored simple syrup, and a small container of fresh nutmeg that she kept in the bar fridge just for Christmas and Gasparilla.

She mixed the drink as she continued chatting with the couple, asking where they were from (Ohio), if this was their first visit (yes, but not their last!), and which attractions they'd visited (Busch Gardens and Sunken Gardens so far, but they wanted to see the manatees).

Then she served the drink, anticipating that the husband would want one in five minutes. *Maybe I should mix up a larger batch*, she considered. *If anyone else asks what they're drinking, then I'll definitely make a pitcher.*

She made the rounds to the tables in her section, who mostly wanted beer, and quickly served them. As she returned to the counter, Carlos walked up and put his elbows on the bar.

"Hey, you," she chirped happily. "Now that we're working together again, I never see you anymore."

She knew that was because she was reliable and had friendly, even-tempered regulars on the day shift. But it still made her a little sad. She missed the old nights when they wrangled crazy twenty-somethings and shouted over the loud music until they were hoarse. But only a little.

"I got a call on the office phone for you. He didn't want to wait for me to get you, so he left a message," Carlos told her, handing over a pink note slip.

"A call for me?" Kallie asked, making a quizzical face. Tess and her dad knew she couldn't take calls during her shift, and if it was an emergency, Marcy or Carlos would have run out to grab her. *Who else would call me here?*

Kallie read the note, and her brow furrowed in confusion. "'You can stop looking now,'" she read out loud. She flipped over the paper, but the back was blank. "This was the whole message?"

"That's what he said," Carlos replied with a nod. "I figured you'd know what it meant."

Kallie smiled crookedly and shook her head, looking at the note again. "No idea. Are you sure it was meant for me?"

"He said your name, Kal," Carlos answered. "Actually, he called you Kalliope."

Kallie felt her heart jump a little but wasn't sure

163

why. Instinct? Intuition? Too many buffalo wings during her lunch break?

"Nobody really calls me that, Carlos. Are you sure?" She asked. After a moment's thought, she added, "Was it Morrison? He sometimes—"

"Kal, I *know* Detective Morrison, remember?" Carlos had met Morrison at the same time Kallie met him, at this very bar a few years earlier, when he was interviewing them both after a murder. "I would've told you if it was him. I didn't recognize this guy's voice."

The beginnings of icy fingers were starting to crawl up Kallie's spine, but she still wasn't sure why – and it annoyed her. She picked up a coaster and tapped it on the bar, thinking, then looked up at Carlos. "Stop looking?"

Carlos was a very calm, stoic person, yet she could see that he was a tiny bit alarmed too. "I thought it must be the guy who asked you to make him a perfect Mai Tai," he added.

"Oh, sure," Kallie answered after a moment's thought. She laughed at herself and nodded. "*Sure*, that's probably right. Maybe he found someone else in town with the old recipe, and they got the reward."

"Do you think that's it?" Carlos asked apprehensively. "Because it suddenly seems..."

Kallie nodded. "Sure. I think we're both a little on edge—"

"You *think*?" Carlos replied with a jagged laugh.

"But that makes much more sense than some random, murderous stalker calling me at work, when we can easily have his phone number traced—"

"And I was *just* going to write that down," Carlos answered, hurrying back to the office to copy the caller's phone number. "Just in case!" he yelled back to Kallie.

Chapter Twelve

Kallie was still a little disappointed about the call at work, when she got home. She'd really hoped to get that reward, but she remembered her promise to Tess about looking for a cut-rate private investigator. She wasn't expecting much, but she sat down at her laptop with a bowl of pretzels and a diet coke, ready to give it a try.

After checking the daily newspapers from Tampa and St Petersburg, two job websites, and a confusing and drawn-out web search, Kallie never found a private investigator who would work for less than a hundred dollars an hour.

They must have rich clients, Kallie thought. *We could barely afford to hire them for one hour. And they couldn't even write up our contract in that much time.*

She gave up, resigned to tell Tess that it wasn't possible. If there was anyone out there who worked cheap, they probably couldn't afford to advertise on the internet. That was just a matter of conflicting resources – and she wouldn't know where to even start looking, offline.

Would a P.I. leave his business card tacked to the notice board at Publix? Probably not.

Kallie was about to close the laptop and start fixing dinner, when she remembered that she'd told her dad that she'd look for a tripod for his old camera. She wasn't sure he'd be able to find any actual, old-fashioned film anywhere, but finding a used stand should be pretty easy.

She opened her browser again and navigated to Bob's List, which she considered the want ads section of the internet. She rarely used it unless she was looking for something retro and inexpensive, like her vintage dresses or vinyl records for Anna's dance classes.

She was scrolling down to the Products and Services section marked "Photography," and trying not to get absorbed by other sections as they swept past — she really needed to start dinner — when she saw it.

The "Private Investigators" section.

Seriously? On Bob's List?

She would never have thought to look here. But, if ever there was going to be a P.I. who worked for peanuts, this would surely be the place to find him.

She right clicked the "Photography" link to open it in a new tab, so she wouldn't forget her initial intention after this distraction, and then hesitantly clicked the "Private Investigators" link.

I'm only looking for five minutes. Seriously.

But there it was, right at the top.

"Husband cheating? Employees using drugs? Need an affordable way to find out?"

Affordable?

Holding her breath, Kallie clicked the link.

Reggie T. Cornwallis, Private Investigator. Three stars, no credentials. Twenty bucks an hour, plus costs.

Sold!

Kallie immediately texted Tess at work, hoping to catch her before she left for the day. "Found an affordable investigator online. Could you ask Winchester if he's heard of Reggie Cornwallis?"

Tess simply texted back, "ok," so she must be busy. Kallie knew she was working on an important case, so she didn't expect to hear back until Tess got home around eight o'clock. She finally closed the laptop and set it on the dining room sideboard, then walked to the kitchen. After some consideration, she took a few potatoes out of a basket in the pantry.

"Whatcha fixin', kiddo?" her dad asked, walking into the kitchen a few minutes later. "Can I help?"

"I put a roast in the slow cooker this morning, but I was going to fix French fries to go with it. Can you scrub the potatoes?"

"Yum, you bet." They both liked fries with the skins left on, so Benny started scrubbing the potatoes to get any dirt and eyes off.

I'll find that tripod later, she reminded herself, glad she'd left the new tab open.

* * * * *

"So, getting into more trouble this weekend? Stalking anyone I know?" Morrison asked over their early breakfast the next morning.

The latest cold snap had passed, so they were sitting outside – but February in central Florida is still February, after all, and they were both wearing jackets and sitting in a sunny spot. Morrison took a bracing swig of his hot coffee and smiled.

"But my intuition is always right, Morrison," Kallie sighed. "I just *knew* it was Brockaway."

Her friend looked at her quizzically. "Your intuition is *never* right, Kallie."

"Are you kidding? I figured out the Owhiro Murder!"

"After about twenty other guesses," Morrison replied, looking slightly exasperated at the memory. "And you stalked so many innocent people, you're lucky you didn't get sued. Or shot."

Kallie blushed. "Okay, well it's not *always* wrong."

"Fine, I will accept that your intuition is

sometimes right eventually," he conceded, diplomatically. But he rolled his eyes.

"Anyway, I was really *sure* this time. I just—"

Justine brought their breakfast and placed it on the sunny, outdoor table. Morrison ordered the same thing — bacon, homestyle potatoes, and toast — almost every time they ate at the little cafe. Kallie had her favorites, but she always seemed to make slight variations.

"You know you're a regular when the waitress just says, 'The Usual?'" Morrison joked, after Justine walked back inside.

"Nobody ever says that to me," Kallie responded, seeming a little dejected.

"She could probably guess by now," Morrison told her. "If she guessed blueberry pancakes, she'd be right about half the time."

"My mother tells me I'm fickle," Kallie sighed.

"*What?!*" Morrison responded, leaning forward. He seemed to sense her discomfort. "Kallie, no. You're not fickle at all, you're just... *variable.*"

"That's the same thing," she pouted.

"No, it's not. Because you're only variable about *food.*" He smiled and added, "And occasionally murder suspects." She poked her hash browns sadly and didn't look up, so he continued, seriously, "Fickle implies a lack of concern for others' feelings. The blueberry pancakes are *not* going to be depressed if you order a waffle."

"Are you sure?"

He paused and considered it. Finally, he gestured with a crispy strip of bacon to emphasize his conclusion, "If the blueberry pancakes become sentient, we have a bigger problem. So I'm going with yes, I'm sure."

Kallie still looked a little sad, but she answered, trying to smile, "I will accept that determination, minus the self-aware pancakes."

"But you're not remotely fickle about your friends and family," Morrison added, bending down to look into her lowered face. "You're the most steadfast, supportive person I've ever met."

Her green eyes got all shiny for a second and he laughed, and added, "Don't you dare start crying. Eat your waffle before it starts attracting bees."

"That's the nicest thing anyone's said about me in ages," she whispered, cracking a smile but still tearing up even more.

"I can go back to criticizing your intuition, if it will make you stop crying," he joked.

"My intuition works perfectly," she laughed, cutting a chunk out of her strawberry-laden waffle, as advised. "It's just a little *delayed* sometimes."

"And it makes some terrible choices along the

way."

"Oh! Speaking of bad decisions," Kallie suddenly remembered what she wanted to ask him, "Have you ever heard of a private detective named Cornwallis?"

"Like the British General?"

"You're killing me today, Morrison. The British General?"

"War of Independence," he added, waving it off. "I've never heard of a P.I. named Cornwallis, I don't think. Why?"

Suddenly, telling Morrison about their idea seemed like a questionable choice. He'd just tell them to mind their own business, and stop nosing around. Probably also say it was foolish and dangerous.

Kallie poked at her waffle while she quickly, furiously considered whether to spill the beans or not. *Should I admit our plans or—*

"You're thinking about hiring him, aren't you?"

Dang it!

"How do you *do* that? Are you reading my mind?"

Morrison smiled. "I just think to myself, 'If I were trying to poke my nose into the most insane, foolhardy, dangerous situation in town, what would I do?' And that's usually what you're planning."

"It's not *that* dangerous," she pouted.

"You're so predictable," he laughed.

"It's safer to hire someone than to do it ourselves," Kallie added, stabbing at her waffle this time, disappointed.

"It's *definitely* safer than doing it yourselves, which is why I'm not yelling at you right now. So how did you pick this Cornwallis guy?"

"He was—"

"The cheapest," Morrison finished the sentence for her. "That was a dumb question. So does he have any references or anything?"

"Not really," Kallie mumbled.

"Okay, but please let me check into him before you give him any money—" Kallie started to interrupt, but he continued, "Just to make sure he's not a scam artist."

She nodded grumpily in agreement, but it really didn't sound like a bad idea.

"If he's just inept, I have no problem with you wasting your money. But I'm not going to let him rob you blind."

"Okay," she acquiesced with a sigh. "Thank you."

"I know you and Tess are going to keep gnawing on this like a rawhide bone. And since I *also* know I can't stop it, I'd much rather have this guy poking around in downtown Tampa, looking for a killer, instead of you."

Kallie nodded, still waiting for the other shoe to drop.

"I know you think this is all a game, but if you hire this P.I. and he somehow manages to find something useful, you go to the *sheriff* with it. Promise me you won't do anything dangerous."

"We'll try. But the sheriff isn't going to take my call if we find something. He doesn't even know me."

"He does now," Morrison replied with a chuckle. "I've known the sheriff since he was a beat cop, and he'll remember you. But you're right, he won't know it's you calling. I can put you in touch with him if necessary."

"Really?"

"We'll worry about that when it happens. But if you get into trouble, you call 9-1-1 first. Not me."

Kallie nodded again. He was making sense, but she could tell he didn't believe they'd find anything.

"No trespassing. No confronting crazy people. And for right now, please just sit tight for another day, and let me do a background check on your *alleged* private eye."

"Fine, but we can't afford anyone else."

"Then I guess we'll both have to hope he's legit, won't we?" His voice sounded firm, but he gave her a concerned look that only lasted a moment, then he added, "Or whatever passes for 'legit' when you get your

P.I. license off the back of a cereal box."

"Okay, okay. We'll wait," she agreed. Then she tilted her head and added hopefully, "You know, you could help us, if you don't want us hiring some stranger."

"Not my jurisdiction, I'm afraid. I'd get in trouble with the Tampa cops. But I'm fine with reviewing whatever you find. As long as you do it safely."

"You'd help us?"

"If the Tampa cops crowd the killer out, Pinellas County is the first place he'll go. I want him caught and off the streets before he can mess up *my* day, too," he answered with a nod. "Besides, I want to clear your name too. We all know you weren't involved, but that arrest is going to hang over you until the case is solved."

"Tess keeps saying that too. But I don't feel like a criminal. No one's watching me anymore."

No one except some crazy people who spend too much time on the internet, anyway.

"That's because you haven't tried to buy a plane ticket. Or renew your passport. Or buy a car. One day, when state or national security's involved, and you've forgotten all about it, then it'll come back to bite you."

"Great."

"But for now, don't worry," he reassured her. "Your waffle is going to be all soggy now. Do you want my toast?"

She poked the waffle one last time and saw that he was right. The strawberry syrup had soaked into it like a sponge. "Gross," she sighed, and reached over to grab a toast triangle and the pot of marmalade. "Thanks."

Chapter Thirteen

Kallie and Tess decided to meet the private investigator before they made an official move to hire him, and he agreed on an appointment at noon on Friday – but the first interview didn't go *exactly* as Kallie had hoped.

"I'll be honest with you," he confessed, "I'm not the world's best private eye."

Kallie groaned quietly and slumped back in the rotting old chair in his office. The chair groaned back, a little louder.

Great start, Sherlock.

"You don't say!" Tess replied cheerfully, sarcasm dripping from every word.

"But I work cheap," he finished, flourishing a little sarcasm himself, which seemed to impress Tess. "And I don't need a notebook full of clues to know that's why you hired me."

"Did we?" Tess asked hesitantly, looking at Kallie. "Did we hire him?"

"We discussed it," Kallie clarified. "Money hasn't changed hands yet."

The office was depressingly dark, lit only by a desk lamp with what appeared to be a 20-watt bulb. Every time Cornwallis moved, a cloud of dust sprang from his chair, dimming the air more and more. Kallie was fighting a sneeze, and she thought she saw a family of spiders hunkered down in the bookshelf.

"But you're here," he added with a seemingly genuine smile. "So let me convince you."

"Could we go outside?" Tess asked, stifling a cough. "It's a little... oppressive in here."

Kallie was always surprised at her best friend's way with diplomacy. For someone so naturally sarcastic, she never intentionally hurt anyone's feelings. Unless they *deserved* it – in which case, she'd eviscerate them.

I couldn't have been that kind, Kallie thought to herself. *This place is ripe.*

"Sure, sure," he replied, pronouncing the word with two syllables. *Shoo-ah, shoo-ah.* "There's a bench in the courtyard outside." He opened the dingy office door, yanking it when it stuck, and led them back to the stairwell.

Kallie and Tess followed him back down the three flights of stairs, and they found that there was another door in the back of the building. The room smelled like rotten cabbage soup, and Kallie held her breath until Cornwallis managed to force this door open, too.

Calling the outdoor space a courtyard was a grave exaggeration. The door opened onto a small, square space with a black metal bench, mostly held together with rust, and a derelict trash can. The rest of the space was weedy dirt, filled with an array of old soda cans and chip bags which apparently missed the antique trash can.

Cornwallis steered them to the bench, which turned out to be just as uncomfortable as it looked. Kallie wondered absently when she'd had her last tetanus shot.

She looked around for an exit, in case they needed to make a run for it, but there was no door to the outside. The courtyard was completely surrounded by the exterior walls of buildings. If their prospective P.I. became a problem, they'd have to go back the way they came. Or try the matching door on the other side.

That door might go anywhere. Escape? Maybe. Grandmother's kitchen? Basement dungeon? Purgatory?

"You were going to convince us to hire you, Reggie?" Tess reminded him, politely.

The investigator turned toward Tess and raised one eyebrow.

Okay, so not 'Reggie.'

Tess blushed uncharacteristically, and corrected herself, "Cornwallis."

Wow, she must really want to hire someone,

Kallie thought. *If she's still talking to this wackadoodle.*

"My father was a cop," the P.I. began, abruptly. "Wanted me to be one too, but I couldn't bear to think of it. No money, and 110% stress. Plus, I didn't want to turn out like him." He paused, seemingly considering the memory, then he shrugged. "But I learned enough from him to be useful."

Tess nodded, silently, still listening.

"After he died, a friend of his called me and asked for help with one of his old cases. Off the books."

"Is that even legal?" Tess asked.

"Sure, I didn't have the old police files, and neither did he. We started from scratch. And it was just an old theft case. He told me the details, and I found the stolen item. It was in a pawn shop in North Tampa, simple as that."

Semple as dat – Kallie couldn't place his accent. *Northeastern, but not New York. Massachusetts or Maine, and something else. Irish? Swedish? Welsh?*

"Never found the thief, but he didn't care." Cornwallis kicked at a clump of weeds and paused for a minute. "I was working as a mechanic in an old body shop, barely making my rent every month. I'd never wanted to do that kind of work, my father's work — but by the time that first case was solved, I had the bug for it. Well and good."

"Your rates don't sound like they could pay the rent either," Tess interjected.

"That guy paid me well. The next few cases paid well, too. But you need a reputation in this business, and I didn't have one. The money dried up, and I told myself I'd quit and go back to fixing cars."

"But you didn't?" Kallie asked, finding her interest piqued after all.

"Nah. I liked it. After all those years of thinking my old man was crazy, I finally got why he did it."

"All this background information is poignant, I guess," Tess managed to say it rather nicely, even though she was apparently getting discouraged. "But if we're going to hire you, we need evidence that you have some skill."

"Sure. I mostly do tails and photography, just because that's what people *need* the most. Cheating spouses, addict spouses, addict employees. Addict kids. I can't even tell you how many drug deals and horse races I've photographed."

"Okay, that's within the realm of what we need," Tess agreed, sounding relieved. "Go on."

"I found a missing kid once. Kidnapped from daycare by her dad and carried off to Oklahoma."

"*What?!* Isn't that a job for the police?" Kallie sputtered.

"The FBI, actually," Tess corrected.

"That's what I said, too," Cornwallis agreed, with an appreciative nod at Tess. "The mom was my sister's best friend from high school. Afraid to go to the police because the kid's dad was a psycho. She was convinced that he'd kill her daughter if he saw any cops. That case was a little different. But I checked the custody records myself. And I found the mom's hospital records, too, where he'd almost killed her once before. Six broken ribs, fractured arm, and a busted eye socket."

"Wow," Kallie breathed.

"I did that case for free, but that ain't normal. It was a special case, like I said."

"We're not asking you to work for free," Tess added, quietly.

"It might be dangerous though," Kallie added.

"They're all dangerous," he laughed, jaggedly. "I had a little old granny swing a tire iron at me, when she caught me watching her buy meth. Woulda busted my head open if I hadn't seen it coming. You never know who the crazy ones are gonna be."

Kallie looked at Tess and raised her eyebrows. Tess nodded back.

"We're looking for the Gasparilla killer," Kallie said plainly.

He shook his head. "Nope. Cops are already working on that. I'm not stepping foot in their way." He leaned back with finality, looking convinced, but disappointed to lose the job, then added, "And didn't they already identify the killer, anyway? They just need to catch her."

"It's a different..." Kallie began to explain, "We have information that it was a different killer. And a second victim."

Cornwallis leaned forward again. "Information from who? A reliable witness?"

"Not remotely reliable," Tess replied with a smirk. "But we believe him anyway."

"Ah, exactly my kind of witness," the P.I. responded with a satisfied nod. "Wouldn't talk to the cops, huh?"

"Not a peep."

"Okay, give me the details, then."

Kallie and Tess looked at each other again, unsure.

"You've got my rates, and my history, and you're still here. So let's talk about your mysterious victim."

* * * * *

"So you actually want to hire that guy?" Kallie asked as they were driving home.

"We don't have any other leads," Tess answered. "And frankly, I like the idea of someone *else* walking into the lion's den this time. Instead of you."

"Me? I don't get into trouble, Tess." Kallie looked at her best friend with wide-eyed innocence.

"You almost sound like you *believe* that." Tess laughed. "I can't watch your back every hour of the day, Kal. Hopefully this guy can handle his *own* trouble."

"You think he's going to watch my back?"

"No, but if he's the one antagonizing the killer — for a change — then no one will *need* to watch your back."

"I really don't think I get into that much trouble," Kallie replied with a pout.

Tess glanced over at Kallie with an incredulous look — but she let it drop, in favor of a better argument. "You could let that cute detective watch your back, you know," she teased.

"It's not like that, Tess."

"It *could* be like that," she added, growing sincere. "It wouldn't kill you to try."

Kallie just shook her head.

"Okay, well, that's your call. I know your last boyfriend turned out to be a real jerk, so I'm not going to twist your arm." After a moment of silence, Tess added, with her eyes still on the road, "But don't come crying to me when Morrison gives up on winning your heart and moves on."

"What? Winning my—?" Kallie began, but she clammed up. "I don't want to talk about it."

Tess sighed. "Okay, then let's talk about our weird – but seemingly very competent – deep-discount private investigator. How much does he want?"

"He asked for five hours up front to start," Kallie replied. "But that's only a hundred bucks."

"Only?"

"I mean, that's a lot for my budget, but compared to any of the other guys I checked—"

"Yeah, okay. You said Morrison checked him out, and he doesn't have a criminal record, right? He's not going to rip us off?" Tess asked, and then added with a smirk, "Skip off to Monte Carlo with our hundred bucks and retire?"

"He doesn't exactly have a Better Business Bureau gold star rating, but no lawsuits against him either."

"And he's not going to spend the five hours in a library or scouring the internet, right?" Tess asked. "Because we can do that ourselves."

"Nope, he said he's all about footwork downtown – searching the streets, not the web — working a camera and talking to a few shady contacts who might've heard something on the crime grapevine."

Tess nodded. "Okay, I'm sold. I'll split the first five hours with you."

"You don't have to do that, Tess. Talking to him was my crazy idea."

"Well, I've been encouraging you," Tess

explained. "We'll pay for the first five hours and see what he finds. If he's useless, we can pull the plug and you'll only be out one night's tips."

"Okay, that's a deal. I'll call him and let him know."

"I'm sure he'll be positively gleeful," Tess replied with a smirk.

"It must be better than sitting in that smelly office all day," Kallie added with a laugh.

"Ugh, anything would be."

Kallie dialed the investigator's number and let him know they were planning to hire him. Cornwallis didn't sound gleeful, but he didn't sound particularly surprised either. He agreed to meet them at a coffee shop near the crime scene the next morning. They could discuss any outstanding details and sign the very basic paperwork explaining his responsibilities.

"He has a *contract*?" Tess asked when Kallie told her.

"I was surprised too. He must've had a bad experience in the past. It might be written on the back of a cocktail napkin, but it's not a bad idea."

Chapter Fourteen

Kallie was watering the plants in her yard when Tess arrived the next day for their meeting with Cornwallis, and she couldn't help laughing at her best friend's arrival. "What are you *doing* with that thing?" she asked with a grin.

"It's for your dad. His birthday's tomorrow, right?" Tess answered, like nothing was amiss.

On the contrary, Tess was holding an enormous triple-decker chocolate cake with an overwhelming spray of white chocolate roses down one side. It was as big as a wedding cake, with ten times the frosting. It must've weighed fifty pounds, and Tess could barely balance it, but she grinned around the side at Kallie. "It's great, right?"

"He's going to faint when he sees it," Kallie answered, shaking her head. "And then all of his teeth will fall out."

"Now that he's dating Anna, all of those local women have stopped stalking him with desserts. I thought I'd make up for it," Tess explained. "Could you get the door? This thing weighs a ton!"

"It's bigger than you are," Kallie chirped, running up the stairs to open the door.

Benny Brooks had been the most eligible senior bachelor in Owhiro for years after splitting from Kallie's mother. And though he'd been oblivious of his popularity with the ladies, their kitchen had been perpetually flooded with decadent cakes and pies from his admirers.

"I wanted to sneak it in while he's out at the dance rehearsal. The bakery isn't open tomorrow, so I had to pick it up today," Tess explained, then she looked around the kitchen. "I wish we could *hide* it."

"A full-grown person could jump out of that thing," Kallie answered. "The only place you could hide it is behind a small planet."

"Not a *whole* grown person," Tess countered, setting the enormous confection on the kitchen counter and stepping back to admire it. "It could *maybe* hold a five-year old."

"Slide it back so it doesn't break the edge of the counter off," Kallie joked.

"I think it's amazing."

"It's *completely* amazing, Tess. He's going to love it," Kallie gushed. "Thank you so much for getting it, and for remembering his birthday."

"Aww, I love your dad to bits, you know that. He's like my second father," Tess answered. "Closer than my actual father, sometimes."

"He thinks you're pretty great too." She hugged Tess, and then looked at the clock. "Now let's hurry downtown to sign that contract before my dad gets back. I want to be here when he sees it!"

* * * * *

"What in the *world*?" Anna's voice suddenly lilted through the living room, only ten minutes after they'd returned.

"Wow, that's as pretty as a picture!" Benny Brooks had walked in behind them with his girlfriend, and he laughed out loud. "That masterpiece has Tess's name all over it. No one else would get me three-hundred pounds of sugar for my birthday."

"Good guess, Mister B! Happy birthday!"

"A picture or a dental x-ray?" Anna added with a laugh, as she admired the huge, lovely cake. "This is really beautiful, Tess. Did you have it custom made?"

"I did!" Tess replied with a smile. "We have an old school pal who just opened her own bakery in Ybor City. She did an even better job than I imagined."

"Do we have to wait for tomorrow?" Benny asked hopefully.

"It's your cake, Mister B. You can eat it whenever you want," Tess answered with a grin, and then whispered conspiratorially, "I don't mean to be a bad influence, but it will be fresher if you eat it now."

189

"That's the best excuse I've heard all day," Benny replied with a smile. He quickly opened a kitchen drawer and pulled out a handful of forks. Passing them around, he added, "That's the *only* good thing about being a grownup. You can eat dessert before dinner! Let's dig in."

* * * * *

"Sherman, put down the turtle."

Kallie's dog smiled up at her and wagged his tail happily, holding his new toy proudly in his mouth.

"Not again. Drop it!" she repeated in the serious mom voice, and he put the poor creature back down on the grass, gently, and then pouted.

Kallie stood and watched for a minute, until the small turtle eased his head back out of his shell, checking for attackers. "You're okay, little guy. I won't let him hurt you."

Before they started off again, Kallie pulled a stuffed squeaky toy out of her bag and handed it to Sherman, for him to carry instead, and he stopped looking quite so disappointed.

"Some of those turtles can bite back, buddy," she cooed while scratching his ears. "Not a good idea."

"He's such a smart boy," her dad noted, as they continued down the walkway around the lake. It was early in the morning, and there weren't many other people around. "He might be slightly obsessed with those turtles, but he never hurts them."

"He never hurts the cats either, but they all think he's psychotic too," Kallie replied with a laugh. "He just doesn't know when he's playing too rough for another species."

Benny took a sip from his water bottle. "Have you heard back from your detective friend, kiddo?"

"I talked to him on Thursday. Why, did Morrison say he was going to contact me? Did he find out something dodgy about the investigator?"

"Huh? What investigator?" Benny asked, looking confused. "I think he was just going to ask if you wanted to go snorkeling on his day off."

Kallie caught herself — she hadn't mentioned the private eye to her dad, and she didn't want to bring it up until they saw some actual results. She quickly pivoted to his second statement. "We almost never have the same time off, now that I'm working the day shift, Dad. But I'd love to go. He knows all the best snorkeling spots on this coast! You should come with us, you'd love it."

"I don't want to be a third wheel," her father replied.

"Now you sound like Tess, Dad. He's not my boyfriend, and you won't be a third wheel."

Her father mumbled something that she didn't catch.

"What was that, Dad?"

"Oh, I was just telling Sherman to pay attention," he replied, blushing a little. "Isn't that right Sherman? Everything's obvious if you just pay attention to what's going on around you."

Sherman and Kallie both look confused at that seemingly tangential statement, and Kallie changed the subject back to snorkeling. "Tess comes with us sometimes. There's no heavy equipment or anything. You and Anna could both come."

"Sure, kiddo. I'll talk to him about it."

They continued in silence along the rest of the walkway until they reached the southern end of the lake. A black and red Muscovy duck crossed the sidewalk with about a dozen tiny ducklings peeping along behind her, and Sherman stared at them curiously. He leaned forward to sniff the air but didn't bother them.

"See, he never barks at them or chases them," Kallie's dad pointed out as the roly-poly, fluffy little ducklings disappeared behind one of the houses.

"He knows when something's dangerous, though. If that mama duck came snapping at you or me, he'd chase it away."

"A *duck*? They wouldn't do that."

"Those ducks can be aggressive, Dad. Especially the ones that've been fed too often. And the males can be fifteen pounds – that's a lot of angry waterfowl coming at you, and they can bite. I wouldn't get too close to her babies."

Her father turned to face the dog. "Would you protect us from a mean old mama duck, Sherman?"

Sherm's face lit up as his human friend spoke to him and scratched his ears, and his tail wagged cheerfully – but Kallie knew he could be protective if they needed it.

But she'd never let him take a risk for her. She'd protect them both if it came to that.

* * * * *

A text from Tess chimed on Kallie's phone as they walked back into the house. She hung up Sherman's leash and then checked the message – surprised to hear from her so early in the morning.

Seeing that it was about Cornwallis, she set the phone down. Her heart was jumping, but she wanted to keep it private for now.

"Dad, could you go get a cold bottle of water for Sherman from the garage?"

When her father stepped into the garage with a nod, she snatched her phone off the counter and quickly slipped into the bathroom.

Honestly, you're acting like a lunatic, Kalliope. It's a text from your best friend, not the nuclear launch codes.

> Cornwallis found something already. Told him we both have to work, but he's going to send photos.

Her phone dinged again, and she saw that there was a voicemail waiting. She touched the play button, and listened.

"Hey, Miss Brooks, it's your private investigator," Cornwallis's message began. "I wanted to let you know that I talked to a friend downtown and got some interesting information. I'll email my notes and a few photographs to you right now, and let you have a look. Call me later if you have questions."

Kallie smiled, feeling more nervous but also relieved. She quickly replied to Tess, saying that they could meet after work to go see Cornwallis, then slipped the phone into her pocket. Feeling a little silly for hiding in the bathroom from her own father, she still washed her hands for effect, then returned to the kitchen – to find her dad giving Sherman a slice of cheese.

"We're busted, pal," Benny whispered, looking guilty.

"I'm going to get ready for work, Dad," she sighed. "Please try not to feed him the whole block of cheese."

Her father saluted, but the way Sherman followed him to the couch, Kallie knew they were still conspiring.

* * * * *

"What did you do to your leg?" Tess asked when they met with the investigator at a diner near Tampa that evening, after work.

"Oh, nothing, I just twisted my ankle," he answered, sitting down quickly and looking a little embarrassed. "Slipped on a wet patch next to one of those splash pads in the park."

"While you were working on our case?"

"Finishing up another case. Deadbeat parent," he answered, pulling his leg under the table awkwardly. "But it's fine. I'm not going to sue them or anything. Danger is part of the job."

"I was thinking the danger would be more like shady villains who were mad about you following them. Not slipping in a kids' play zone," Kallie replied.

"So was I, actually. But I *greatly* prefer a twisted ankle to a sucking chest wound."

"Understandably," Kallie added with a nod. "And the cane?"

He held up the heavy wood and brass cane and spun it, theatrically, showing a carved dragon wrapped around the handle. "Pretty cool, right? I bought it for an undercover gig about fifteen years ago, but I was glad I had it today. Do you have any aspirin, by the way?"

"So what did you have to show us?" Tess asked, opening her purse and taking out a small bottle of ibuprofen, which she handed over. "You found something important, Corny?"

Kallie looked at Tess like she'd grown a second head. *What is she doing?!*

Cornwallis chuckled but shook his head, *absolutely not.*

"I have some pretty good connections in town," he explained. "Some folks who exist in the invisible class. They work for cheap and see everything."

"The invisible class? Like our ghost, Elijah?" Kallie asked, confused.

"Yeah, that's not a bad description. Some are homeless, or jobless. Others are just antisocial. Some are just kids who wanted to escape from a bad home life. Sometimes I can get the right shop owner in the right neighborhood to talk, if he's worried about the crime rate. I even have a sociology student working on his dissertation, who just listens really well. Quite a few are veterans. But my contacts are all reliable and honest, if sometimes motivated by less-than-perfect goals," he added with a shrug. "They can watch without being seen, and I like being able to help them, when I can."

"And one of them saw our guy? Our killer?"

Kallie asked curiously.

"He didn't see the murder, but he saw the girl earlier. Recognized her from the sketch, and saw her being chased by a guy who sounded mad."

"Hmm. An ex-boyfriend?" Tess asked.

"That's exactly what I said, but it doesn't sound like it," Cornwallis answered. "He said the guy was yelling about something he wanted her to give him. Sounded like money."

"Oh, so maybe she was a prostitute?" Tess asked. "Or he was her drug dealer?"

"We're completely guessing," Kallie added with a shrug. She looked around apprehensively, wondering if the other customers were listening to their odd conversation, but they all seemed unconcerned. "Did your contact say he hurt her?"

"Grabbed her, he said, and yelled," the investigator clarified. "Didn't sound like he hit her or anything. He would've mentioned that — a girl being hit."

Kallie tilted her head in curiosity.

"He ran away from home to protect his little sister from their mom's boyfriend." Cornwallis thought for a moment and then explained, "All of my contacts have different interests and skills – because they're *humans*, even if they aren't always treated that way. I've never met his sister, but they're both over eighteen now, and I know they're staying in a week-to-week motel.

He's still taking care of her, and I'm confident that he would've mentioned it if this girl had been attacked."

Kallie nodded, convinced, and looked at Tess, who was watching Cornwallis with an odd expression on her face.

Cornwallis took out his notes and scanned over them, adding, "He said the guy yelled something like, 'You know I'll find them.'"

"Find them?" Tess asked, frowning. "That doesn't sound like money. Was she hiding something from him?"

"Or *someone*?" Kallie added. "Maybe a child custody thing? But you said it didn't sound like an ex."

"I wanted to record his story, but he said no," Cornwallis complained.

"We had that problem too," Kallie replied with a nod.

"So all I have is my notes," the investigator continued. "But he said they didn't sound like a bickering couple."

"The cops are still working on this, day and night," Tess mentioned. "If this conversation happened near the murder scene, and the guy killed her, they would've found her."

"The places he goes aren't very public, and don't have so many cameras," the investigator explained. "He tries to stay away from them, all the time."

"So maybe she was buying drugs, somewhere hidden?"

"Or selling them?" Tess added. "And that angry guy was her supplier?"

"Could be," Cornwallis nodded. "If she was low-level and stealing from him, it might make more sense for him to make her a cautionary tale."

They thanked him, glad to be back on track. They didn't have anyone to check out yet, but Cornwallis was already proving to be a useful ally.

Chapter Fifteen

When Kallie returned to the police station, this time without an orange jumpsuit, she approached the main desk to ask for her case worker and was quickly shown to his desk.

"Good morning, Miss Brooks," he greeted her, gesturing for her to sit down. "We're waiting for an update on your case from the judge, but he has a pretty full docket today. I'm going to check right now. Can I get you a bottle of water?"

Kallie was strangely disappointed that her case hadn't been magically dismissed – even though she knew that was unlikely to happen until Allbright's killer was caught – but she smiled and accepted the offer.

While she waited for him to return with, hopefully, news from the judge, Kallie took out her phone and checked her messages. Nothing from Tess or Cornwallis. Tess had been called in to work by Winchester at the last minute, but she promised to check in with Kallie whenever she had a break.

Kallie's phone batteries were low, so she sighed and grudgingly put it away.

The buzz of conversations came from every direction. A woman reporting her son's stolen bike, the second one this year. A man complaining about his neighbor mowing the yard at 7:30 a.m. A tearful woman with a black eye, leaning on a companion who looked like her twin sister. Two cocky young men, keeping silent as they were asked about street racing.

"Her husband hits her every time he comes home from the bars. You need to make him stop before—"

"He needs his bike to get to school, because the bus doesn't come out to our neighborhood. I can't afford to keep buying him more—"

"I'm going to blow up that stupid lawnmower, if he does it again on Saturday. I have to work until midnight—"

Tess would love this! Every crime in town, from the smallest to the most horrific, all in one room.

"No, I hadn't spoken to her in the few weeks before she disappeared. But if she was fighting with someone, she would have told me. Complained to me, I mean. But everything seemed to be going well for her, recently. Finally—"

"Having a rich daddy isn't going to get you out of jail anymore, boys. You're over eighteen now, and racing over a hundred miles an hour on the bridge is a felony—"

"I brought in this recording of my neighbors

having a party until four a.m. You can hear how loud it is, and no one will stop them, so—"

Kallie considered recording the buzz for Tess, because she'd never believe it. She felt like she was swimming in Tess's favorite crime blogs. But she didn't want to invade anyone's privacy – she pushed the thought aside.

But there's nothing else to do until my case worker gets back, she sighed to herself, bored and wishing her phone was fully charged.

"Well, you know how young girls are. She had a string of lousy boyfriends that her father and I didn't like. A few dead-end jobs—"

The woman sitting right behind Kallie was talking about her daughter, and her voice was rough and scratchy, like she'd been crying. Kallie immediately felt bad for her – the only person in this room full of problems who was actually weeping.

Ugh, I hate crying in public. Poor lady.

"She just started a new job a few months ago, and she was dating a decent guy. It seemed like a miracle that she finally liked a guy with a job and an education, instead of tattoos and bad financial decisions."

"Any drugs or drinking?" the interviewer asked.

"Not since high school—"

"So I couldn't get a response from the judge,"

her case manager said, returning to the desk and jerking Kallie out of her sympathetic eavesdropping. "But his clerk wrote you up a continuance for two weeks." He slid a sheet of paper across the desk to Kallie.

She quickly, slightly guiltily, picked up the paper and glanced over the page, which seemed to be written in a foreign language. "I don't speak Legal," she answered awkwardly. "Is a continuance a good thing?"

He smiled at her choice of words. "In your case, it mostly just means a delay. It could give your lawyer time to find witnesses or do research, or it could give the prosecution time to scour your background for troubling precedents—"

"Oh, I'm not even sure what my lawyer's doing," Kallie admitted.

"But this is such an unusual case, I think Judge Anderson just wants to give the police more time. He mentioned that he'd like to speak with you, but you'd definitely want your lawyer present for that."

Kallie choked at that, her heart leaping into her throat. "The *judge* wants to talk to me? About the murder?" She took a deep breath to try to calm herself but started coughing more instead. "I thought this was almost over," she croaked.

Her case manager looked alarmed at her reaction and coughing fit and glanced around his desk. "I forgot your water when I was talking to the clerk. Let me go get it for you." He ran off to get her a drink.

Kallie breathed through her nose until she could stop coughing, but her heart was still racing.

Morrison and the sheriff both said the judge was on our side. Now he wants to talk with me directly? Does he expect me to crack and admit that I'm a killer?

Calm down, Kalliope. Maybe he just wants to tell you he believes you. Heck, maybe he loves the food at the Lazy Gecko. Don't assume the worst!

She took another deep breath, dabbing at her eyes to make sure she wasn't teary, and waited for her case manager to return. She felt a little calmer already.

"You don't know if she went to a nightclub that evening?" Kallie heard the interviewer at the desk behind her continue.

"I hadn't spoken to her, but she loved to go to the parade every year. I doubt she would go to a club, when there's such a big party in the streets."

Parade?!

The woman being interviewed paused and then added, "Unless Tabitha wanted to go to a club."

"Tabitha?" the interviewer asked.

"Tabitha's been her best friend since they were in high school. If she went to the parade, then Tab would have been with her."

Kallie's head jerked halfway-around at the

surprise information, and it took sheer force of will to straighten up, keep her eyes forward, and not stare. *That's the same woman with the missing kid who was talking before. Her daughter disappeared from the parade?!*

Instead she took out her phone again, grimacing at the low battery indicator. She tapped on the screen, and then set it on the desk – mentally crossing her fingers.

Don't you dare feel guilty, Kalliope. This is important. I just know it.

Kallie heard the interviewer's fingers tapping on the computer keys. "Do you have Tabitha's last name?"

Kallie glanced over her shoulder as casually as possible, pretending to check out the front door, and saw the woman take an old, folded-up photograph out of her wallet. She handed it over carefully to the interviewing officer. "Tabitha Chr—"

A loud crash made Kallie jump as a woman nearby knocked over her chair. "Don't you *dare* tell me to calm down!" she yelled at the man sitting next to her. "It's your fault the car was stolen!"

Dang it! Work with me, people!

The angry woman's assigned officer quickly resolved the shouting match, but it was too late.

"This is the two of them from a few years ago," the worried mother continued, seemingly unaffected by the racket. "She looks about the same now, except her hair's longer."

The interviewer picked up a tablet from her desk and used it to take a picture of the photo, then handed it back. She paused to type something quickly on the tablet. *Presumably cataloging it with the missing persons case and adding the friend's name*, Kallie thought to herself.

Kallie couldn't see the photo or the woman's face from that angle, and she turned back forward in her seat with a sigh.

"Thank you, we'll need to find her and ask her some questions. You haven't spoken to Tabitha in the past week, either?" the officer asked. "Since the parade?"

"No, I was actually worried about her too, but my son said he saw her at—"

"Well, you sound better, at least," Kallie's case worker stated with a chuckle as he sat back down at the desk, handing over the bottle of water. "I thought I'd scared you to death."

Not now! I just found a decent clue!

Kallie smiled cheerfully, wishing he'd taken another thirty seconds to return. She opened the water bottle and took a sip.

"Excellent news, Miss Brooks. When I went back for your water, Judge Anderson was just coming out of his chambers. I asked about your case, and he signed the dismissal for you." Her case worker smiled and slid a small stack of papers across the desk.

"Oh, that's..." Kallie forced herself to stop being nosey and refocus her attention on the news at hand. She smiled back, genuinely, in surprise. "Wow, that's great news. I didn't expect—"

"He apologized for the delay, but it took a while for the restaurant's security company to return the footage from that night, with an exact timestamp."

Kallie's attention was torn between her obvious relief at the judge's decision, and the jumble of conversation behind her.

Did she just say her daughter was in rehab? Or did she say taxi cab? Wait, sleep lab?

Kalliope, focus!

"What do I do now?" she asked, politely. "Will my lawyer be notified?"

"All you have to do is go home," he responded with a smile. "You're free to go, and your bail collateral will be released. Your attorney will close out the case for you."

Kallie thanked him, and collected her purse and coat, and began gathering up the papers she'd received.

The woman behind her was still talking, though, so Kallie carefully folded the papers, slowly putting them in her purse. Her case worker looked at her strangely but didn't comment on her slow-motion act.

"They usually make it a girls' outing. But it's

possible that her new boyfriend would've gone with them," the woman added, as Kallie lingered for a few last words. "Most guys wouldn't want their girlfriend down there alone."

"No," the interviewer agreed. "I don't think many of them would."

Kallie bent down to tie her shoes, which were already tied securely.

You can never be too sure about correctly-tied shoelaces, she told herself, ignoring her own nosiness. *I wouldn't want to trip in the parking lot.*

"I just gave her my mother's pearls," the woman finally added, quietly.

"Sorry?" the interviewer replied.

Kallie also wondered if she'd misheard her. *Pearls?*

"I really don't want to have to bury her with them," she sighed.

Kallie sighed, too, and silently made her way to the exit as the interviewer told the woman not to worry too much, just yet. Young women could be forgetful when they were out having fun – but Kallie had a bad feeling about this one.

* * * * *

Thirty minutes later – after driving home and

208

plugging in her phone to charge – Kallie dialed her best friend's number. Tess's phone picked up with a small click, and Kallie started talking immediately.

"Oh my gosh, Tess, I found us another lead."

"*What?* Wait, hang on," Tess replied quickly, and Kallie heard some typing in the background. She suddenly heard Winchester's voice, and then both of them talking for a few minutes. Then Tess came back. "Sorry, what happened?"

"I didn't know Winchester was back in town."

"He's not, he was on the speakerphone, and I was taking notes. I thought he was done when I picked up your call, but he had one more question for me. Now *what* happened?"

"I went down to the police station, and I think I saw the girl's mom."

"What? Kal, you totally lost me. *Whose* mom?"

"The victim. The girl we've been looking for."

"Her *mom?*" Tess asked incredulously. "We don't even know who she was. What makes you think it was her mom?"

"She was talking about her missing daughter, and said she went to the parade with her best friend. And she showed the cop a photo of her daughter and said they hadn't spoken in a few weeks. So something happened to her daughter at the parade."

"And if the police knew about it, they wouldn't

need a picture," Tess finished Kallie's thought quietly. "So she wasn't there about an open case."

"I mean, it's *possible* that more than one girl disappeared that night," Kallie acquiesced, not believing a word of it, but making the valid suggestion.

"*Totally* possible," Tess agreed. "And her daughter might just be hiding away with her boyfriend in a sordid little love shack in Brandon, or something."

"She could be completely fine somewhere, madly in love, drinking cheap gas station wine and eating Fritos. If they hadn't spoken in weeks, she wouldn't expect her mom to even be looking for her."

"It might be completely unrelated," Tess replied with apparent finality.

"But we both know it isn't."

"*Nope*," Tess agreed. "Did you catch her name?"

"No," Kallie sighed. "They were already talking, and the room was so noisy that I missed the beginning of the interview. But her best friend is named Tabitha something."

"Okay, that's a start," Tess replied, and Kallie heard tapping on the computer again. "Someone on social media would have mentioned a missing girl by now. I wish we had that photo."

"They were directly behind me, so I couldn't see it," Kallie explained. "Unless I gave up all hope of subtlety, and snatched the picture out of her hand—"

"Which you considered—"

"*No...*"

"Briefly?"

"Okay, maybe *briefly,*" Kallie replied with an embarrassed laugh. "Can you imagine me jumping over the desk and grabbing the tattered old photo out of the officer's hand?"

"Vividly," Tess replied, choking back a laugh.

"She probably would've tased me," Kallie grumbled. "Anyway, I may not have *seen* anything, but—"

"But?" Tess asked, and Kallie could hear the expectant grin in her voice.

She took the phone away from her ear and switched to the camera roll. Pressing play, the recording started. The screen was all black from sitting camera-down on the desk, but the tinny conversation began mid-sentence, "—you have Tabitha's last name?"

"You *didn't*. In the *police station?*" Tess groaned, stifling a laugh. "You're insane, Kal."

"I didn't get much, because my case worker and I were talking over most of it. And then the battery died. But I'll email it to you."

"I mean, there's no expectation of privacy in a police station," Tess rationalized. "And we were never going to use it as evidence. So it's mostly just *rude*, not illegal."

211

"That's the story of my life, lately," Kallie replied, rolling her eyes. "Rude but not illegal."

"You should get that tattooed on your ankle," Tess replied with a laugh. "Send me the video, and I'll see what I can find. I'll come by your house after work with takeout from Thai One On. And I know Marcy gave you the morning off so you could go downtown, but now you're going to be late."

Kallie looked at the kitchen clock in surprise. "Yikes, it's *so* late. Thanks, sweetie. I'll see you after work!"

* * * * *

That evening, after eating their takeout Thai dinner with Kallie's dad, Tess took the phone and listened to the video again – holding the phone up to her ear in case there was something that had been inaudible in the emailed version. "I wish you'd been able to film the speaker, but this is a good start. I mean, if there was *another* girl missing from the parade, it would be on the news."

"Definitely," Kallie replied, feeling more certain by the hour that this was related to their current obsession.

"We can definitely use this to link back to the speaker, if we find the name of the missing girl. And maybe Cornwallis could get some info from that interviewing officer. I'm sure he'll recognize her voice."

"Good point; he seems to know them all."

"Now what did they say about the boyfriend?" Tess asked. "There isn't much on here, but you heard more of the conversation?"

"She didn't think the boyfriend went with them to the parade. She said it was usually a girls' night out."

"But she *had* a boyfriend," Tess replied, tapping thoughtfully on the back of Kallie's phone. "So for right now, I'm calling him a suspect. Until we find out otherwise."

"That sounds like a reasonable plan," Kallie agreed with a shrug. "Should we play this for Cornwallis?"

"Definitely. Could you call him and ask him to meet us for lunch tomorrow? I didn't have much time to research this, while I was at work. Winchester's case in Louisiana is getting more complicated, and he needed me to check some local records for him."

Kallie took her phone back, while Tess commandeered the laptop and started searching social media, using their new information.

There was no response on their P.I.'s phone, so Kallie left a brief voicemail and then immediately texted him, asking to meet the next day before work.

"Wow, that was easy," Tess mumbled from the dining room table.

"You *didn't* find her already."

"I knew her best friend would've posted about it, if she was missing. And Tabitha's a pretty uncommon name."

"Wasn't that the baby's name on *Bewitched*?"

"That's the only place I've ever heard it," Tess answered with a nod. "There were about fifty users with that name in their profile, but only three of them specifically say they're in Florida. *This* Tabitha is clearly the best friend of the missing girl from the police station."

Kallie's phone chimed, but it wasn't Cornwallis, so she turned back to Tess. "How can you tell? What did she say?" she asked.

"Apparently they got separated at the parade, and Tabitha was afraid she was mad, because she wasn't returning her calls or texts."

Kallie walked over and stood behind her friend, so she could see the screen. Tess pointed out where she was reading. "This post is from the day after Gasparilla. It just says, 'I know you're mad, and I shouldn't have left, but I couldn't find you and my phone was dead. Please just let me know you're okay.'"

"Oh, that's depressing." Kallie sighed. "Did she tag her in the post?"

"Not in this one."

"I'm *barely* on social media, and even I tag

people when I want them to respond."

"She was probably still hungover," Tess grumbled. "And she must've been feeling really guilty. She probably didn't want to broadcast to the whole world that she ditched her best friend."

"True," Kallie agreed.

"Even with just this short note, some of the comments are brutal," Tess added.

Kallie leaned forward so she could see the comments section, and frowned. *You abandoned her... Some BFF... Might be dead... Worst friend ever...* And worse. Much worse.

Wow, I thought people were being mean to me, and those were strangers. Aren't these people supposed to be her friends?

"Anyway, it's too cryptic to tell who she's talking to," Tess continued. "But I think we're safe to presume it's that missing girl – since Tabitha's name, the location, and the timeline all match. And it gets worse."

"I'll never understand why some people like social media—" Kallie replied, turning away.

"Oh, wait!" Tess called to her. "The next post says, 'I'm starting to really worry about you, Kelsey, and your mom wants to hear from you, too. Please contact one of us.'"

"Kelsey," Kallie repeated, quietly. "That fits with the woman at the station saying she hadn't spoken to her daughter," she added. "Tabitha must feel awful. She couldn't have known her friend would disappear, but what a nightmare."

"If she feels guilty now, she's going to feel so much worse when the whole story comes out." She started to type a direct message to Tabitha, asking for more information.

"Tess, no." Kallie stopped her. "We can't talk to her yet."

Tess thought for a minute and then agreed. "You're right. She shouldn't hear it from us. And she wouldn't believe us, anyway."

"If we find anything concrete to tie this girl to our victim, I'll pass it on to Morrison. The Tampa cops might not believe there was a second victim, but Morrison will listen to us, if we find something real."

"We can't be sure that she's talking about our mystery murder victim, but I'm starting to feel like we're on the right track. I doubt there are *two* missing girls from the parade, and *neither* of them have been publicly reported or found yet. But it's possible."

"Well, this one's name is Kelsey," Kallie sighed, glad to finally have a verified name, at least.

If this is even our victim, she thought to herself, automatically. But she was sure this was the right track too. *No way there's this big of a coincidence.*

"What's her last name?" she added, leaning forward to read the screen.

Tess scrolled a little more and then shook her head. "No luck. Let me check Tabitha's 'Followers' list, maybe she'll be in there." She clicked on the link to see the list of accounts that followed Tabitha, and then groaned. "Gee, only two thousand followers. No problem."

"It could be worse."

"True, at least she's not a major influencer. Then there could be a million."

"How does the 'Following' list look?" Kallie suggested, referring to the accounts that Tabitha herself followed.

"Only three hundred," Tess replied with a shrug.

"That's a little better. And she'll be in that list, if they were old friends."

"Three hundred will still take a while, but I can probably eliminate a bunch of them — all of the guys and all of the celebrities."

Kallie looked at her watch. "I'm getting ice cream. You want some? It's coffee chocolate chip."

"Sure, sounds good," Tess replied absently, opening multiple windows at once and closing most of them as she eliminated them.

Kallie took the ice cream out of the freezer and started a pot of decaf coffee, since it seemed like they'd be researching for a while.

"I think I found her," Tess mumbled. "I jumped

down to the K's on a hunch. Her screen name is @kellokello and... Whoa. I think you need to look at this, Kallie."

"One sec, let me just get some bowls and spoons out."

"Kallie, *seriously*. Come look."

Something about Tess's tone made Kallie close the silverware drawer.

"Okay, what is it?" she asked, walking back over to the table for a look. She saw a photograph blown up on the laptop screen, and suddenly felt a little ill. "Oh."

She was an attractive young blonde – pouting a little too hard, wearing too much mascara and bright lipstick — in a typical glamour selfie. It could've been any twenty-something girl in America, looking pretty for the uncaring eye of social media. But Kallie recognized her in an instant.

"Isn't that—?" Tess started to ask.

"Yep," Kallie replied, shaking off her initial shock. "That's the girl who fell on me. Outside the restaurant. That's the girl with the knife."

"So our second murder victim is—"

"The cops' missing *suspect*," Kallie finished. "The Killer Wench. I'll call Morrison." She picked up her phone again and opened the favorites list.

"Wait, Kal." Tess looked over to the muted television and pointed. "I don't think she's missing anymore."

Chapter Sixteen

Kallie grabbed the remote and un-muted the television, where a grainy still frame of Kallie and the strange woman outside the restaurant was plastered on the screen. A moment later, the black and white witness sketch replaced the image – this time stamped dramatically with the word "FOUND" in red letters.

"—have identified the body of the woman who was found in Tampa Bay this afternoon, as the Allbright murder suspect," the news anchor began, midsentence. "We haven't received much information, but the sheriff has scheduled a press conference for eight o'clock, and Tampa News Twelve will be there to cover it for you."

The station cut back to other local news and Kallie muted the television again. "That's only twenty minutes from now. Do you want to stay and watch it?"

"What kind of *crazy* question is that?" Tess laughed with a snort. "I'll fix milkshakes. Mocha ok, Mister B? I'll have to combine the coffee and chocolate flavors, so there's enough for three."

"Mocha is utterly perfect, Tess. I'll make popcorn," Kallie's dad, who had returned from the garage when he heard the television, answered cheerfully. They both walked into the kitchen, Tess heading for the freezer, and Benny taking out a dutch oven and a stick of butter from the refrigerator.

Kallie watched them with an amused grin, baffled by what they'd found online, and trying not to obsess about it until the press conference started. Trying to ignore the unpleasant lurch in her stomach. "But how can she be both—?" Kallie asked, just as Tess started the noisy blender and the frozen mocha concoction spun wildly.

A minute passed and Tess stopped the blender, sticking a spoon into the milkshake to taste it. "What was that, Kal?"

"I was just wondering how this girl could be both—?"

The large pot on the stove suddenly started popping loudly, as Kallie's dad tended to his part of the late-night snack offering. The smell of melted butter and fresh popcorn filled the house and Kallie gave up.

I guess we'll find out in a few minutes, anyway, Kallie thought to herself, reaching into the highest shelf of the kitchen cabinet for some extra-large dessert glasses that were rarely used.

"Those are perfect," Tess shouted over the noise as Kallie next reached for the biggest mixing bowl, on the top shelf of the pantry, for the popcorn.

"This should clear everything up, right?" Kallie

shouted, as the metal cookpot cracked and pinged loudly.

"*What?* Oh, yeah," Tess replied, and then laughed. "Or confuse it even more."

"At least the sheriff will finally believe that there was a second victim."

"Maybe. We'll see," Tess replied.

"Oh, it's starting," Benny noted, pointing at the television, as the popcorn commotion finally started to dim. "Turn it up, would you?"

Kallie hurried to pick up the remote, as her dad continued rocking the pot, to keep the popcorn from burning. She un-muted the television just as the public affairs officer for the Tampa police was leaving the podium.

"Hey, there's your friend the sheriff," Tess teased.

"Good evening," Sheriff McReed began. "We don't usually hold these press conferences so late in the evening, but we wanted to get this information out before the weekend."

One of the reporters said something Kallie couldn't hear clearly, and the sheriff briefly smiled. The expression left his face, and he began his announcement. "The owners of a local parasailing company called in to the Coast Guard this morning around eight o'clock, requesting assistance. When the Coast Guard arrived, they found the body of a young female in the water. I'll let the City of Tampa medical examiner give you the details."

The sheriff left the podium and a petite young woman with a serious expression entered the screen. Tess quickly poured the milkshakes into three glasses and grabbed a few treats for Sherman, hurrying to finish before she missed anything. Benny had taken the fresh popcorn off the stove and dumped it quickly into the mixing bowl, so they all gathered on the couch.

"My name is Dr. Britney Tran," the speaker began, and spelled her name. "I'm the chief medical examiner for the City of Tampa. My examination is complete, but the DNA results in this case are still pending. The state and dress of the drowning victim have left the department confident that she is the knife-wielding young woman seen in the video from Gasparilla. The woman currently being sought as the presumed killer of Marcus Allbright."

There was an audible buzz, as the reporters began whispering and several phones chimed. The medical examiner glared silently at the crowd through her dark-rimmed spectacles, and they settled back down.

Kallie couldn't tear her eyes from the screen, but she felt Tess take her hand.

"I'll have a further report when we have the DNA results. But I want to manage expectations. There's no guarantee that a genetic match will be on file, or even that it will match any of the findings from the crime scene." She closed her notes abruptly and turned to leave, but stopped when she made eye contact with someone offscreen.

Then she visibly sighed and stepped back to the podium. "I've been asked to take a few questions," she added. Clearly not someone who thrived on publicity, at least not this kind, she understood the rules of her job. Shouts rang out around her, and she silently pointed to one of the reporters at random.

"Why do you think this is the Killer Wench?" a man's voice called out, using the nickname that the tabloids had coined for the presumed murderer.

The medical examiner grimaced at the nickname but didn't comment on it. "After a week in the water, she wasn't identifiable, and fingerprints weren't viable. But her clothing was recognizable and there was a small tattoo visible in the video which matched the body. I can't give you any more information on that at this time."

Tess frowned and took out her phone, tapped a few times, and then leaned toward the screen, squinting. "How did they see a tattoo? I don't see a tattoo," she muttered in surprise.

Kallie leaned over and looked at the phone, which was showing a still shot of the woman stumbling against Kallie. "You have this stored on your phone?"

"Well, yeah," Tess replied with an embarrassed

laugh. "I don't know how they saw a tattoo in this grainy video."

"They must have a different video." Kallie reached over and expanded the picture. "Even the police probably didn't notice it, until they had a body to compare."

"I doubt that," Tess replied with a chuckle, "but thank you for trying to make me feel better."

Benny shushed them. "I want to hear this."

Kallie smiled at her dad's interest, but also wished he didn't have to hear it at all. *How has my life become so crazy?*

Another reporter was asking, "Was anything found with the body?"

"The boaters who found her were a mile or two out in Hillsborough Bay, so nothing was located with the body – and the murder weapon was already found near the scene. But I've been told that dive teams are searching the area. The sheriff can give you more information on that. One more question?" She pointed to a woman in the second row.

"You called her a drowning victim. Is that how she died? Do you know how she ended up in the water, after we saw her running down the sidewalk? Wasn't she headed away from the Bay?"

"I can confirm that drowning was the cause of death. I can't divulge any additional information since it's an ongoing case. But I don't know how she made her way to the water. Hopefully the police can determine that when they resolve the rest of the murder. It's still an active investigation." She gathered up her paperwork and added, "Thank you."

As Dr. Tran walked away, the sheriff stopped her and shook her hand warmly, saying something quietly, and then returned to the podium.

"As the medical examiner noted, this is still a very active case. You'll see our police boat out in Hillsborough Bay, and we've sent a sketch of the tattoo to the local news stations. We're hoping someone will recognize it. We just ask, as always – if you see something, say something. There's a $2500 reward for information, and we've been told that the NFL will be increasing the reward money. You can report anonymously at the local tip line and still receive the reward. Thank you for coming."

The publicity officer returned to the podium, but the station cut away before she started talking. The anchor began, "So, to recap, that was the press conference revealing that a body—"

Kallie muted the television again. "What now?"

"Well, we've already told them everything we know. All we can do is wait for the DNA analysis to come back and see if they identify her as Kelsey."

"If the medical examiner did an autopsy, she would've been able to tell if she was murdered, right?" Kallie asked.

"That's probably what she meant when she said she couldn't divulge anything else," Tess answered with a nod. "It also means Kelsey was still alive when she entered the water. Hopefully she was unconscious."

* * * * *

Kallie was just loading a tray, to bring a cute couple from Vermont their drinks, the following day before the lunch rush, when Marcy showed up at the bar. Kallie did a double take, surprised to see her boss outside of her office.

"Hi Marcy," she greeted her, hesitantly. "What's up?"

"You need to see this," Marcy whispered. She was carrying the remote control for the wall-mounted televisions. There was a stock car race playing on most of the screens, but it wasn't crowded and no one was watching it – they weren't really a sports bar, after all.

Kallie delivered the drinks with a smile and left two menus, and then looked up, curiously. Marcy changed the closest television to Tampa News Twelve, leaving the others on the race channel.

"Sure, what is it?" she asked, setting the empty tray on the bar.

"—We'll check back with you soon, Rebecca," the anchor was saying, apparently to one of their many on-scene reporters. He directed his attention back to the main camera, and continued, "Again, if you're just joining us, we're covering a breaking news story from TPD. The body of the young woman found yesterday in Hillsborough Bay has been matched with an open missing persons report."

Kallie leaned back against the bar as her knees went weak. She slumped onto a barstool.

"The TPD public affairs officer informed us that once a possible match for the drowning victim was found, the medical examiner was able to use her dental records for positive confirmation," the anchor continued. He paused for a moment, then added, "We've just been notified that a press conference has been scheduled for three o'clock. Let's go back to Rebecca, who's outside the police station, and we'll cut to the press conference when they're ready to start."

The station returned to their reporter, who was standing in a sunny spot across the street from the main Tampa police station. Marcy muted the television.

"Well, I guess I know what I'm doing after work." Kallie smiled at Marcy crookedly.

"That's after the lunch rush; we can watch it here. When the press conference comes on, I'll let you know," Marcy answered, giving Kallie's shoulder a squeeze. "But you know those things are never on time."

Kallie raised an eyebrow.

"You're such a bad influence!" Marcy joked, realizing what she'd just said. "I swear, in my fifty-four years of life, I never *once* watched a police press conference. Not one! What kind of true-crime junkie are you making of me?"

Kallie smiled back at her friend and boss. Then, realizing that she was literally sitting down on the job, she sat up straight and looked around.

No one was waiting for a drink, fortunately. They were all still glued to the screen, even though the reporter was muted, reading the closed captioning. Some of the regulars knew that Kallie was involved with the Gasparilla murder – but even the tourists were engrossed by the story. It was national news. Probably international, by now.

Kallie stood up, recovered from her initial surprise, and returned to her spot behind the bar.

We told them there was another victim, and they didn't believe us, she thought to herself, starting to feel vindicated. *This should either confirm our story, or—*

She didn't want to think about the other possibility. She didn't know Sheriff McReed very well yet, but she admired him. And she certainly didn't want him to think she was stupid. Or nuts.

She left the television muted and turned the music on. No need to ruin the Lazy Gecko's cheerful beach vibe with murder news. There was plenty of misery outside these walls. She was ready to hear her regulars laughing again.

There's plenty of time to worry later, Kalliope. It's a beautiful day and the people here care about you. Just relax until there's something to worry about.

Three women sitting at a table by the window laughed, as if on cue, and Kallie smiled. She walked over to their table and took an order for another round of wine and a slice of raspberry cheesecake to share.

She had calmed down by the time the lunch rush started, and was soon too busy with filling orders, and the chatter of happy diners, to give the news another thought. Then, with the longer weekend lunch service officially over at two, she returned to her regulars. Barry ordered another beer, and the Vermont couple, still lingering by the windows, ordered more drinks and a blackberry crumble with ice cream.

Kallie served a few more rounds of drinks to her customers and was starting to tap her toes to a Sheryl Crow song playing on the stereo, when Marcy came back.

"Do you want to watch it?" she asked.

Kallie sighed. "Yes. I mean, no. But I need to hear what they found." She grudgingly turned the music back down as Marcy unmuted the television. It wasn't a loud, active crowd, and no one complained.

"—I'll turn it back over to Dr. Tran," the public relations agent was saying, as Kallie sat down on the barstool again, where she could see.

The medical examiner walked to the podium

230

and introduced herself again, even though it had been less than twenty-four hours since the last press conference. This was a major case, and she'd be quoted in news articles all over the country. "We were notified this morning of a missing persons case that was filed last week. A woman in Seminole Heights had reported that her adult daughter was missing and hadn't been seen since the Gasparilla parade. Luckily, we were able to reach her right away. The DNA results will take another few weeks, but she was able to give us the name of her daughter's dentist."

A police officer silently carried a portable easel into frame, leaving it for the medical examiner. Dr. Tran acknowledged her with a nod of thanks.

"I was able to verify the identity of our victim from Hillsborough Bay, tentatively believed to be the woman seen at Gasparilla with the knife used to kill Allbright, as Kelsey Ann Majors." She removed a covering from the easel and displayed a photo of a young woman.

Unlike the picture that Tess found online, this one appeared to be from a family event. Maybe a Thanksgiving dinner. Kelsey was seated at a table with other people, who were cropped out of the photo, and her hands were visible, as if the photographer had caught her while talking. Laughing.

Tess was right, she doesn't really look that much like me...

The woman was younger than Kallie, and her hair was a sandy blonde color. The shape of her face was similar, and Kallie knew they were about the same height – but that was where the likeness ended. Kelsey's eyes were brown, and had a little sadness to them, even though she was smiling in the picture. Dr. Tran uncovered the next photo, which must've been taken on the morning of the parade. In it, Kelsey was wearing an identical version of Kallie's now-ruined blouse, corset, and hat.

Kallie shivered, and saw that a few of the Lazy Gecko regulars were looking over at her.

After several seconds of quiet, one of the reporters asked a question, and then several more called out. Dr. Tran silently gestured to her left, offscreen, and the sheriff quickly joined her at the podium. They spoke for a moment, and then she left. The photograph remained on the easel.

"Go ahead, Barbara," Sheriff McReed pointed at one reporter without further comment.

"What else do you know about Kelsey Majors? Does she have a past criminal history?" the local reporter asked.

"Kelsey Majors was twenty-four years old and a Tampa native," the sheriff replied, adding, "She attended high school in Seminole Heights and went to USF for two years. She was currently living and working in downtown Tampa." He looked at his notes on the podium, flipping between pages. "She had a minor criminal record, mostly petty theft and misdemeanor drug possession. Breaking and entering. Nothing violent. Her juvenile record is sealed."

I did overhear her mother saying she was into drugs in high school. I guess her problem got worse, not better. Sounds like she was in a lot of trouble, and it got her killed.

"Her mother gave us a phone number for her employer," the sheriff continued, "but we haven't been able to reach them yet."

"How did she know Allbright?" another reporter asked.

"We haven't determined how, or even if, she knew him, at this point. Her mother said she never mentioned him, and she didn't even care about football. But it might have been a recent meeting," the sheriff concluded. "Or she may not have known him at all. I can't speculate at this time."

"So she didn't leave any kind of manifesto or confession?" a popular reporter from a national channel called from the left.

"I believe—" He waved at someone offscreen, and a law enforcement officer in uniform approached the podium. "This is Officer Flannery. He was on the team that checked her apartment. I'll let him answer that question."

Officer Flannery took his place at the podium

and began, "The victim's apartment was searched, but there was no journal or manifesto found. Written confessions aren't common in cases like this. Our forensics unit is checking the other evidence, and we'll have an update on their findings in the next few days."

Kallie found herself relieved that the officer had called Kelsey a victim, and not the suspect. Although she appeared to be both. Kallie wasn't even sure why she cared.

Because they're treating you like a suspect too, Kalliope. Both of you held that knife, what if it belonged to someone else, entirely?

The officer continued, "And there was nothing on her public social media accounts about Allbright, or any criminal plans for Gasparilla – nothing but the usual revelry."

"What about her personal life?" a female reporter called out. "Where does she live? Does she have kids? A boyfriend?"

The sheriff returned to the officer's side and ran interference, "We're not releasing that information at this time. It's still a very active investigation, and we're interviewing several people who knew Miss Majors. We should be able to give you some more details in the morning. That's all for now."

McReed and the officer left the podium, and Kelsey could see the sheriff pat him encouragingly on the shoulder. The public relations officer returned, and

Marcy muted the television again.

"Thanks, Marcy."

Kallie was still looking at the silent television, thinking about everything she'd heard. After a moment, she returned to the bar, turned the music back on, and took out her phone. She tapped a quick text to Tess and Cornwallis, watched for a reply, and then went back to work.

At least now we have another lead. Or two. Or twelve.

Chapter Seventeen

Kallie poked at her chocolate chip pancakes, the breakfast special of the day, as she joined Morrison at their café the next morning.

She tried to sound utterly nonchalant as she asked, "So I was watching the press conference, and the sheriff said Kelsey's juvenile record was sealed—"

The detective was carefully applying the perfect amount of hot sauce to his home-fried potatoes, and he replied without even looking up, "I'm not asking him for any information from her juvie file."

How does he do that?!

"But Morrison!"

"Absolutely not. I've already used up all of my good will with the sheriff. I'm not asking him for legally protected information."

"He's really nice, though," Kallie continued sweetly. "And he *likes* me—"

Morrison laughed. "Yes, he does. And he likes *me* too. Let's not ruin that, please."

"But it might help us figure out who killed her!"

Morrison finally looked up from his potatoes and gave her a huge smile, which made her stomach flip over twice.

"Your complete and utter insanity is really refreshing," he replied teasingly. "But you're overestimating his kindness, Kallie. Juvenile records are sealed for a good reason."

"Yeah, and that's why I should—"

"He's not even in my jurisdiction, and I *still* think he'd find a way to get me fired if I asked him that. He'd at least put me on a psych hold."

"I'd come visit you in prison," Kallie answered, batting her eyelashes cutely.

Morrison laughed out loud.

"Fine, no juvenile records," Kallie sighed. "We'll solve it some other way."

"I never had a moment's doubt," Morrison replied with a smile, reaching for the orange marmalade.

* * * * *

After breakfast, Kallie drove to Tess's house, stopping only to pick up a pair of pantyhose at the drug store. Then she walked tentatively into her best friend's house like it was a torture chamber that she might never escape.

Tess was waiting with an arsenal of makeup, hair products, and some business clothes that she hoped would fit Kallie. She rubbed her hands together like a mad scientist, and practically cackled. "I've always wanted to do this!"

Kallie grimaced and backed away toward the door.

"Don't panic, it won't hurt," her best friend reassured her. "Well, my *shoes* would hurt you. We'll have to get you some sensible pumps at Target or something."

"True, I'd have to cut my toes off to get into your shoes. And I only have two pairs of heels, and neither of them is remotely sensible," Kallie agreed. "So what did Cornwallis say?"

Kallie had sent the text about the press conference to both of them the previous afternoon, but her friend and the P.I. had continued the conversation on the phone.

"I was able to find Kelsey's boss with some creative googling," Tess explained. "She won an Employee of the Month award, believe it or not. It was on her boss's business page, but it didn't list the company."

"Employee of the month? That doesn't sound like a drug dealer or criminal."

"Drug dealers probably *have* an employee of the month, but I doubt they get an award," Tess agreed with a smirk.

"Exactly," Kallie nodded.

"Cornwallis tried to get some information on Kelsey from his connection at the police station, but they're all locked up tight on this one. They wouldn't even release her address."

Kallie sighed. "Well, we'll work with what we have. Who's her boss?"

"Her name's Esmerelda Collins. She apparently controls a handful of local companies, and her website doesn't really differentiate between them very well."

"So we visit all of them until we find someone who knew her?" Kallie asked hesitantly.

"I think we should go straight to the source, instead," Tess smiled, raising an eyebrow. "Now sit down and let me do your hair."

Kallie sat tensely in a dining room chair, trying not to whimper, and Tess started combing and pinning her hair into what felt suspiciously like a wedding photo creation.

"Why do I need grown-up hair?" she whined. "I hate grown-up hair."

Tess laughed and stepped in front of her, explaining slowly like she was a toddler, "We need grown-up hair so we look like grown-ups, Kalliope. We're going to see a very rich and powerful lady, and she's not going to give important information to a couple of hoodlums."

Kallie pouted and slumped in her chair, but nodded.

"Would you feel better about your *very attractive* chignon if I get you a Pop Tart?"

Now Kallie couldn't resist laughing. "Yes, please. Do you have the blue kind? With frosting?"

"Of course I do," Tess answered with a smirk. "It's the only kind you'll eat." She set down the comb and hair spray and walked to the pantry. "Do you want it toasted?"

"No, cold is fine." She accepted the bribe and tore open the packet. "So we're going to see Esmerelda Collins? Did you have Winchester make an appointment with her assistant or something?"

"I have a better idea," Tess replied, continuing with Kallie's hair. She stepped back to check her progress and nodded, clearly impressed with her work, then started on her makeup.

Kallie reached for her phone and turned on some music, while she ate her Pop Tart and tried to sit still for her makeover. She stopped when Tess needed to do her lipstick, and then she was done.

"Go look," Tess ordered, pointing toward the bathroom.

Kallie sighed and went to check out her new look in the full-length mirror, calling back, "I'd better still look like myself."

But what she saw stunned her into silence. She blinked a few times and then leaned back out the bathroom door. "Tess? Who am I?"

"You're an elegant, professional woman. You look gorgeous."

Kallie laughed and pointed at her reflection in the mirror. "*That* lady's gorgeous. But I don't recognize her." Her hair, as advertised, was in an elegant chignon, and her makeup was perfect but understated. It was all completely mismatched with her jeans and Converse tennis shoes.

"It's just for today, Kal. I love you just the way you are, but we need to convince Mrs. Collins to help us. Even Cornwallis is out of ideas."

"Got it," Kallie nodded. "We're in disguise. Undercover!"

"We can't pretend to be cops. They lock you up for that. We just need to look professional and serious," Tess corrected her. Then she sighed and added, "Hopefully she'll think we're working with the state prosecutor or something, and she won't ask too many questions."

"That's not as much fun as being undercover."

"I know," Tess agreed. "Come on, let's find you a pencil skirt and pretend it's Halloween."

* * * * *

"Excuse me, Mrs. Collins?" Tess called out cheerfully to the well-dressed woman in the driveway. They'd parked Tess's car and arrived at the mogul's home on foot, just as she returned. "We were hoping to find you."

The older woman turned away from the trunk of her Mercedes, and looked at Kallie and Tess like they were a pair of slugs on her favorite rose. "Why would you hope for that, young lady?"

"We wanted to ask you about Kelsey," Kallie replied.

The blood rushed out of the woman's face, and she suddenly looked deathly pale under her perfect makeup, but she kept her calm. "Well, bless your heart," she oozed. "I guess you'd better come inside."

Without another word, Mrs. Collins turned on her elegant Louboutin heel and headed toward the house. Like an immaculately-dressed thoroughbred, she walked quickly to the door and unlocked it, while Tess and Kallie hurried to catch up with her.

Tess whispered, "Bless your heart. That's what southern women say when they mean—"

"Shhh," Kallie shushed her, stifling a laugh. "I know, I've heard your mom say it."

Tess picked up the last two grocery bags from the top step, so their host wouldn't have to come back for them.

"You're *helping* her?" Kallie whispered.

"Well, it's only polite. We did interrupt her while she was emptying the car."

As she loaded the frozen food into the freezer, Mrs. Collins said, "I've told the police everything I know about Kelsey. I've heard some rumors that she had troubles in her past, but she was a good employee. She never caused any problems, and the customers loved her."

"Loved her?" Tess asked, eyebrows raised.

"You wouldn't think it'd be a very touchy-feely business, since most of our customers already know what they're buying. But everyone likes a good listener," their host replied, leaning on the kitchen counter, and suddenly looking like a shrewd businesswoman. "Someone who makes them feel important. Most employees don't really listen to the customers."

Wait, we don't even know which of her businesses Kelsey worked for. How can we—

"You're so right," Tess agreed with a sensible nod. "I wouldn't think it would matter in your business."

Smooth, Tess.

"*Exactly*. No one does," Mrs. Collins agreed. She turned away again, placing a carton of orange juice in the refrigerator and closing the door. "To be honest, you don't really even notice that it's a missing quality in your staff, until you find someone like Kelsey."

"So you don't know anyone who'd want to hurt her?" Kallie asked.

"The police asked me that, too. I can't think of anyone who didn't like her." She paused and gave herself another moment to think. "She was charming but not cloying. Had innate business sense without being pompous," she seemed to be thinking out loud. "Heck, even my other *employees* liked her. And they work on commission."

"She never poached anyone else's clients?" Kallie asked.

"She didn't have to. She had all the business she could manage."

"So she was making a lot of money?" Tess asked, looking for a caveat. "A sudden windfall can get people into trouble."

Mrs. Collins shrugged. "She was our highest earner for the last few months, but I don't know anything about her personal life."

"You did a background check on her before you hired her?" Tess asked.

"Yes, of course. That's our standard procedure, since our products are so expensive," their host answered with a pragmatic nod, adding, "Not that anyone could sneak one out the door, but there are plenty of con artists willing to try. I gave a copy of that report to the police, too. When I hired Kelsey, she didn't have any extensive debt — just the normal stuff, a couple of credit cards and a student loan — and no felonies." She shrugged. "We don't repeat the check unless something specific comes to our attention, and there were absolutely zero red flags with Kelsey. So if she got into trouble after she was hired, I wasn't privy to it."

Kallie glanced at Tess, feeling pretty convinced. Her best friend seemed surprised and persuaded too.

This lady doesn't seem like an easy woman to fool. So was Kelsey really a drug user with a shady past, or did someone start that rumor just to take her down a notch at work?

Or to make her death less intriguing to the public? And maybe to the police?

"Could we ask your other employees about Kelsey?" Kallie asked their host, confused and out of ideas.

"You could try, but I don't think any of them knew her personally, either." Mrs. Collins shook her head. "She'd go to lunch with them sometimes, but I don't think she socialized with any of them outside of work."

"Did you ever meet her boyfriend?" Tess asked.

"Her boyfriend?" she half-smiled, looking a little embarrassed. "No, I didn't even know she had one. At that age, most of them parade their love interests around the shop like well-bred poodles." She sighed, obviously considering the talent she'd lost. "You could ask Tiffany about that — she's the shift manager. I don't think they were close, but she'd remember if he ever called the store, or visited Kelsey at work."

Kallie wrote that down. "We'll do that. Thank you."

"Of course. I hope I don't seem disinterested, but I barely knew her. She certainly seemed like a fine young woman, so I hope you'll be able to find her killer."

They thanked Mrs. Collins again and made their exit. As they left the house, Kallie whispered, "I can't believe she didn't ask us for ID or anything."

"See," Tess replied, "That's what happens when you have grown-up hair and wear a pencil skirt."

By the time they reached Tess's car, though, Kallie's feet were aching from her three-inch heels, and she was stumped about their conversation with Esmerelda Collins.

"Did we even learn anything?" Kallie asked, slumping into the passenger seat and wrenching off her shoes.

"Sure," Tess answered with a smile. "She said no one could just walk out with their products, which narrows it down..." She took out her phone, and added, "And the manager is named Tiffany." She tapped on her phone for a minute or two, then put the phone down and started the car. "Got it. And it's less than five miles from here."

* * * * *

"Hi, welcome to Smitty's," a pretty salesgirl swooped in on Kallie and Tess as soon as they entered the door. "Can I show you around?"

Kallie was astounded by the building they'd just entered and stared awkwardly around the room. It looked like a car dealership showroom, but instead of shiny new coupes and sedans placed strategically around the room, there was earth-moving equipment that looked bigger than her house.

The lifting arm of a massive yellow machine rose above her head – the scoop at the top looked like it could catch the moon.

"Actually, we're here to see Tiffany," Tess replied, giving Kallie another moment to take it all in. "Is she here?"

"Oh, sure," the girl, who looked like she was about sixteen, replied, sounding crestfallen. "I'll get her." She turned to walk toward the office.

"Ugh, I hate it when salespeople do that," Kallie whispered. "No wonder Kelsey was doing well, if the rest of them act like vultures."

"I think some people like it," Tess replied with a shrug. "It makes them feel visible. Wanted."

"The only thing that girl *wants* is her commission," Kallie answered, rolling her eyes. "Even in a bar, you have to give people five seconds to look around before you pounce."

"I think this is Tiffany," Tess whispered, nudging Kallie, as a woman only slightly older than the first approached them. "Are they all in high school?"

"Welcome to Smitty's," the shift manager greeted them. "I heard you wanted to see me? Did you have a problem with a purchase?"

"No," Kallie replied, stepping forward. "Actually we spoke with Mrs. Collins earlier, and she said you might be able to tell us something about Kelsey."

"Oh, Kelsey," the young manager repeated, quietly. Her face fell. "Sure. I didn't know her very well, but I can show you her timecards and stuff, if you need it. Come on into the office."

Wow, people are really trusting around here, Kallie thought to herself. *Just handing over names and timecards to strangers.*

Then, for just a moment, she caught her reflection in the front window of the office and saw that she *did* look rather like a detective. Or a lawyer.

I do look like a genuine grown-up. I think it's the hair, though, not the suit.

After passing through two locked doors, Kallie and Tess found themselves in a surprisingly formal office. Tiffany immediately opened a small filing cabinet and pulled out a thin file.

"You keep your records on paper?" Tess asked, surprised.

"Mr. Collins doesn't like computers," Tiffany replied.

Kallie and Tess looked at each other for a moment. "We weren't aware that there was a *Mister* Collins," Kallie added.

"I mean, there isn't, *anymore,*" the manager answered. "Not really. They got divorced and she got the company."

"Then why—?"

"I guess she'd have to hire someone to put it all in the computer," Tiffany answered with a shrug. "I can't even type." She set the thin file on the desk and pushed it toward them. "This is all of Kelsey's timecards. She wasn't here for very long."

Tess sat down in the guest chair and picked up the file but didn't look at it. Instead, she asked, "Did you know Kelsey's boyfriend?"

"No, I didn't really even know Kelsey, much less any of her friends," she answered. She turned and locked the filing cabinet, and then added, "I might've seen him one time, though. Now that you mention it."

"Do you remember what he looked like?" Tess asked.

"Not really. She went home sick one day, and a

guy picked her up because she was too sick to drive."

"Wow, that's pretty sick," Kallie replied.

I'm not sure I've ever been too sick to drive. Maybe she went to the emergency room?

"I noticed because he opened the car door for her, and helped her get in. It seemed pretty sweet. You know, old fashioned." She blushed a little. "No guy's ever done that for me. It was a nice car, too. A grey Range Rover."

Kallie looked at Tess, who was frowning.

Her mother told the officer that she was dating a nice guy, but surely she would've mentioned it if he was rich.

"Is it important? I think Terri recognized him, because she said something like 'I didn't think he liked nice girls.'"

This time Tess looked at Kallie and made a weird face. *Who is this guy?*

"It is important, actually. Is Terri here today? Could we please talk to her?" Kallie asked.

"Sure, if you think it'll help. Let me just make sure she's not with a customer." Tiffany yanked the filing cabinet handle again to make sure it was locked, and left the office.

"A rich guy who likes bad girls?" Tess asked, shaking her head. "This case has more mixed signals than a high school homecoming dance. Is this girl a drug mule or a straight-laced Pollyanna?"

"Hopefully Terri can tell us. I'm lost," Kallie agreed.

Tiffany walked back into the room with a petite blonde, who had a cute demeanor, but hard, unkind eyes. She didn't wait for an introduction but immediately asked, "You had a question about Kelsey?"

"Yes," Tess replied, standing back up. "Tiffany said you knew Kelsey's boyfriend?"

"Oh, I don't *know* him. He was only here one time, and I never spoke to him. But I recognized his face from social media."

"Oh, is he an influencer or something?" Tess asked.

"No, he's just always at the big events in town. Usually with rich party girls," Terri added with an eye roll. Kallie noticed that she seemed a little snarky about his wealth, for someone who presumably made a ton of money in commissions, working with rich customers all day and handling huge sales.

"And that's who picked up Kelsey when she was sick?"

"Yeah. He's apparently pretty well-off. I haven't lived here long enough to know all of the big names in the area, but I think his father's somebody important."

"Like, a politician or something?" Kallie asked.

"Maybe. I think, like, his family is the Florida

251

version of the Kennedys."

Tess nodded, apparently realizing what she meant. "Politically or financially like the Kennedys?" she asked.

"Probably both. They seem to go hand-in-hand most of the time."

Again, so jaded. Where is this coming from?

"Do you know his name?" Kallie asked.

She shook her head, no. "I might remember it, if I heard it again, though. It wasn't a name that I associate with rich people's kids — like Chandler or Winston. Or *Brock*," she rolled her eyes again. "I think it was... Cheyenne, or Phoenix, or something."

"Oh," Tess stated simply. "Was his name Dakota?"

"Yeah... I think that *was* it, actually," the salesgirl replied.

Kallie shook her head in confusion and looked at Tess questioningly.

"Dakota Abernathy."

"Yes!" Terri yelped. "How did you *know* that?"

"Lucky guess," Tess sighed, covering her eyes. "The Abernathys are one of the richest families in town. Old money, I mean. And you're right, they're involved in local politics too. Deep philanthropic roots — multiple charities. Dakota was famously troubled when he was in his teens, but he went to college and came

252

back... different. Better."

Kallie looked at Tess, baffled. She wasn't the type to follow local drama.

"He's Winchester's nephew," Tess explained. "Or, his ex-wife's nephew, I guess."

"Do you remember anything else about him?" Kallie asked.

"Not off the top of my head, but Winchester told me all the gory details a few years ago. Local bad boy makes good. I'll ask him what he knows about Dakota's recent history when I talk to him tomorrow, but Kelsey's mom was right. Kelsey could've done a lot worse."

"So we don't think he's the killer?" Kallie asked, trying not to sound disappointed.

"Oh, I'm not giving him a free pass just because he's rich and reformed," Tess replied with a rather jaded laugh, herself. She quickly reverted to the task at hand, "Terri, do you remember anything else?"

She shook her head. "No, Kelsey never talked about him. I just knew he was rich," she added. "And the local gossip never said anything about him being '*reformed*,' as you say."

"Why? What *did* they say?" Tess asked.

"That he was a druggie and a thief, basically," Terri sniffed.

"Well that stirs up the pot a little, doesn't it?"

Kallie mumbled.

"So the paparazzi either know a lot more than *we* do... Or a lot less," Tess observed.

"We'll check him out either way," Kallie agreed.

They thanked Tiffany and Terri and let them get back to work. There were several more people in the showroom when they exited the office, and there was money to be made.

"So how will we know where to find this Dakota person?" Kallie asked as they walked to Tess's car. "The Abernathys aren't going to just open their mansion doors for us."

"That's one of the great things about stalking the rich and famous," Tess answered with a smirk. "We don't have to find him — we'll let the internet show us the way." She started the car and turned on the heater, then took out her phone.

Kallie peeked over her best friend's shoulder as she opened the browser and typed 'Dakota Abernathy,' and then paused. The autofill on the search bar gave a list of possible searches:

> Dakota Abernathy dating
> Dakota Abernathy TMZ
> Dakota Abernathy net worth
> Dakota Abernathy father
> Dakota Abernathy hot pictures
> Dakota Abernathy art gallery
> Dakota Abernathy college

"That's interesting," Tess mumbled.

"What?" Kallie leaned over to look at the list more closely as Tess clicked an option near the bottom.

"Coronado Art Gallery," Tess read when the search popped up. "Out on Clearwater Beach."

"He has a job? In *retail*?" Kallie asked. "Ugh, *why?*"

"Winchester says he's really changed," Tess replied with a shrug. "I guess part of that is making your own living, even when your family has a jet and private pilot on speed-dial."

Chapter Eighteen

The bright yellow and blue transit bus to Clearwater Beach pulled into the parking lot just as Tess was locking the doors of her car.

"Oh, the shuttle's here," Kallie noted. "Let's run for it, so we don't have to wait for the next one."

Clearwater Beach was freakishly popular during the winter months, but its location on a barrier island slightly off the coast, accessible only by a bridge, made it frustrating to reach by car. Parking was both rare and expensive. Luckily there was a convenient shuttle service from the nearby mainland towns.

Kallie and Tess sprinted across the parking lot and hopped up the stairs of the shuttle, thanking the driver. It was still fairly early in the morning, so the ride wasn't overly crowded. It would be standing room only, by noon.

"I love the tourists when they're buying drinks and tipping well at my bar, but not when they're all driving on my streets," Kallie quipped. The tourists were usually friendly and polite, really. A few bad apples made the news, of course, but most locals didn't mind them.

"I love this shuttle," Tess sighed, leaning back in her seat as the bus pulled into the famously crazy roundabout, headed for the beach. "I never get to see the view when I'm driving, and it's so pretty out here."

"The gallery is at the south end, right?" Kallie asked.

"Yeah, we can get off at the last stop, and it'll be a short walk."

"Can we go to Clearwater Marine Aquarium after we talk to Dakota? I haven't been there in years, and I'd love to see the dolphins."

"If we finish early, sure," Tess agreed. "I haven't been there in a few years either. But I don't want to fight the crowds."

Being a coastal community, the Tampa Bay area had three major aquariums. Clearwater Marine Aquarium was the most famous and popular, even though they were more focused on animal rehabilitation than tourism.

"Why don't we ever come out here outside of tourist season?" Kallie asked with a laugh. "It's only about five miles from my house."

"They say seventy-five percent of the people who live in New York City have never been to the top of the Empire State Building," Tess shrugged. "I guess it's like that."

"Well I'm putting it on my calendar," Kallie replied, taking out her phone. "We're coming out here for lunch next week, to really visit. It's after the holiday rush, and before spring break."

A few minutes later, the shuttle stopped at the southernmost end of the route. Kallie and Tess climbed off, thanking their friendly driver again, and verifying that he'd be back every half hour.

"Okay, the gallery should be down here on the right, if this online map is correct," Kallie pointed.

"Man, it must be a nice place," Tess observed, looking around at the posh boutiques, restaurants, and art galleries. "I'll bet rental space in this neighborhood costs an arm and a leg."

"I don't think we're going to trick anyone here into talking to us without showing a badge, Tess," Kallie said nervously. "We'd better come up with another plan."

"Well, we're both still dressed nicely, so let's just start by window shopping, and see what we overhear," Tess suggested.

Kallie shrugged in agreement. *Can't hurt to try. Hopefully.*

Crossing Coronado Drive, they stepped under the pretty but eclectic awning of the gallery, and briefly admired the nearest pieces through the window. "Whoa, Kelsey's boyfriend works at this place?" Kallie whispered. "That sculpture says it's almost ten thousand bucks."

"Come along, *dahling*," Tess teased. "Mama needs a new knickknack for the hearth, and that will do *nicely*." She opened the gallery door and swept in like she owned the place.

"But it's a carving of a mouse," Kallie added, still staring at the small sculpture. "Why is it ten thousand dollars?"

* * * * *

Kallie followed Tess into the gallery a moment later, after one last confused look at the mouse — telling herself repeatedly not to bump into anything. Tess, of course, was as comfortable in a gallery full of priceless art as she would've been in a redneck bar, drinking beer and eating boiled peanuts.

The elegantly sparse and pale gallery was beautifully sunlit by windows high above them, where the exquisite artwork wouldn't be damaged by direct light. They circled the room, admiring the pieces on display and whispering about which ones they couldn't *possibly* live without.

A handsome young man approached them and mentioned politely that he could answer any questions they might have. He was about to drift back toward the counter when Tess stopped him.

See, that's so much nicer, No vulture action

here.

"Are you Dakota?" she asked politely.

He looked surprised. "Yes, I'm Dakota. Do I know you?"

"No," Kallie replied. "We wanted to talk to you about Kelsey."

After a moment of visible shock, his eyes teared up a little, but he nodded calmly. "Of course. Let me speak to my manager for a second, and we can step outside to talk."

It was as quiet as a church in the gallery, even though there were other people in sight, so Kallie thought his suggestion made sense. None of the other patrons needed to hear their conversation.

The young man returned a few minutes later, and gently guided them back to the door — with the air of someone much older than his years.

They sat on a decorative bench outside and Dakota began, bluntly but not aggressively, "You're not with the police. How are you involved?"

Kallie's heart sank, feeling like they'd been busted as complete phonies – but Tess wasn't fazed. "We're working with a private detective on the case, who has been hired to investigate the circumstances *behind* the murder," she replied coolly.

Wow, that was some serious flim-flam, Kallie thought to herself, impressed by her best friend.

Completely true, and yet completely bamboozling.

Dakota nodded. He hadn't refused to answer their questions, and he didn't seem defensive. Kallie didn't think they'd *tricked* him, exactly; he was just grateful for a reasonable explanation. "Of course, I'll be happy to help if I can."

Kallie began, "We've been told that you were dating Kelsey. How long did you know her?"

"We'd only been dating for about two months," he explained. "But I felt like I'd known her my whole life."

"You seem like you're from two different worlds—" Tess mentioned.

"And our parents couldn't have been more upset about it," he completed her thought and nodded with a sigh. "My parents actually liked Kelsey, but they said she wasn't 'our type,' and that I should forget about her. That our differences would only cause problems later."

"And *her* parents?" Tess asked.

"I never met Kelsey's father. Her mother was nice enough, but she was always very defensive. Like she was waiting for the other shoe to drop."

"She thought you'd grow up and forget her daughter," Kallie concluded.

"I suppose," he nodded.

"Did you love her?" Tess asked bluntly.

Kallie's head whipped around in shock at the

question, but Dakota just smiled sadly. "My mother said two months was too soon to know. But yes. We weren't going to *elope* or anything, but..." He paused for a painful moment, then added, "She loved me too. That's what she said."

"When did you last see her?" Tess asked, gently changing the subject.

"On that Friday afternoon. I wanted to go to the parade with her, but there was no one else to cover for me at work."

Kallie couldn't imagine this young princeling dressed up like a pirate and fighting through the crowds in downtown Tampa, but people could surprise you.

"Her friend Tabby doesn't like me, anyway. She thinks I'm 'fake and superficial,'" he sighed. "We were going to meet later that night, when I got off work. But then I heard from her mother that she hadn't come home from the parade."

"You didn't hear anything from her after you saw her on Friday? No calls or texts before the parade on Saturday?"

"No, but I knew they were dressing up. That costume stuff takes time. And we didn't text each other constantly, like some couples."

"No?" Kallie asked, a little surprised.

Dakota smiled at her reaction. "I know it's old-fashioned, but I think it ruins the romance. You never get a chance to miss each other, if you're chattering about nothing all day long."

"How old are you?" Tess blurted out.

He laughed. "I know, it's weird. She thought it was odd at first too, but I think it's why we were so close. We actually looked forward to seeing each other."

"So how did you meet her? It doesn't seem like your paths would have crossed much."

"We met at a hockey game, of all places," Dakota replied. "We both had to go to the game for work, and neither of us wanted to be there."

"You don't like *hockey*?" Tess asked.

"What kind of a *sociopath* doesn't like hockey?" Kallie added, momentarily baffled. "I mean, watching a Lightning game when it's 90 degrees outside? Is there anything better?"

Dakota chuckled at their banter. "Well we like it *now*, obviously. We're not heathens." He paused at his mistake in tense, and closed his eyes for a moment but didn't bother correcting it. "Neither of us had ever seen a game before — even on TV — and frankly, we were coerced. She was there for a mandatory team-building exercise, and I had to go for the boss's birthday."

"Okay, I'll accept that coercion is the wrong way to convert hearts," Kallie agreed, uncomfortably.

"Anyway, we met at one of the concession stands before the game. She looked pretty miserable, and I was feeling pretty grumpy myself. Honestly, I was drawn to her like a magnet."

"Misery loves company?" Kallie asked.

"Well yeah, but besides that. There was just something *magnetic* about her. She was pretty, but there were plenty of pretty girls there. And, honestly, I don't have a problem attracting women."

Tess coughed, clearly suppressing a scathing comment. Kallie smirked.

He blushed and quickly clarified, "Jeez, I sound like an egotistical playboy. I just meant... it wasn't about her looks. I really felt like I was meant to know her. Like she was standing in a million-watt spotlight that only I could see." Dakota looked at Kallie and Tess and added, "I didn't even care if I got her number. She wasn't a conquest – I just wanted to meet her."

Either this guy is the best liar we've ever interviewed, or these two were made for each other.

Tess nodded, and he continued, "She'd ordered a veggie burger and fries, and I swooped in like a lunatic to pay for them. I was babbling 'are you sure you don't want a soda?' and 'how about a glass of wine? a cup of wine?' and then 'how about an ice cream cone?' I'm surprised she didn't take out a restraining order."

Kallie cringed in sympathetic embarrassment, but Tess laughed out loud. "Girls like a doofus," she replied.

"I have generally *not* found that to be the case," he answered, blushing even more. "But at least she didn't pepper spray me."

"And it was all hearts and flowers from that moment on?" Kallie asked.

"I'm afraid not. She accepted the offer to pay for her dinner, and she thanked me, but that was all. She didn't give me her number, or even her name."

"Please tell me you didn't do anything creepy to find her again," Tess groaned.

"I seriously considered it. I could've used my connections to find out where she was sitting. My father's a big donor to the team's charity foundation. I could've gotten her name, or at least her employer's name, from the reservations system."

"But you didn't?"

"I didn't have to, as it turned out. One of her co-workers had seen us at the concession stand, and he recognized me. When Kelsey mentioned to her manager that 'some cute guy' bought her dinner, because she hadn't had a chance to eat before the game, he overheard them, and told her my name."

"Did he not warn her about your reputation? We heard you had quite a sordid past, Dakota," Tess added with a smile.

The young man blushed a little more and laughed. "I swear, a guy runs away from home *one time*, when he's sixteen, and everyone calls him a rebel."

"Winchester mentioned that," Tess responded.

"Sounds like you scared your family pretty badly."

"I didn't think it was that big of a deal, at the time, but I guess it made the local news."

"The *local* news?!" Tess chuckled. "TMZ was here in Pinellas county for a week, covering the story."

"Yeah, my father had just become a state senator. I guess I didn't factor that into the plan," he winced.

"Winchester said they dredged every lake in town for your body and searched for your car. Checked every morgue within fifty miles, in case you'd overdosed. There were even rumors that you'd been kidnapped by foreign terrorists."

"Yeah, *oops*," Dakota added, shaking his head.

Kallie was impressed that he had the decency to look mortified about it. She and Tess had done plenty of stupid things at sixteen, too, but none of them made the national news.

"But I was never into drugs," he quickly added. "That was just a rumor that developed when the media was trying to suggest where I'd gone. I even kept up with my homework while I was squatting in an abandoned house."

Interesting. He knows we aren't cops, and he has a reasonable alibi, but he's still trying to clear his name. And make sure we know he's a good guy. Is that guilt or just rebounding childhood trauma?

"But my parents put me in therapy when I got back," Dakota continued. "Daily. And that was the best thing that could ever have happened to me."

"How do you mean?" Kallie asked.

"I think everyone that grows up rich has some degree of entitlement, and I was no exception. I had no concept of how lucky I was, and how I needed to pay it forward," he answered, and then added, "Or at least try."

"And you got that from *therapy*?" Tess asked, sounding skeptical.

"Not overnight. I got part of it from my roommate in college, who was so rich he made me look like a pauper. His folks took him to volunteer, starting when he was little – first at animal rescues and the library, and later building homes for injured veterans and serving dinners at homeless shelters. Teaching kids to read. All kinds of stuff like that." Dakota shook his head and added, "He couldn't have been less like me, but he never gave me any kind of guilt trip."

Kallie nodded, but she saw that Tess was looking at him differently now. She was watching his face intently, and Kallie knew she was trying to decide if this was all an elaborate lie.

Nah, this guy's a good one. Good guy, good catch, Kallie thought to herself.

I hope.

"He just pointed out things I could do

differently, and I could see for myself how badly I'd treated some people, and how I needed to do better. Before the Christmas break, he took me shopping, and we bought a ton of Christmas presents for kids who wouldn't otherwise get any. Toys, and clothes, and books and stuff. Bikes. Sports equipment. Even one of those old-fashioned wooden rocking horses." He chuckled and shook his head. "We filled up the whole back half of his Maserati SUV and had the rest delivered. And honestly, it was the coolest thing I ever remember doing." He seemed stuck in the memory for a second – lost in a past where he wasn't sitting on a chilly bench and recalling his murdered young girlfriend — but then he looked up at them, and came back to the ugly present. The slight smile left his face, and he shrugged, adding, "I'm not saying I'm some angel or hero. I just try to be less of a jerk."

They both regarded him silently for a minute, and then Kallie asked, "And that's why you meshed so well with Kelsey?"

"Yes and no. Kelsey had never been in my position, but I swear she could make *anyone* into a better person. She's kind and respectful, and she's the most beautiful, gentle—" he stopped himself. "*Was. Was* the most genuine soul I've ever met."

Kallie watched as he leaned back on the bench and seemed to fold away into himself. She looked at Tess and sighed.

"Do you know if she had any enemies?" Tess

asked, clearly trying to stay on topic.

"She told me she was kind of a wild child when she was in high school. Nothing major, I guess; she wasn't a criminal. But Tabitha got her into party drugs..." he trailed off and frowned. "Tabitha was a bad influence, but Kelsey cleaned up when she went to college. She was embarrassed about it. If this was a targeted attack, and not random – then I guess it might've been related to something back then."

"She didn't mention a dealer or anything?"

"No, and I didn't ask," he admitted. "She was really embarrassed, and it seemed like she was just clearing her conscience. I didn't want to pry. Or sound like I was judging her." He looked heartbroken again. "Now I wish I'd asked."

"You don't think she got back into that lifestyle when she came home? When she was back with Tabitha?" Tess asked. She sounded kind, but Kallie didn't think she was convinced by any of this.

"No way," Dakota answered quickly. "I would've been able to tell. And she wouldn't have been so great at her job, if she was partying and getting into trouble. She was really proud of that job."

Tess nodded, noncommittally.

"The police said she had an arrest for breaking and entering," Kallie added. "Do you know anything about that?"

"That's actually on her adult arrest record,"

Dakota answered with a frown. "Tabitha and her boyfriend thought it'd be cute to break into their high school on graduation night as a prank, and Kelsey was the one who got caught." He looked angry, suddenly.

He's blaming a lot of this on Tabitha. Is he right, or is he making excuses for a girl with a lot of problems?

"And you haven't heard about her getting into any trouble lately?" Kallie continued. "You didn't get any sense that she was having setbacks?"

"She seemed stressed out sometimes, but I'm sure she would've told me if she was in trouble." His face fell again. "I hope she would've told me. Maybe I could've helped her."

"She wouldn't want you to be sad," Tess mumbled, and then closed her eyes. Kallie knew she didn't mean to sound trite, but it sounded like she still wasn't quite buying his story. She added a little archly, "And she wouldn't want you to get into any trouble, either."

"I'm not going to get in trouble. That's all in my past – the fast cars, the parties, the gold-digging girls. I just thought... I really thought she was my *forever*. She knew my past, had her own past, and showed me that I could get beyond the tabloids and drama. I didn't have to date the rich, shallow girls that my parents wanted. I had the *real thing*."

"I'm so sorry," Tess mumbled. She looked at

Kallie and they both stood up. "We'll let you get back to work."

He nodded and stood up too. "You'll let me know when your investigator catches the guy who killed her, right?"

"Sure," Tess replied with a nod. "Of course."

"I can't fix it, or undo it, but I need to see it concluded. And I know my dad will do everything he can, to make sure the guy never sees freedom again. He might not have wanted me to marry Kelsey, but he really liked her. And she liked him."

"We'll keep you informed," Tess replied. "Can we talk to you again, if we have more questions?"

"Of course." He took a business card out of his shirt pocket and flipped it over to write on the back. "That's my direct cell number," he added, handing it to Tess. "Call me anytime."

"Thank you," Kallie replied, feeling awful for him, and grateful at the same time.

Tess and Kallie walked back to the shuttle stop without speaking, both deep in thought. They'd seen several murders in the past few years, and they'd all been tragic, but this interview felt so personal and private. Like they'd shone a glaring flashlight into his soul.

"I don't want to go to the Aquarium right now," Tess said when they were almost to the bus stop.

"No, me neither," Kallie agreed. "I'm not in the mood anymore."

"We'll probably need to come out here again anyway. We can go next time."

"Sure," Kallie nodded, feeling morose. "Next time."

Chapter Nineteen

"Are you *sure* that's not blood?"

"Do I look like an expert on blood?' Tess asked with a sigh, peering closer at the sidewalk. They had returned to the scene of the crime, for one more look, since the interview with Dakota had been a bust. "*That* part's spray paint," she added, pointing at one side. "This part could be anything. But blood has that very specific coppery smell, and I think it would be even worse after all this time in the sun."

"A stronger smell than pee?" Kallie's nose crinkled.

"I know they cleaned the streets after the parade, but you're right. It does still smell like pee out here," Tess frowned. "We really need a good rain. But yes, I think weeks-old blood sitting in the sun would smell stronger than pee."

"I think it's blood."

"Well, it's not the yogurt that you pointed out the other day. It might be blood." She sniffed the air and looked slightly ill. "Why does everything smell so disgusting today? I want to go home and smell chocolate chip cookies baking or something."

"Look at the way it's pooled over here."

"*Everything* pools, though. Blood, wine, gasoline, hot sauce. Maple syrup. And even if it *is* blood, it's not like we have a handy crime lab in your garage where we can run a DNA test on it," Tess replied, sounding dejected and frustrated. "The police already did a full crime scene investigation. So if it's blood, and it's from the night of the parade, then they already have it sampled and logged."

Kallie looked disappointed for a minute, but then nodded. "I can accept that. So where do we go next?"

"Beats me," Tess sighed. "I'm out of ideas. Let's get lunch and brainstorm."

They walked back up to the riverfront and picked their lunch spots from the dozen or so pop-up restaurants, all housed in brightly-colored shipping containers. Kallie got Cajun scallops at one take-out spot, and Tess got a cheeseburger and onion rings at another, and they walked out to sit by the water and eat.

"So we know the murdered guy was a football star," Tess began between bites. "Young and crazy but apparently financially stable. Plenty of enemies, but no one that seemed ready to kill him."

"And there was full news coverage on that, and multiple press conferences," Kallie added, "so we already know everything the police are willing to share with the public."

"But who was Kelsey, really? And how was she involved in the first murder? How did she get the knife? Did she try to *save* Allbright?"

Kallie grimaced at that thought. The descriptions about Kelsey were so varied, it might be totally in her nature to save a stranger, if they believed Dakota – or it might be a ridiculous suggestion, akin to an orca saving a penguin, if they believed all of the other rumors.

"And is that why he attacked her? Did she manage to take it from the killer while he was attacking her?" Tess continued, thinking out loud. "Or was Allbright just collateral damage, like Elijah said? Are we going all-in on Elijah's statement?"

"The police immediately assumed that a woman in a pirate costume was the killer, before they even found us," Kallie added. "So maybe someone who saw his attack said the killer was a woman."

Tess considered that, dunking a delicious-looking onion ring thoughtfully into a pool of barbeque sauce, until Kallie was provoked to steal one from her plate. "The police wouldn't have stopped to discuss it with bystanders at that moment," she added, "so maybe someone just pointed and yelled, "she went that-a-way."

Tess laughed as she nabbed a crispy hush puppy from Kallie's lunch in retribution, "That-a-way? Was

Elmer Fudd one of the witnesses?"

"Absolutely," Kallie replied sincerely. "I saw him myself. Silly wabbit."

Tess rolled her eyes with a grin, and then returned to concentrating on her lunch. She was obviously still considering the murder, though, because she soon abruptly added, "There must have been a 9-1-1 caller!"

"Of *course* there would be, in that crowd," Kallie agreed immediately. "So that's probably who tipped them off about it being a woman."

"But there were thousands of random women with knives, in that crowd of well-armed mutineers and scallywags." Tess mused. "Was it Kelsey or someone else? Or was it just a mistaken identity?"

"*Another* mistaken identity, you mean?" Kallie asked, sarcastically. "Besides me?"

"Or was it the killer, trying to throw the cops off the chase?" Tess continued.

"Oh, that's a good one."

"Kelsey and the football player *couldn't* have known each other, right?" Tess asked, sounding frustrated again. "They were in completely different worlds. She was just a kid starting out, and Allbright was a rich and jaded sports star."

"They probably weren't *friends*. But you never know where two people's paths might intersect. Maybe he knew Tabitha – she was more of a party girl."

Tess nodded noncommittally.

"Oh, or maybe Allbright knew *Dakota*," Kallie added, sounding intrigued.

Tess looked up from her burger. "That's *way* less farfetched. Actually, that's not much of a stretch at all. They certainly wouldn't be hanging out together, sipping prosecco on the dock at daddy's house, but I'd bet money they have mutual friends."

"But then how does *Kelsey* end up doing the stabbing?"

"*Aaaaand* we're back to the million-dollar question. But young love has made girls do dumber things. Maybe Dakota put her up to it."

"Okay, that's possible. But why?"

"I have no idea," Tess sighed, taking a bite of her burger.

"But you still think he did it," Kallie stated, not a question.

Tess nodded. "I don't know the why or the how, but I really get a bad feeling from Dakota. I can *tell* he's lying about something, and I don't know which part – so as far as I'm concerned, his whole story is a sham. I don't believe a word of it."

I think he's nice, Kallie thought to herself. *But Tess is a really good judge of people.*

"I wish they'd play that 9-1-1 call on the news,"

Kallie added. "I'll bet that would explain everything."

"They probably will, eventually. That's great for ratings, everyone wants to hear the gory details. But it's too risky for the police to name a witness right now and make them a revenge target."

"Yeah, that's a good point. But it makes perfect sense. Of course the 9-1-1 operator would've asked the caller what they saw — *who* they saw. And of course the attacker would've been dressed like a pirate. In a sea of pirates, that could confuse anyone."

"It'd be weirder if the killer *wasn't* dressed like a pirate." Tess agreed. They both sat quietly for a while, finishing their lunch and pondering everything they'd discussed. Finally Tess asked, "I think it's time for me to send that DM now, don't you?"

Kallie nodded. "I think we've heard her name too many times now. Go ahead and contact Tabitha. I doubt she'll answer us, but give it a try."

Tess took out her phone, tapped a few times, and then typed a short message. "Okay, we'll see what happens," she added with a shrug.

* * * * *

"Wow, it really smells terrible over here," Tess complained as they walked back toward the parking lot where they'd left her car.

"We should go back and stand near the

restaurants again. It smelled like the cake shop exploded." They'd gone back to get iced coffee and cake pops before leaving the riverfront, and the coffee-caramel smell was still dancing in their heads.

"It's not like we live in seventeenth century London, why does it stink over here?" Tess groaned. "The city keeps everything clean."

"Maybe there's something that they missed when they were cleaning up?"

"Something *dead*?" Tess asked sarcastically, and then choked. "Oh no. I was kidding. *Please not* something dead."

"I don't think it smells quite that bad," Kallie answered quickly, grabbing her friend's hand. "Don't worry."

"It's pretty bad."

Kallie laughed awkwardly. "I don't want to be the one who stumbles on another dead body down here. I'll end up in front of a firing squad. Let's go home and leave it to Cornwallis."

"Yeah, one more dead body and they're going to lock you up just for public safety," Tess agreed, turning back toward the parking lot.

They walked back down the sidewalk, starting to window shop as the nasty smell faded away – but Tess paused before their turn. "Let's just go back for one minute."

"Seriously?" Kallie asked. "I thought you were going to start gagging."

"So did I. But I need to find out what's making that smell."

"Tess..."

"I'll make it quick," Tess urged, still looking back down the street. "We can't keep paying that investigator for everything, and we're already *down here.*"

"Fine," Kallie sighed, starting to feel a familiar twist in her stomach. "But just for a minute."

She's right, though. Even at twenty bucks an hour, we're going to run out of cash soon.

They hurried back to the smelly location, close to where the football player had been killed.

"See, this is such a nice, clean area," Tess mumbled, turning slowly in a circle, analyzing everything. Kallie knew she was waiting for some clue to jump out at her. "I can't believe the shop owners haven't complained about the smell yet."

"There isn't a sewer drain right here," Kallie noted, looking around. "And everything's clean. I guess the smell could be in one of the apartments up there," she looked up at the windows and balconies on the buildings above them.

"A stench like that, coming from these million-dollar apartments?"

"Maybe someone went on vacation and forgot something in the trash?"

"Like a spleen?" Tess asked, making Kallie snort back a laugh. "Help me think, Kal. What else is there? There's nothing else around here. No dumpsters, no trash piles, no animal nests."

"They don't even have trash cans out here," Kallie added, looking around.

Tess turned slowly in a circle again, eyes hunting for something she seemed to know was there. "Wait. The police would've checked that, right?"

"What?"

Tess pointed. "That big flower planter."

Kallie looked where she was pointing, and noticed a huge, industrial-looking concrete planter outside one of the restaurants, spilling over with split-leaf philodendrons and bright tropical flowers. "Across the street? I doubt it. It's too far away, and Kelsey ran that way." Kallie pointed down the opposite direction.

"I'm checking it," Tess announced, stoically. But she stood still.

"What? Why?" Kallie asked, but she took a step toward the street anyway, agreeably planning to cross — until Tess grabbed her arm.

"I don't want to look," Tess whispered.

Kallie turned back, surprised. Her best friend looked haunted and tired, and Kallie grasped Tess's

281

hand, where it was still holding her arm. "Hey, that's fine, sweetie. We don't have to look. Seriously, let's just go home."

They turned around again, for what felt like the twentieth time, starting toward the car — but Tess suddenly made a dash for the flower planter. Kallie watched as she ran headlong toward the restaurant, afraid or not, determined to know the answer.

Hurrying to catch up with her, Kallie saw Tess carefully but determinedly pushing the plants aside, to see what was hidden underneath. But by the time she caught up, Tess's shoulders had slumped in exhausted disappointment.

"It's nothing. Nothing but plants."

"Well, good," Kallie replied. "And as a bonus, it doesn't smell so bad over here either."

"Great, well then..." Tess stopped, staring across the street.

"Oh," Kallie whispered when she saw what Tess was looking at. "Well, that explains the smell."

"Gross, no kidding."

Hanging halfway off the balcony across the street was a giant fish. *Most* of a giant fish.

"I don't even want to know what that's doing up there," Kallie said, not sure whether to gag or laugh. "Think someone was trying to make sushi for the first time and failed?"

"It's probably from an Osprey," Tess replied, covering her nose and mouth with the top of her blouse. "They grab fish out of the water, but if they get startled and drop it, they can't pick it back up."

"I wonder how long it's been sitting there?"

"Too long," Tess answered, looking a little green. "I'll admit, I thought we might be onto another dead body, but I don't think the police are going to be interested in Mr. Limpit, up there." She started to walk back to the car, looking disappointed and annoyed.

"The owners must be out of town or something, if they haven't noticed the stench," Kallie noted. She started to follow Tess, but something caught her eye, and she looked closer. "Hey, Tess. The fish isn't the only thing up there."

"What?"

Kallie, who was much taller, had a better view of the balcony. "There's a security camera up there. And it's pointing right down here."

* * * * *

Morrison called Kallie back before they got home, and Kallie put him on speakerphone so Tess could listen. "I called the sheriff's office when I got your text," he told them. "Grayson wasn't available, but I talked to the lead on the case, and asked if they checked that apartment."

"He calls the sheriff 'Grayson,'" Tess whispered with a laugh. Kallie grinned but shushed her.

"He said they were trying to get access, but the owner's out of the country. The landlord wouldn't let them in without talking to him first, and no one's been able to reach him. They didn't see the camera, though. The officer said he's going to run back down there and see if the camera you mentioned is visible. If so, that might be enough to get a warrant."

"See, it's good when we go hunting for clues," Kallie teased him.

"I have no problem with you and Tess looking for clues, *Kalliope*," he sighed, sounding exasperated. "I just don't want you getting into dangerous situations."

"We're—"

"Or interfering with police business. Or contaminating crime scenes."

"We don't—"

"But thank you," he added.

Tess and Kallie both sat in shocked silence for a moment.

"This might actually be a big help," Morrison continued. "I'll let you know."

"Oh, you're welcome," Kallie replied sheepishly, still a little stunned.

Did he really just thank us?

"We're glad to help," Tess added quietly.

Kallie hung up, and they stared at each other until they both started laughing.

"We're actually getting pretty good at this," Kallie said, between giggling fits.

"I can't believe he thanked us," Tess added.

Their phones both chimed at the same time, making them both laugh again. They looked at their messages, and then at each other.

➢ Witness wants to talk to you. Pick you up at 4?

"When it rains, it pours!" Kallie concluded, shaking her head. "Cornwallis has something too?"

* * * * *

"Who are you taking us to see?" Kallie asked, as Cornwallis pulled into a parking spot in downtown St Petersburg. "This is pretty far from the crime scene."

"This guy's usually one of my contacts in St Pete, but he was up in Tampa for Gasparilla," the investigator explained, climbing out and leading them down the sidewalk a short distance. Much of St Pete was a pretty expensive city, overall, but their surroundings were quickly growing less affluent as they walked.

"Some party guy?" Kallie asked.

"Do I look like I use party guys?" Cornwallis

asked with a raised eyebrow. "My contacts don't use drugs – they'd be useless to me if they did. He's a professional panhandler."

"Really? Isn't that a long way to go for panhandling?" Tess asked. "It's at least half an hour by car."

"He took the bus with a few other guys. Gasparilla is one of the best-paying events all year, they tell me. Unless the Super Bowl's in town."

"Wow, okay. I had no idea there was so much coordination involved in panhandling," Tess replied.

"The police keep them off the parade route, but there's a lot of money to be made on the side streets."

The investigator stopped at a dilapidated old building and slowly pushed the front door open. He took a glance around the dark entryway to make sure it was empty. The place looked long-since abandoned, but clearly wasn't. Kallie heard a door slam on a higher floor, and then it was silent again.

"I've been here dozens of times," Cornwallis whispered. "It's not pretty, but it's safe."

Kallie wasn't convinced, but when she looked at Tess, her best friend seemed relaxed.

Am I really the only person who's ever scared? This place feels like a bad horror movie, where you're screaming 'Don't go in there, stupid!' at the TV screen.

"He wouldn't tell me what he saw," Cornwallis

explained. "He wants to talk to you. He's a manipulative and angry guy, but he's been a consistently great informant. I'm confident that he has legitimate information."

Tess and Kallie both stood silently, and he smiled.

"I won't let him bully you. And he's not dangerous, he just likes mind games," Cornwallis explained. "Don't answer any of his questions until I tell you it's okay."

"I'm not sure about this—" Kallie started to answer, voice trembling a little.

I must look and sound pitiful.

"Hey, no, that's okay," the investigator replied, stepping back toward the door and leading her away, suddenly aware of her discomfort. "I can try to find another witness."

"No, let's do this." Tess answered, shaking her head. "We're already here. And you said he's not dangerous, right, Wally?" She took Kallie's hand, supportively.

Wally?

Later, Kalliope. Focus. We can unpack that later.

Cornwallis nodded, looking back and forth between his clients. Kallie could tell he didn't want to push her, but he also really wanted the information this witness had.

"If he thinks he's going to intimidate us, he picked the wrong chicks," Tess added quietly to the investigator, conversationally, and with the hint of a smile.

"After only meeting you in person three times, I actually believe that," Cornwallis replied with a laugh. "Nobody's ever called my office *'oppressive'* before."

Tess raised an eyebrow.

"I bought an air freshener," he added.

Kallie grinned at them and took a deep breath. She knew Tess was right, and her nerves started to calm down.

Tess will probably have this bully crying for his mommy by the time we're done.

After a moment, they walked back inside, and the investigator stopped at the first door on the right. Tess nodded, and he tapped on it quietly. After a few moments, he pushed the rotten old door open a little and leaned in, "Badger, are you here?"

"*Badger?*" Kallie mumbled.

A voice called out from the darkness, inaudible.

"That's him. Let's go," Cornwallis added, pushing the door open a little more. Then he paused, turned, and checked out both girls briefly. After a quick scan, he took off his old plaid shirt and handed it to Tess.

"What?" she asked, taking the overshirt from him hesitantly.

"Put that on. Your neckline's a little low cut."

Tess looked down at her clothes, which seemed perfectly modest to Kallie, and started to respond, defensively, "It's not that low—" After just a second of consideration, though, she added, "You know what? Thanks." She slung the overshirt around herself and fastened the top button as high as it would go on her neck.

She made eye contact with Kallie, who nodded in agreement.

If he wants to protect us, we need to take his advice. He obviously knows something we don't.

Cornwallis gave them one more appraising look and then opened the door, leading them inside. It felt like they were walking into a lion's den, but once Kallie's eyes had adjusted, she could see that it was a pretty large studio apartment. It had once been beautiful, she could tell, with high ceilings and elegant woodwork around the doors and windows. The original hardware was long gone – probably sold or stolen decades ago – from the doors and windows, and the walls were covered in grime and water stains.

There was a sleeping bag on one side of the room, and a man was sitting on the floor near the dirty window, working on something in his lap. Boxes and cans of food were stacked behind him. For an apparent squatting nest, it was practically a penthouse.

"Badger, these are my clients. They're the ones who wanted to ask about the girl you saw."

The man looked up from his work, where he was drawing with a sharpie marker on a pair of old shoes. The canvas was smudged and well-worn, but even from far away, Kallie could see that it was intricate work.

She made eye contact with the man called Badger, and instantly wished she hadn't. The vicious look in his eyes made Kallie's blood run cold.

"Why you wanna help that girl?" he asked bluntly, in a tone that sounded perfectly normal, but his icy stare didn't change. Kallie suddenly wished she had an overshirt too.

Cornwallis nodded at Tess.

"We saw her before she died," Tess replied calmly. "She handed my friend the bloody knife."

"That don't make her your responsibility," he grunted, impatiently.

"No, but it's the right thing to do," she answered simply, coolly.

"Can you tell them what you saw, Badger? They came all the way out here because you said you'd tell them."

"Where's my payment?"

The investigator didn't approach him, but held up the bag he was carrying, and then tossed it to the man on the floor. It slid the last foot or two across the warped hardwood boards. Opening the shopping bag, Badger pulled out a twin-pack of new black markers and a cheap white baseball cap. He nodded his thanks and began to speak.

"I seen that girl with a *man*," he started, oozing the last word like Kelsey should've been wearing a scarlet letter on her chest. His angry eyes flashed a watery blue. "They thought they was alone, but Mickey and me was sittin' in the doorway, and we saw 'em."

Kallie wanted to ask a question, but she remembered the warning Cornwallis had given them, and she stayed silent.

"What did you see, Badger?" the investigator repeated, urging him to continue.

"He was standin' real close to her, and she kept turnin' her head away, like she wanted to leave. But she stayed."

This is just the same guy that Cornwallis's witness saw, yelling at her, Kallie thought to herself. *We're wasting our time. And I don't want to leave this place after dark.*

"Could you hear what he said?" Cornwallis asked.

"He said she should just give it to him, an' then she'd be safe. But she said she couldn't get it. She didn't have it." The man called Badger shook his head, and started inspecting the pristine new baseball cap like it was made of gold. "Me an' Mickey thought it must be a lotta money. 'Cause he was real mad. I could see him open and close his fist like he was tryin' not to hit 'er."

"Was the money for drugs, Badger?"

"Nah, I seen all them drug girlies." Badger shook his head in annoyance, like Cornwallis had asked a stupid question. "I wouldn'a told you, if she was one o' them."

"What, then?"

"Dunno. I thought maybe he just gave her money," he replied. "An' her loan came due. But he didn't say so."

She must've given him some kind of collateral then, Kallie thought, afraid to say it out loud. *A back-alley loan shark doesn't lend money out of the goodness of his heart. But maybe she lost the collateral.*

"She said somethin' like, 'I ain't followin' you, so you don't gotta follow me.'"

"What? Why would—" Kallie blurted out, and then quickly covered her mouth with both hands and shut up.

Cornwallis and Badger both turned to look at her like she'd startled them, but the investigator continued, "Why would she be following him, Badger?"

His contact looked back at his tennis shoe and continued drawing, silently, for a few minutes, but Cornwallis waited.

"You thought that was important, right, Badger? Was she trying to convince him that she wasn't following him?"

"Sounded to me like maybe she saw somethin', or heard somethin'. An' she wanted him to know that she was lettin' it go," he finally answered, without looking up.

Wow, he really wants to help us. For all that ferocity, he must really trust Cornwallis, to tell us this story.

"And the man was considering her offer, but he wanted her to *pay* for his good will, right? But she couldn't afford it? What did he say she should do?" Cornwallis sounded like he already knew the answer to this, and he was just asking for their benefit.

"Said she should ask her rich boyfriend," Badger replied with a chuckle.

Oh man. He knew about Dakota. So how—

Cornwallis interrupted her train of thought, "Why is that funny?"

"Because he's plenty rich too, that guy," Badger sneered. "He don't need that money from no pirate girl."

Cornwallis looked surprised, "You know him, Badger?"

"Nah, I don't know him."

"Then how do you know he's rich?"

"'Cause he made that movie with them fancy fighter planes. That 'need for speed' movie."

Cornwallis looked baffled and turned to Kallie and Tess with an eyebrow raised.

One of my dad's favorite movies from the 80s – he made me watch it a dozen times as a kid. Kallie made a curious face and mouthed the words, "*Top Gun*?!"

Cornwallis's face fell in disappointment. "Tom Cruise? The dead girl was being threatened by *Tom Cruise*, Badger?"

"That's him!" Badger nodded, managing to look happy and frighteningly angry at the same time. "Imagine him askin' some pirate girl for money."

Cornwallis shook his head, "Badger, I don't think—"

But Badger turned and fixed his savage, ruthless eyes straight at Kallie, snarling, "Don't you go near him, girl." He leaned forward, glaring fiercely, and added, "He'll kill *you* just like he killed them others."

Chapter Twenty

"What in the heck was *that* supposed to be?" Tess grumbled as they walked back down the sidewalk toward their car.

"I'm so sorry, Tess." Cornwallis shook his head again. "I know he's a tough case, but he's always been a good informant. Very reliable and tight with the details."

Kallie and Tess looked at him, waiting for him to go on. It was getting dark, and they were walking faster.

"Maybe he's losing his mind. Maybe he's been eating lead paint chips in that old house. Who knows?"

"So you don't think Allbright was murdered by Tom Cruise?" Kallie asked with a smile.

Cornwallis looked mortified and didn't answer.

"You were so brave to go in there, Kallie," Tess grabbed her hand. "I'm sorry this was all a waste of time."

"I'm not billing you for these hours, obviously," Cornwallis reassured them. "Let me talk to some more of my contacts. Maybe someone else saw something. I can check with more of the shop clerks down there too."

He unlocked his car and they drove back to his office in an uncomfortable silence.

* * * * *

"Well that was pointless," Tess growled, throwing her purse down on the couch in annoyance. She'd grown more and more irritated as they drove home to Owhiro.

"Pointless and dangerous," Kallie agreed with a sigh.

"Have we completely misjudged this guy?" Tess snapped. "I mean, we're *paying* him. Is he just pulling random people off the street, to pretend to be witnesses?"

"I'm not—"

"Is he ripping us off? Messing with our heads?" Tess steamed.

"Maybe it's—"

"I mean, what a joke. All that time, and the fact that he actually got our *hopes* up. He sounded so sincere, and worried about us, and then—"

"What if that guy was right?" Kallie interrupted, almost shouting.

Tess turned and looked at her like she was a

cockroach, making Kallie flinch a little, and then rolled her eyes. "You think Kelsey was killed by *Tom Cruise*."

"Well, yeah." Kallie shook her head. "I mean, no. Obviously not. Tom Cruise wasn't even in Tampa."

Tess laughed in spite of herself.

"But what if he saw someone who looked just like Tom Cruise? Cornwallis said he's super-observant, but maybe his day-to-day—"

"Sanity?" Tess suggested with a grin.

"*Discernment*," Kallie emphasized, "isn't quite at one hundred percent. He might've seen someone who looked like Tom Cruise lurking around at the parade. Maybe someone who even yelled at Kelsey, like he said."

Tess groaned, accepting the possibility. "Fine. Cornwallis said he's not charging us for any of the time he spent with that Badger guy." Her lip twitched in an annoyed sneer, as she repressed her disgust at the afternoon's events. "Go ahead and text him with your idea."

Kallie jumped up and grabbed her phone. "Okay, just one more try." She quickly typed a message to their investigator and sent it.

"Honestly, I think we're trusting this guy way too much," Tess added with a sigh.

"You think I'm trusting Dakota too much, too," Kallie mumbled.

"Yes, that too," Tess replied. "I'm still convinced that Dakota's in on this, somehow. But we do have to look at every angle, and I really don't mind you being the trusting one. I'm okay with being the bad cop."

Kallie smiled. "Well, if this Tom Cruise thing falls flat, we can go back to investigating—" Her phone dinged, and then dinged again. "Whoa, he answered already." She tapped on the message. "He says, 'Way ahead of you. Give me five minutes.' Sounds like he had the same idea."

"Even a broken watch is right twice a day," Tess grumbled.

"Don't say that," Kallie responded, sympathetically. "He's been great so far."

"We'll see."

Kallie went to the kitchen and turned on the oven to preheat for a frozen pizza, while they waited for the update from Cornwallis. In the meantime, she carried hummus and tortilla chips to the living room. They were both hungry, and that wasn't helping their moods.

The phone dinged again as they were snacking, and Kallie grabbed it. "He's coming out here," she read from the screen. "He'll be here in twenty minutes with some photos and news."

"You're kidding. It's barely been an hour since we left his office."

"He did seem like he felt really bad about letting

us down."

"And are you okay with him coming here?" Tess asked, looking wary again.

"I mean, sure." Kallie paused, considering. "He already has my address. He could show up any time, if he was a psycho."

"Sherman will protect us, if he turns out to be dangerous," Tess suggested jokingly.

"Absolutely not," Kallie replied seriously, remembering her earlier thought. "No way."

Tess leaned over and took Kallie's hand, smiling crookedly. "Agreed. I'll go get one of your dad's big claw hammers from the garage. Sherman can nap in your room, while we receive our unexpected guest." Sherman picked his head up off the couch when he heard his name, and Tess scratched his ears. "C'mon, sweet boy."

* * * * *

The private investigator arrived twenty minutes later, as he'd predicted – giving Kallie and Tess time to eat their frozen pizza – and promptly leaned his dragon-wrapped cane against the wall and plopped down on the couch. He took an old laptop computer out of his backpack and opened it quickly.

"I had the same idea," he began. "Badger might've seen someone who looked remarkably like

Tom Cruise."

Kallie and Tess both nodded.

"And I doubt the real Tom Cruise has time in his busy schedule for parades. Even really good ones in warm climates," Cornwallis continued. "Besides, *Top Gun* was Tom Cruise circa, like, 1985. A completely different look. I thought facial recognition software would be perfect for this, but I can't afford anything like that with my rates." He smiled at them and opened the laptop. "Luckily, my sister is dating a computer nerd."

"We could've just gone to the police," Tess suggested, still feeling grumpy.

"I thought of that, but it would take forever. Their backlog is over a month long. My sister owes me a favor, so I sent an old picture of Tom Cruise to Bobby – that's her boyfriend – and asked him to scan all of the uploaded Gasparilla videos on YouTube."

"Seriously?" Tess asked. "Just like that?"

"He thought I was kidding, at first. But he's been experimenting with an open-source facial recognition system in his spare time, and it's a pretty cool test, right?" Cornwallis asked, sounding impressed. "Obviously, our famous movie star didn't jump into a time machine and attend the parade with a younger face. So either Bobby's homegrown recognition software pulls up three hundred random guys, or no one at all."

Tess nodded. She tended toward nerdy herself,

at times. "So he was curious about how it would work in a real-world test."

"Exactly," Cornwallis agreed. "And so, I have good news and bad news."

"He didn't find anyone?" Kallie asked, anticipating the bad news first.

So why are you here? Just to make us even more irritable and frustrated?

"On the contrary," the investigator replied. He clicked a few keys and turned the laptop around. On the screen was a clear photo of Tom Cruise in a pirate costume.

"What the—?" Kallic asked breathlessly.

"You've got to be *kidding* me," Tess agreed.

Cornwallis tapped a few more keys. "It's not him. But it sure looks enough like him to fool me. Much less a bunch of drunk pirates."

"Much less a snarky, half-mad informant hiding in the shadows," Tess added with a grudgingly acquiescent nod. "Although, to be fair, that guy might've fooled me too."

Cornwallis tapped another key, and the next photo showed Kelsey in the frame with the doppelganger. They all looked at it silently.

"I'm afraid to ask for the bad news," Kallie added hesitantly.

"Right," Cornwallis sighed. He tapped a few

more keys and another photo popped up. Tom Cruise was in the background, here, and it showed another young man in profile. Not a pirate, but surrounded by costumed revelers. Kallie and Tess both recognized him immediately.

"That's Dakota," Kallie whispered, and then went silent as her mind raced. "He was at the parade?"

Tess looked at Kallie, raised one eyebrow, and somehow managed to not say, "Told you so."

"What's he *doing* there?" Kallie wondered aloud.

"Not to burst your bubble, ladies, but Bobby was looking for Tom Cruise. So let's start there."

Kallie shook her head, baffled, and replied flatly, "Sure. I need to process this, anyway. What happened with Tom Cruise?"

"Obviously, the police were working non-stop on the Allbright case. There are terabytes of facial recognition footage on everyone who was within a block of him that night. For our girl Kelsey, not so much. That official research just started, after finding her body in the Bay, and it hasn't progressed much."

Kallie sighed and started to argue, "We still need to—"

"Not that she's unimportant," Cornwallis interjected quickly. "But the first forty-eight hours had already passed. The evidence was probably already washed away, and the furor about *your* arrest has died down. And frankly, there were a lot fewer cameras pointed at her than at the muscular, wealthy bad boy." He stopped to let Kallie continue, but she nodded for him to go ahead. "As I mentioned, my sister's beau was able to run a scan, and send me these results quickly."

"Do you know who he is?" Kallie asked.

"Once we'd established that he was a real person, and not a figment of Badger's imagination, and that he attended Gasparilla and the post-parade revelry, Bobby was able to use these pictures to run a search against social media pretty easily, within specific hashtags. With the presumption that he lives in the Tampa Bay area – which was a bit of a stretch, frankly – he found his identity within a few minutes."

Tess turned to Kallie and whispered, "Remind me to take *all* of my photos off of social media tomorrow, Kal."

"I hereby present to you, Grant Forsythe," Cornwallis announced, with a bow and a minor flourish toward the screen. He was obviously exhausted from their earlier hunt, too, but enjoying the reveal. He tapped a few more keys, and a recent arrest mugshot from nearby Polk County popped up on the screen, with Forsythe's name at the bottom.

Disorderly conduct, Kallie read from the screen. *Not exactly Jack the Ripper*.

More tapping by Cornwallis, and a social media profile appeared, with photos of the same man in a red velvet frock coat that would've made Captain Hook envious. His black feathered cap finished the look.

Tess let out a long whistle. "Wow, nice job."

"Now, how do we find him?" Kallie asked.

Cornwallis poked one last key on the laptop, and a directory page popped up with the man's name and home address.

"Holy cow," Kallie whispered.

"That's terrifying," Tess agreed.

"If not for the arrest record, I don't think we could've found him, to be honest." The investigator shrugged. "Drivers' license photos aren't publicly available or searchable, but most mugshots are posted on police websites, for public safety reasons. We got lucky. Want me to go check him out tomorrow?"

"Yes!" Kallie and Tess both answered, grinning. "But take us with you," Tess added. "We'll check out Dakota again, too," she told Kallie, who nodded, "But your friend Badger's batting a thousand now, Wally."

"Forsythe lives out this way," Cornwallis replied with a nod and a tiny crooked smile. "In Palm Harbor. Pick you up at eight?"

So we're sticking with Wally, apparently. And Tess has officially lost her mind.

"Absolutely," Kallie agreed. "Eight o'clock. Could you email all of those photos to us?"

"As soon as I get home. See you in the morning."

"So how are we going to do this?" Kallie asked from the back seat of Cornwallis's beat up Ford Falcon, the next morning. The sun had just cracked the horizon, and the three of them drove north toward the nearby town of Palm Harbor.

"I did a little more research on our doppelganger when I got home last night," Cornwallis replied, "and I think I should be the one to approach him. Forsythe started out as a basic, low-level drug dealer, selling pot to teenagers, but he's really escalated in the past few years. Increasingly harder and nastier drugs, dealing in stolen firearms, even human trafficking – but he's clever and never leaves any evidence that points back to him. My contact at the station said they know he's guilty, but they can't prove it yet – and his cohorts are too afraid to roll on him."

"Lovely," Kallie answered.

"The only thing the police have ever managed to catch him on was that old disorderly conduct charge," Cornwallis added. "That charge really *should* have been dropped – it looks like he just got singled out at a noisy party in a rental house. But I'm glad we had it for the ID. They're mostly non-violent offenses, but I'd rather handle it, if you're okay with that. I can just stop him, and ask where he was after the parade," their investigator suggested, looking at Kallie in the rearview mirror.

"We shouldn't alert him that we're checking him out," Tess considered aloud. "If the police haven't questioned him about the murder, then he probably thinks he's still flying under the radar."

"He looks so devious," Kallie squinted at the printed photo in her hands, captured and cropped from a video taken after the parade. "The way he's watching Kelsey."

"We can be devious too," Tess answered her with a grim smile. "You cover our backs, and we'll try to strike up a conversation with him," she advised Cornwallis.

The investigator took his foot off the gas briefly, and slipped a hand down to his ankle, and then nodded at Tess. Kallie realized with surprise that he was probably checking for a hidden handgun. Her heart skipped a beat, but she found herself a little relieved, too.

"You're running this show," he agreed. "We can try it your way. But if anything goes pear-shaped, I'm taking over."

They both agreed.

I did tell Morrison that it'd be safer if we hired someone. Cornwallis can handle anything scary – that's why we pay him the big bucks.

The investigator made good time, and they arrived at Forsythe's condo just before 8:30 a.m. They were cruising the street casually, and just starting to discuss their next steps, when the front door of his building opened. A handsome young man stepped outside, walking a beautiful Golden Retriever on a leash.

"Is that him?" Tess hissed.

"Definitely," Cornwallis nodded.

"A young Tom Cruise with a Golden Retriever. If he was looking for a girl to drug and murder, that's like luring kids into a white panel van with candy," Kallie agreed with a whimper.

"Drop us at the corner," Tess suddenly insisted. She turned to look at Kallie in the back seat, adding, "Let's do this."

"Okay, but don't walk fast. I'll try to keep up with you, in case you need help." The investigator drove cautiously up the street, trying not to draw attention, and stopped at the corner to let them out.

"Thanks for the lift!" Tess called to him as they jumped out of the car. "I'll give you five stars!"

Cornwallis played along, waving to them as they hurried away in the chilly, February morning air. He pretended to be checking his phone for his next rideshare fare. Kallie tried not to look back, trusting that he'd stay nearby.

"I can't believe Cathy wouldn't drive us home," Tess continued shrilly, ranting like a disappointed party girl, as they approached their latest murder suspect.

"She had plenty of time, and it's not like she had to go to *work*," she added with a jaded sniff.

Forsythe, their erstwhile Tom Cruise, stared down the walkway as they approached him like a small tidal wave. He tightened his grasp on the Golden Retriever's leash, and nervously pulled her off the sidewalk, into the grass, out of their way.

"Oh, what a cute doggy!" Tess suddenly gushed, loudly. Kallie looked at her normally reserved best friend in surprise, but Tess was on a roll. "Can I pet him?"

Kallie suspected she'd mixed up the dog's gender intentionally, hoping to pull Forsythe into a conversation. *Everyone wants to talk about their dog. She's so smart.*

"Oh, sure," Forsythe replied uncertainly. "She loves people."

Tess knelt down and snuggled the strange dog affectionately – this part wasn't an act, Kallie knew – and looked up at their suspect. "You're so sweet to take her for a walk, in this cold weather."

Most men were enraptured by Tess's beauty, but Forsythe just blushed and looked awkward. "She's my best friend," he answered shyly, showing none of the boldness they expected. The adorable dog spun around happily, waiting for Tess to pet her again, and her owner smiled innocently. "Thank you for playing with her. She loves meeting new people, but... Well, I don't have that many friends." He lowered his face, embarrassed, and moved away from them.

Kallie made eye contact with Tess and tilted her head in confusion.

This is our psychotic killer?

Tess went out on a limb, obviously just as bewildered as Kallie, but determined to clear this up. "We're going to the Gasparilla Arts Festival tomorrow. We're visiting a friend on this street who's showing his work. Do you know where he lives?"

Their suspect shook his head silently, blushing again.

"You don't know any artists on this street?"

He put his hand out and touched the dog, who nuzzled him back. Shook his head again.

Timid, awkward. Childlike, even. This guy's no killer.

"Have you ever been to Gasparilla?" Tess asked, smiling gently.

He turned to her and nodded, cheerfully. "I went to the Gasparilla. I went with my mom." He looked at Kallie, and his eyes lit up. "There were pirates."

"You bet there were," Kallie replied with a smile. "Did you get to dress up like a pirate?"

He nodded happily again.

"That's awesome. Well, you have a great day, sweetie," Tess told their former suspect, giving the dog one last scratch. "We'll find our artist friend, don't you worry."

As they walked back toward the car, Forsythe waved at them again, and Tess kicked a rock down the sidewalk in frustration. "Okay, we'll go see Dakota again on Sunday."

Kallie nodded, feeling bad that they'd followed this guy, suspecting him of murder. Cornwallis met them at the opposite end of the street, looking relieved that they were safe.

"Another dead end," Tess growled, as they got back into his car. She slammed the door loudly.

"You're kidding?" he asked, sounding shocked as he stared at Tess in the passenger seat. His eyes flicked to Kallie in the back seat. "Nothing?"

They described the conversation that had just happened, and Cornwallis continued to look confused. "No... No, I didn't see anything like that in his files." He shook his head and looked horrified.

"Looks like your buddy's software still has some serious bugs," Tess grumbled, angrily.

"I'll check my research when I get back to the office," the investigator answered, awkwardly. "There's no *way* I messed this one up."

They drove back to Kallie's house in tense silence.

Kallie and Tess walked into the house, both still feeling grumpy, and Tess sat down with a sigh. "What a mess. And that poor Forsythe guy must think we're crazy."

"Well, he's not totally wrong," Kallie replied with a slight smile, which quickly turned into a frown. "Oh, we definitely have to see Cornwallis one more time, anyway."

"Why?" Tess asked. "Apart from the fact that we paid him, I mean?"

"Because he left his cane," Kallie grumbled, pointing to where it was still leaning against the wall. "I'll move it so we don't forget it."

She picked it up just as Tess's phone dinged. Her friend checked it angrily, obviously expecting a message from Cornwallis, but then grabbed Kallie's arm. "It's from *Tabitha*!"

"I can't believe she answered you! What did she say?"

"I told her we were working with a detective on Kelsey's murder, and we'd like to speak with her," Tess replied. "She said she's out of town, but she'll help us if she can. And she sent her phone number!"

"It's not even noon yet. Do you want to try calling her now?"

Tess nodded and tossed her purse onto the

311

couch, then sat down at the table, as Kallie poured them each a glass of lemonade. "Ready?"

Tess dialed the number and put the phone on speaker. It rang four times, and Tess was about to hang up, when a woman's voice answered, "Hello?" Loud music was playing in the background, and she sounded like she'd been running.

"Tabitha?" Tess asked. "I sent you a message yesterday. We're calling about Kelsey."

"Oh, hi. Give me one minute." They heard a door shut, and the music became much quieter. "I talked to the police, but I didn't see anything that night. I'm not sure if I can help you."

"We know you and Kelsey got separated at the parade. We just wanted to ask you a few other questions. How was she acting in the few days before her death?"

"She was fine. Why?" Kelsey's friend sounded defensive and confused. She was trying to sound tough, but Kallie felt awful for her.

"We think she might've been targeted," Tess continued. "Did she say anything about—?"

"Targeted? I thought she just got caught in the middle of that other murder."

"We're not sure yet; that's why we need your help," Kallie explained. "Was she acting unusual?"

"Well she'd been dating a new guy, so she was

acting all lovestruck. She just started a new job too, so I didn't see her that much." Her voice cracked a little and Kallie sighed.

"Do you know if she was in any trouble?"

"She was making tons of money at work, and dating a guy she—" she paused.

"Yes?"

"A guy she loved," she finished. "I didn't like him, to be honest. But she was crazy about him."

"Why didn't you like him?" Tess asked.

"I was happy for her, at first. But he never wanted her to hang out with me. He's super rich, and he didn't think I was good enough," she sniffed.

Dakota sounded like he was protecting Kallie from Tabitha's bad influence. Which one of them is lying?

"Oh, so you hadn't talked to her in the days before she was killed?" Kallie tried not to sound disappointed.

"I talked to her; I just didn't see her." Tabitha clarified. "She mostly talked about him, though. And I know when you're in love, that's all you want to talk about. I've been there too," she added with a sad laugh. "But I wanted to talk about *us*. About our costumes for the parade and who we were going to party with—"

"Did she party a lot?" Tess asked.

"Nah, not anymore," Tabitha answered. "It had

been a couple months since we went out, and she's clean now. She barely even drinks."

Tess and Kallie looked at each other, both a little surprised.

"Actually, she did say something about that last time we went out. When we talked on Friday night, the night before the parade, she said she wanted to show me a funny picture. She was going through the photos on her phone, looking for a selfie of us to post, and found a shot of someone we knew."

"Do you think it's important?" Kallie asked. "Did she sound worried?"

"Not at all," Tabitha answered. "She was happy. She said, 'I found some pictures of Marty. I'll show you tomorrow.' But we both forgot about it while we were getting ready for the parade."

"Who's Marty? An old boyfriend?" Tess asked.

"Just a guy we used to party with when we were younger. He was nice, and he played the guitar. Everyone liked him."

"Was?" Tess asked.

"Yeah, he died back in January," Tabitha answered.

Kallie looked at Tess again and raised an eyebrow.

Are we looking at the wrong suspects for this murder? A lot of people suddenly seem to be dying around Tabitha.

"Are you going to be back in Tampa, Tabitha?" Kallie asked. "We'd love to meet with you."

"Nah, I don't want to be there right now. It's too depressing," Tabitha answered with a sigh. "I'm staying with my brother in Jacksonville."

"Okay, well, thank you for your help. We'll get in touch with you, if we have any other questions," Kallie replied.

"Miss Poirot, I believe we have a new suspect," Tess noted, after they hung up.

"I was thinking the same thing," Kallie agreed. "I'll call Morrison; you tell Cornwallis."

Chapter Twenty-One

Kallie called Tess on her cell phone as she was leaving work the next day. She'd had another idea and wanted to meet in downtown Tampa.

"I'm sorry, Kal. I can't. Winchester is still on that big case in New Orleans, and I need to be available while he needs me," she explained. "Can we go tomorrow before work?"

"I don't want to cut it close for my shift at work again. I was late last time we tried that," Kallie replied, feeling bad for disrespecting Marcy's time. "I'll just run down there right now."

"Okay, but be careful."

"I just want to take a couple pictures. Nothing dangerous, I promise," Kallie agreed. "I'll send them to you as soon as I get home."

They hung up, and Kallie pulled out into Owhiro's evening traffic. Her phone was low on batteries, so she pulled a charger out of the glove compartment and plugged it into the old cigarette lighter in her car's dashboard.

If the guys who made this little old car knew it

would be charging a tiny cordless phone one day, she smiled to herself. *Much less a camera and digital map and email system and video game arcade, all in one...*

Kallie turned on the radio and made the long drive to downtown Tampa – grateful that it was late, and that she was going against traffic. She made good time and pulled into the parking lot nearest the sushi restaurant where they'd been eating after the parade.

Just as she was getting out of the car, though, she heard her phone chime. She sat back down and checked the display – Morrison.

> ➤ Checked with TPD, Tabitha was on trolley when murders happened.

Dang it.

Kallie sighed and texted him back, thanking him for trying. She started to get out of the car again, but was pulled back by another chime.

> ➤ Warrant on balcony video shows Majors followed by someone. Not clear but TPD working on it. Grayson says thank you.

Yes!

Kallie sent a smiley emoji, so glad that the camera she'd seen on the apartment balcony, behind the rotting fish, had usable video. Hopefully the police could find the killer that way.

She just wanted to get a few pictures outside the restaurant, and then a quick video of the path down the street, to where Kelsey would've turned. They were missing something, so they needed to go back to the beginning – and this is where it all started.

Have we really eliminated all of our suspects so far? Tabitha and Brockaway were cleared, and poor Forsythe was so sweet. I guess that proves you can't judge a person by one video.

I mean, look how everyone's judging me by one video...

Dakota's story fell apart, so he's the only one left without a solid alibi.

She continued snapping pictures of her surroundings, reviewing them on her phone screen for lighting and details before she moved on.

Too bad about that facial recognition software not working right. Hopefully they'll get that fixed and we can try it again—

Suddenly she heard a voice nearby say, "Hey, isn't that her?"

The news stations were still sending reporters down here occasionally, even though the Allbright story had stopped being major news. She hoped it wasn't a reporter, recognizing her from the security video. She'd just gotten off work and wasn't feeling particularly pretty after a long shift.

Kallie put her head back down and tried to become invisible – just a lady taking pictures, just a tourist, just an artist who liked old brick buildings. *Invisible.*

She didn't hear the voice again, and finally relaxed, realizing it was probably a coincidence. Focused back on her pictures, she finished the photos she wanted by the restaurant, and started filming the pathway down the street, walking slowly and getting the sidewalk and walls in the shot. Pivoting a little to include the curb and part of the road.

What would Kelsey have seen, as she was stumbling, searching, bleeding?

If I can just get into her head, I know I can figure this out...

She was watching the screen intently, as she approached the corner where the young victim would have turned.

I can't film all the way back to where Allbright was killed. That would take an hour to do properly, and I don't have that much space left on my phone. Besides, it would be a little crazy. If the video is going to help us figure it out, this will be enough.

She had just turned off the camera and dropped it into her pocket, ready to go home, when she felt something brush her arm. Confused, she turned back, just as a hand reached out from around the corner and grabbed the sleeve of her coat.

There was no sound, no voice. And when she leaned forward, there was no one standing at the corner. She took a step back, perplexed, and in an instant, someone was all over her. A hand grabbed her shoulder and tried to get an arm around her waist from behind, silently.

Scream, Kalliope. Make some noise.

But she was too shocked to make a sound. The calm, quiet night seemed so peaceful, and her mind couldn't quite grasp it. Luckily, her father's lifelong lessons to be constantly alert kicked in almost immediately.

Not sure Dad was picturing this scenario. He probably just thought I'd have handsy boyfriends.

She bent her right leg and then swung her foot back as hard as she could, smashing into the knee of whoever was holding her. As he screeched and stumbled in pain, she felt him double over, and braced her arm, confidently. Swinging her elbow back, hard, she heard a satisfying *crack* and a grunt as she made contact with his mouth.

Yanking her arm away, and preparing to run, for an instant she considered taking a picture of the attacker.

They have cameras everywhere, remember? Go!

Without looking back, she ran for her life.

Dodging around corners as fast as her legs would carry her, she zigzagged and ducked behind cars, so she wouldn't be a sitting duck.

That guy wasn't alone, she thought to herself. *You might have incapacitated him, but he was talking to someone else.*

They must have split up before he grabbed you, keep going.

She kept running haphazardly for another few minutes, wishing there was a crowd tonight that could hide her. After another minute or two without hearing footsteps or shouts, though, she thought she might be in the clear. *Hopefully.*

Kallie turned right at the next corner and slowed to a walk, forcing herself to stroll casually – but as quickly as possible – down the sidewalk. Trying not to run, to remain invisible. Looking for a place to hide.

Thank goodness for Isabel's yoga and aerobics classes, she thought to herself, trying to catch her breath. *I think I outran that guy, but I need to get out of these streetlights.*

She pretended to window shop while looking for cover. She already knew there weren't very many alleys in this section of downtown Tampa, but their absence had never been as *annoying* as it was right now.

I'll even take a large dumpster to hide behind, she thought to herself. *Give me something.*

A driveway came up on her right, leading to a

small parking lot ringed by businesses – a rarity in itself – and she stealthily followed it. She leaned against the wall outside a dentist's office, trying to calm down. This was good cover off the street, but the expensive parking lot was lit up like midday, for security.

If anyone saw me turn into that driveway, they'll be back here in a few seconds, and I'll stand out like a prima ballerina under these spotlights. Her mind raced, and she looked around for any possible hiding spot. *Only one car in the parking lot – should I try to hide under it?*

Kallie knew that was her worst-case option, and started moving along the storefronts and offices instead, hoping for a brilliant idea.

Dentist. Coffee shop. Women's apparel. Maybe someone's working late, and they might help me? Smoothies. Eye doctor. Chiropractor. These places must be really popular, and expensive, to afford their own parking lot! Luxury pet supplies. Another coffee shop?

Why are they all closed?

As she swept past the next series of doors, movement caught her eye. On a store up ahead, the dangling 'Closed' sign inside the door was moving, blowing a little in the breeze.

Breeze? Inside the shop?

She hurried toward it and touched the door gently. It opened just a crack.

"Thank you, thank you, thank you," she barely breathed the words, as she cautiously pulled the door open, and glanced behind her to make sure no one was following. The night was silent, and she slipped inside.

Kallie pulled the door closed, and then, after a moment's hesitation, locked the bolt.

Stepping away from the door, she slipped into a small storage room off the entryway, and put her hands on her knees, taking a few deep, thankful breaths. Then she called out quietly, "Hello? Is anyone here?"

No sounds, and the place was dark as midnight. She closed her eyes for thirty seconds – forcing herself to be still – and let them adjust to the lack of light.

Better.

"I'm not robbing you," she called out again. "Is anyone here?"

The storage room was full of cardboard boxes, some kept neatly on shelves and others stacked on the floor. She squinted into the darkness but couldn't see any labels, and she definitely wasn't going to turn on any lights, even if she could find a switch.

I just escaped one psychopath; I don't need to get myself shot by a startled shop clerk.

"Hello," she called again, louder, stepping into the main room of the shop. Huge refrigerators hummed quietly against one wall, and three long rows of shelves sat parallel in the center of the room, crowded with boxes and tins.

Oh, it's some kind of market, she thought to herself. *I wonder why the door was open at this hour?*

She looked around to find an office, thinking the owner might be working overtime on his finances, but didn't see another door.

"Is anyone here?" she called again, even louder this time. Desperate, but trying not to yell.

Okay, no. They must've just forgotten to lock the door. Saving my skinny butt in the process.

She leaned against the counter and slid down to sit on the floor, hoping no one would see her from the street and call the cops. It was late though, and there didn't seem to be many people outside.

Should I call the cops, myself? she considered. *No, I'm in enough trouble. I've already been arrested for murder once in the past month, no need to add breaking and entering to the issue. They'd probably tase me on sight.*

Kallie sat motionless on the floor, impatiently waiting for the coast to be clear.

Could those people still be looking for me?

Yes. But it's a big city, and they'd never be able to find me in here.

Unless they collected their creepy friends to help search. After all, I was on the news every hour for a solid week. Everyone within a hundred miles knows what I look like.

Kallie whined quietly and told her brain to shut up.

Maybe you're overreacting, Kalliope. It could've been a mistake. Let's just hope you didn't incapacitate someone who was just hoping for directions to the waterfront.

She waited for what felt like an hour, but her phone said it had only been ten minutes. Finally, out of curiosity and boredom, she slid over to where she could see the shelves. There was enough light from the street to make out labels in a multitude of foreign languages. German, French, several Asian scripts of which she could only identify Korean. Spanish, Arabic, and Hindi labels — and then Cadbury, Aero bars, and Jelly Babies, which needed no introduction to her sweet tooth.

Oh, this must be that Global Grocery store that opened last year, she thought to herself. *I've been meaning to come down here.*

"Ooh, pocky sticks," she whispered, shocked at her own voice in the silence.

Kallie took a five dollar bill out of her wallet and reached up to place it on the counter – probably overpaying, but she didn't want to risk being seen while checking the price on the shelf. She cautiously leaned forward and slid a box of strawberry pocky off the shelf, trying to remember when she'd last eaten.

Slouching back against the counter with her crunchy treasure, she began eating the first stick, while considering who could've grabbed her.

Could it all have been a mistake? Did I just overreact?

Not a chance, Kalliope. Nobody grabs a stranger like that. It had to be related to the murder. But how?

Maybe he just thought I was someone else? Oh, or maybe he thought I was an easy victim to rob!

How'd that work out for you, robber? Kallie smirked to herself. *That's probably all it was. Bet he won't be making that mistake again soon. Or walking soon. Heck, he's probably still picking up his teeth.*

She pulled another pocky stick out of the box, thoughtfully. She wanted to reconsider their clues, but right now she needed to get home.

It's getting late, and I don't want this store owner to find me lurking in the dark, either.

She closed the box of pocky and crept back toward the rear of the shop, grateful for the dose of sugar. Unlatching the bolt and slipping back outside, she felt much calmer than her earlier moment of panic. That is, until a car door slammed somewhere out in the darkness, and her pulse started racing again.

Okay, go, Kalliope. Fast, but not too fast.

She turned out of the driveway onto the main street, glancing around just once.

Don't look guilty. Don't look behind you. Don't

look scared.

But don't walk blindly into trouble, either.

Wishing again that her brain would shut up, Kallie made her way back toward the parking lot near the restaurant, as calmly as possible. But every voice, every moving car, even a distant sneeze made her jump – and soon she was running in the dark again.

* * * * *

After dodging between streets for ten minutes, the parking lot up ahead looked like a miracle, and Kallie ducked behind the first car she encountered. She didn't see or hear anyone running behind her, but she was sure someone would find her soon. She groped across her pockets quickly for her car keys in the dark, but didn't find them.

Oh no.

She checked her pockets again, then started patting at her jacket in a near-panic – and finally heard the muffled clink of keys. Sighing in relief, she pulled them out of her jacket pocket and darted over to her own car, which was sitting alone in a bright ring of light.

Why did I have to park right under the floodlights?

Kallie unlocked the door and collapsed into the driver's seat of her car, out of breath and streaming tears. A moment later, she pushed down the old-fashioned door lock with her elbow.

Don't relax yet. You're sitting in a spotlight. Get out of here.

Still seeing spots from the glaring security lights outside, she gripped the keys again, jabbing blindly for the ignition.

Calm down, Kalliope. Focus.

She tried to take a deep, calming breath, but failed miserably. Her exhale came out as a choked sob, but the key finally found the ignition. She turned it firmly and immediately put the old car into gear, leaving the headlights off.

The parking lot was dark and blurry through Kallie's tears, and her running mascara burned her eyes. Her ankle hurt vaguely, where she'd twisted it while running for the car, but she couldn't focus on it. She lifted her toes off the brake, gritting her teeth as her ankle protested, and rolled quietly, slowly through the parking lot.

Her temporary calmness was gone, and her brain turned irresistibly back to the murder.

You know that's why they grabbed you, Kalliope.

No, it was just a failed robbery.

Nonsense. And don't touch the gas, yet. Don't draw any attention. They could be anywhere.

Watching and waiting.

When she finally reached the parking lot exit, she was relieved to see that there was still some traffic on the main road. The rearview mirror was broken, as it had been for years, but she took one last glance over her shoulder to see if she was being followed. Her eyes dropped to the back seat, instinctively, but if anyone was back there, they would've already attacked her.

She slammed her foot on the accelerator and pulled recklessly out of the parking lot and into the stream of traffic, leaving her headlights off until she was safely between two cars.

The driver of the second car honked angrily and made a rude gesture, but she could only wave and wish a metric ton of happy blessings upon him. He was between her and her pursuers now, and that was the greatest relief she'd felt in years.

After driving for another quarter mile, hitting nothing but green lights, she wished the still-angry driver behind her a champagne breakfast, three winning lottery tickets, and a pet unicorn.

Her knuckles gripped the steering wheel more loosely, and her teeth gradually clenched less tensely by the mile. Jumping on I-275 toward home, she let out a deep breath, but then grabbed the dangling rearview mirror and watched behind her, just in case.

I might've gotten away clean, but this isn't the most generic-looking car in the world. If they see me, they'll follow me the whole way home.

What makes you think they don't already know where you live, Kalliope? her brain whispered to her sinisterly.

Whoever they are, whoever you've antagonized this time, they're probably already at the house, waiting for you.

With your dad.

Kallie inhaled sharply and dropped the mirror, fumbling for her phone frantically.

Calm down, Kalliope. They don't know where you live.

Are you sure?

She pushed the phone icon to call her dad.

"Hello?" he answered sleepily. Kallie knew he would've been reading on the couch.

"Dad! Oh, thank goodness. Listen, I know it's late, but could you go to Anna's house?"

"What?" he asked, sounding confused. "Sure, I'll go over there in the morning. Do you need me to bring her something?"

"No, Dad. Now. Can you go now?"

"It's after nine o'clock at night, kiddo. What's going on?"

"It's a long story, Dad. Could you please just go over there? I'm probably overreacting, but just to be safe?"

"Are you in trouble?"

"I'm not sure. Maybe."

Her father sighed and mumbled something Kallie couldn't hear. "Okay, I'm going. Should I bring Sherman?"

"Yes," Kallie replied, relieved that he'd thought to mention her sweet dog. "Yes please, Dad. I'll explain later."

Chapter Twenty-Two

Kallie dialed Tess's number next, and her best friend picked up on the first ring.

"Hey, Kal. Did you get the text? I'll pick you up in five minutes."

"What? No—" Kallie clumsily switched screens to check her messages, and saw an urgent text from Cornwallis. "'Found some important evidence. Please come to my office.'" she read out loud. "I'm not at home yet, though, Tess. I'll come to your house, and we can drive over there together."

And I'll tell her what just happened, when we get there.

Tess agreed and met Kallie in the driveway when she arrived a few minutes later, with her own keys in hand. They quickly switched to Tess's car for the drive.

It felt like an hour later when they pulled into the dirty, dark parking lot to see Cornwallis, but the clock on the dash said it had only been twenty minutes. They'd missed the evening traffic, of course, and they made good time once they were off the bridge. Kallie and Tess walked up the stairs to the investigator's office.

Cornwallis greeted them at the door and immediately sat down and opened a manilla envelope on his desk. "My contact said he found this near the crime scene, the day after the parade," he held up a ragged piece of paper, enclosed in a Ziplock bag, but didn't hand it to Kallie and Tess.

Pretty sure sandwich baggies aren't protocol for evidence, but it's better than nothing, I guess.

"What is it?" Tess asked, tilting her head to see it.

"It's part of a letter."

"It's just a scrap of paper. Why did he even bother to pick it up?" Kallie asked, squinting at the writing.

"He has good instincts," Cornwallis replied, and shrugged. "Plus, he knows I'll pay for evidence. He collects a lot of stuff that I don't need, but every once in a while, we both get lucky."

The investigator put the baggie on the desk and slid the lamp over toward it. Kallie and Tess both leaned in for a look, incredulous. He flipped it over, and amidst the other writing that was still legible on the stained and torn ragged slip of paper, part of a word stood out: 'Dakot'.

"Whoa," Tess whispered. "I *knew* he was involved in this." She turned to Kallie, who wasn't convinced, "I told you he was lying." Looking back at Cornwallis, she insisted, "You need to take that to the police. That could be real evidence."

"We don't even know if it's related at all, right now," Cornwallis countered. "It might be a coincidence, or maybe it belonged to someone else entirely." He tilted his head and added, "Someone from Fargo."

"I think that's more likely, actually," Kallie added, morosely. "But that's not for us to decide. The cops can check it out and determine whether it's worth keeping or not."

"Some of these words look like 'trouble' and 'owe me,'" Tess pointed out. "It could be from our girl. Or *to* her."

Kallie tried to reach for the baggie, but Cornwallis pulled it away.

"I'm not saying it's definitely related," Kallie replied, frowning. "But if we keep it, we're interfering with a police investigation."

"We have to take it to the police," Tess stated, and then she smiled. "But we can *read* it first, right?"

"Definitely," Kallie agreed. She glared at Cornwallis, who was still being stingy with the evidence, and added, "We won't touch it. You can just hold it, since your fingerprints are already on it. The cops can exclude you."

"Why should I let you read it?"

"Um, because we're *paying* you?" Tess replied, rolling her eyes.

"Oh, yeah. Good point." Cornwallis moved the desk lamp over a little more, and then took the scrap of paper out of the baggie with a pair of tweezers. Holding it in the middle of the desk, he mumbled, "I got carried away for a second there."

Tess and Kallie ignored him and crowded up to the desk for a look. The oppressiveness of the smelly office faded away as they looked carefully.

"It's not every day you find real evidence in a famous murder case, you know," he continued, mostly to himself.

"It's more than half of a notebook-sized sheet, but it's so filthy... And it's hard to guess what was on the missing part," Tess mused, analyzing the ripped page and reading aloud. "'Don't let me—' This word is probably 'catch' — and then on the next line it says, 'dangerous game'."

"It definitely sounds like it could be related to the case," Cornwallis added. "After all, Badger said he thought she owed the guy money."

"But practically everyone owes someone money," Tess sighed.

"My mortgage company never sent me any letters like this," Kallie added.

Tess laughed, "Only if you were *really* late with a payment. But criminals are more likely to have grumpy friends." She took out her phone and snapped a picture of the letter. After looking at the photo, she took a few more, with and without flash.

"Done?" Kallie smirked.

"Well, if we're giving it to the police, I want to have a good copy. I have a feeling we're going to want to read it again."

Kallie nodded, and then took a quick picture with her own phone. "Just in case," she added. A moment later she asked, "Could you flip it over again?"

Cornwallis silently turned the paper over with the tweezers, and they both took a few more pictures.

"I can't tell what the writer was saying about Dakota," Tess added. "But if Kelsey owed someone money, why didn't she just ask him to help? He's rolling in money."

"Maybe that's what this note is about – telling her to get the money from him," Kallie reasoned. "But she was probably embarrassed. And they'd only been dating for a few months. I'm sure she didn't want him to think she was one of those gold diggers."

Cornwallis didn't add anything to the conversation, but watched them discuss it like he was viewing a tennis match.

"Could it have been anything else?" Tess wondered aloud. "Maybe they were blackmailing him and she was trying to stop it?"

"That sounds like something she would do, but what could he possibly have done to be blackmailed for? He grew up in front of the news cameras, so his life is pretty much an open book."

"Did your guy say there was anything else around this paper?" Tess asked the investigator. "An envelope? A pen?"

"A giant puddle of blood?" Kallie suggested, wryly.

"No, he just said it was by a dumpster," Cornwallis answered. "He's not the dumpster diving type, but I might be able to find someone to check it for you, if you want. It'd take a couple more hours, though."

"Nah, the cops can check the dumpster," Tess replied without looking up. She blew up the photo on her phone to see the scrap in greater detail and squinted. "Hey, check this out. Does this paper look like it has a watermark, to you?"

Kallie leaned over for a better look, and her friend pointed at the screen. "Oh, sure. Yeah, I can see part of a circle here. It's actually easier to see in the stained section." Tilting her head, she asked, "Do criminals and drug dealers have their own stationery these days?"

"Only the entrepreneurial kind," Cornwallis answered.

"It might be from a hotel or a restaurant or something," Kallie noted, taking Tess's phone. "I can't make it out. Anyway, the cops can figure that out too."

"Wait, is that a snake?" Tess asked, grabbing Kallie's arm and scaling the picture back down, so she could see the whole thing.

"A what?" Kallie looked back at the picture and shook her head. "I don't think it's a snake. Can you hold the paper up again, in front of the lamp?" she asked Cornwallis. "Maybe we'll be able to see it better."

Cornwallis picked up the scrap again and held it in front of the dim desk lamp.

"That's no good," Tess sighed. "And it's dark outside, so we can't use sunlight—"

Kallie turned her phone's flashlight on, and handed it to Cornwallis, adding, "Try this."

The investigator nodded, then held the phone in one hand and the paper in the other. After a few minutes of clumsily moving them closer and farther apart, they could finally make out some of the watermark.

"Oh," Kallie concluded. "I think it's a fish hook."

Tess and Cornwallis both squinted, doubtfully.

"Turn it this way," she took the investigator's hand and bent his wrist sideways.

"Oh, I see it now," Tess mumbled. "A fish hook in a circle. Why does that look familiar?"

Kallie shook her head, bemused. "No idea."

"Oh, I think that's the logo from the Fishmonger

in St Pete," Tess clarified after some consideration. "It's near the Dali Museum."

Cornwallis quickly typed on his computer keyboard, scrolled, and then turned the screen toward them. "Is this it?"

They looked at the logo of the trendy Fishmonger Hotel, and then they both leaned over to look at the watermark again, and Tess nodded. "Definitely." She took another few screenshots of the original photo on her phone, trying to get a decent copy of the watermark. Then she took a picture of Cornwallis's computer screen. "What's the address?"

Cornwallis read the address to them, and gently placed the scrap of paper back into the sandwich baggie. Kallie agreed that she would tell Morrison what they'd found, and show him the photos. But taking the evidence to the police, himself, would earn Cornwallis some points with the TPD detectives on the case. And maybe a little respect from them too.

"We'll go down there in the morning—" Tess started to reply, but Kallie cut her off.

"Let's go tonight. I need to talk to you anyway."

"About what—?" Tess started to ask, but then nodded. "Okay, we'll go tonight." She added, to Cornwallis, "We'll check with the concierge at the Fishmonger, and let you know what we find."

"Okay, thanks. Say, you didn't happen to bring my walking stick, did you?" Cornwallis asked Kallie. "I accidentally left it in your living room. I don't really need it anymore," he added, wiggling his foot. "My ankle's okay. I just like the dragons."

"I came straight from work," Kallie replied, bending the truth a little about her evening's activities. "But I did see it after you left. I'll bring it next time we come down here."

Cornwallis walked them back down to the parking lot. "I'll ask my sister's boyfriend if he can run facial recognition from the parade videos against Dakota's picture, while you're in St Pete."

Tess frowned and looked like she was going to decline the offer.

"He's been troubleshooting it, and he said it's working better now. And I really think we need to check Dakota out, after seeing that note." He added, "Sorry, Kallie."

"No, I agree," she responded. "I was *sure* he was innocent. He seemed so nice. But there's too much evidence to the contrary now. Tess is right – he's mixed up in this somehow."

Tess started the car and waved to Cornwallis, and then pulled out of the grimy parking lot onto the dark side street, headed for St Petersburg.

* * * * *

"Hey, I meant to tell you," Tess began as they

merged onto the highway, "I found some information about the original Mai Tai. It was made with this 17-year-old rum from Jamaica, but they don't produce it anymore. That's probably why it didn't taste—" Tess paused, sensing Kallie's tension.

"Sorry, what?" Kallie asked, awkwardly, noticing the silence.

"Nothing, Kal. I'll just email it to you. What did you want to talk about?" Tess asked. "Is it about Morrison?"

"What?" Kallie asked, confused. "Morrison? No... Remember how I asked you to come downtown with me?"

"Oh," Tess replied. "Sure, I had to work."

"Yeah, I was taking pictures down there, trying to get re-focused on the details of the case, and someone grabbed me."

"*What*?" Tess asked, looking away from the road.

"I thought they were attacking me, at the time. That it was related to the murder." She looked over, sheepishly. "But now I think I might've overreacted."

"Grabbed you, *how?*" Tess asked, looking protective and angry.

"I was near the corner, taking pictures, and I wasn't paying attention. Someone grabbed my shoulder, and I kinda freaked out."

Tess was now watching the road again, but she shifted her eyes toward Kallie and smirked.

"I know what you're going to say, but it could have just been a misunderstanding," Kallie backpedaled. "Maybe they just wanted—"

"To rob you? I agree, that's probably more likely. Did you kick the crap out of him?" Tess asked, and a tiny smile was still stuck at the corner of her lips.

"A little," Kallie whispered. She could feel herself blushing.

"Your dad would be so proud. Anyone who grabs a strange woman in public needs to be introduced to better manners," she explained. "Did you use that elbow move he taught us?"

Kallie nodded, silently.

"Good girl. Are you okay?"

"I was pretty scared, but I'm okay now."

"There are a million cameras down there – as we've recently noticed. And it could've been totally innocent, or *not at all*." Tess's expression was both concerned, angry, and amused. "We'll call the police when we get home and file a report."

"Thanks, Tess."

They pulled into the parking lot of the Fishmonger Hotel a few minutes later. It was an expensive, super-trendy spot, restored from an old nineteenth century cigar factory, with a popular nightclub on the second floor. The neighborhood was evolving, but still a little questionable.

Tess parked the car and they walked into the huge, Industrial lobby, with exposed brick and rusty i-beams in the ceiling. Unfortunately, the concierge wasn't available after nine p.m. – and it was after eleven now.

Disappointed, Kallie and Tess left the hotel, planning to return the next day. "I can't believe we didn't think of that," Tess mumbled. "We should've called first."

As they walked across the parking lot, though, Kallie noticed a familiar car in the reserved spots of the front row. She closed her eyes in frustration and asked, "Tess, is that Dakota's Range Rover?"

Checking the license number, Tess nodded.

"I hate him more every minute," Kallie sighed. "I can't believe he tricked me into believing he was such a nice guy."

Tess quickly reminded her, "Just because he's here doesn't mean he's a killer."

"Should he really be out partying right after his true love died?" Kallie grumbled.

"Okay, just because he's here, *and he's an insensitive jerk*, doesn't mean he's a killer," Tess amended.

"You're the one who thought he was the

murderer all along. Now we have a false alibi, an angry note at the crime scene with his name on it, written on stationery with this hotel's watermark. And he just happens to *be here*?"

"Okay, when you add it up like that..." Tess considered.

"That would be a huge coincidence."

Tess tapped one elegant heel on the dingy parking lot asphalt, thinking. "Let's see if we can find him," she finally answered. "He knows we're working with a private investigator, so maybe he'll keep talking to us."

Being a Thursday night, the parking lot wasn't that crowded. They went back inside and found that the nightclub was already mostly empty, and the hotel's privacy rules wouldn't allow the front desk staff to disclose if Dakota was staying there or not. So they left in frustration again.

"We're so close," Tess grumbled. "He must be here, if his car's here. I wish we could force them to tell us."

"I can't think of any way to find out, short of getting a room."

Tess checked her phone quickly and shook her head. "Not without Winchester's expense account."

"Or staying here until morning?" Kallie suggested.

"Eight hours of sleeping in *this* car? No thanks," Tess laughed. "Maybe if we were sleeping in that Range Rover. And he might not check out until eleven a.m., anyway. Or not at all. Let's just go home."

As they returned to Tess's car once more, though, Kallie noticed movement nearby. After her experience downtown, earlier that evening, she was still a little jumpy, and pointed out the motion to Tess.

Another old, statuesque brick warehouse next door was being renovated too, and it was bathed in bright security lights. A familiar figure moved near the side doorway.

"You've got to be kidding me," Tess growled.

"That sure looks like him," Kallie agreed. "And I'd like to knock *his* teeth out with my elbow, too. Let's go get him."

"Hang on," Tess interjected, grabbing Kallie's wrist for a second. "We're telling Cornwallis and Morrison first, before we do anything." She tapped a quick message on her phone.

"Great, now they can't say we're completely crazy," Kallie concluded, pulling her best friend across the field toward the nearby warehouse.

Chapter Twenty-Three

"Shoot, where is he?" Tess whispered. "I can't see him anymore."

They'd watched the figure slip into the building through the deserted construction zone, and cautiously followed a few minutes behind him. They couldn't afford to follow too closely, and risk bumping into him in the dark. The doorway led straight into a narrow old stairwell, and they climbed the rusty steps, cringing at every creak and echo, until they found a metal door standing ajar.

After hesitating to listen for any sound inside, they'd slipped through the doorway silently, quickly ducking down to hide when they saw a figure moving across the huge room.

This was another regal but obsolete nineteenth-century factory – probably some kind of clothing manufacturer, judging from the open space and large windows. It was currently in utter disrepair and appeared to have been deserted for decades.

"I think Dakota went down some stairs over there," Kallie said quietly, pointing toward the distant rear corner of the room. "Can we go now? This place is scary."

"I don't want to turn my back on him," Tess whispered. "Are you sure he went into the stairwell?"

"No, I just thought I heard a door, and feet on metal stairs."

"Why did we even come in here?" Tess groaned. "Let's just back up to the doorway, so he can't sneak up on us."

"Unless he's already behind us..."

"Great. Thanks for that," Tess answered, sarcastically.

"Sorry," Kallie whispered.

Tess took hold of Kallie's forearm and started backing away from their hiding place. Her heels tapped on the floor a little too loudly, and she stopped to take them off.

"Why am I always wearing heels when we get in trouble?" she whispered, annoyed.

Something loud and metallic crashed behind them, and they both snapped to a halt. Kallie whimpered softly.

"Shhh," Tess whispered, ducking and pulling Kallie down into a crouch. After a few minutes of silence, she added, "I really don't think he's behind us. That must've been something else."

"The cops? Please say you think it's the cops."

"I was thinking maybe a cat," Tess mumbled.

"A cat is good," Kallie whispered with a nod. "Cute. Cuddly. I would even accept a raccoon right now. How about a black bear?"

"I don't think we want to wish for a black bear, Kallie."

"They're around here a lot. I saw it on the news. And they're probably nicer than a murderous psycho with a trust fund."

They stayed in their crouch for another minute but didn't hear anything else. "Okay, well." Tess paused. "Either he's gone, and didn't hear that racket... Or he *made* the racket."

Kallie whined again.

"But I can't think of any reason he wouldn't have come running to investigate, so he must be gone," Tess concluded. "We really need to work on our snooping skills, by the way — we're being way too noisy."

Kallie waited for a disembodied voice to say, 'Yes, you really are,' but there was nothing. "Okay, you're right," she whispered. "He's probably gone. Let's go."

They stood up cautiously and continued backing toward the door, eventually bumping noisily into the pile of old, empty butter cookie cans that had fallen across the path, making the previous racket. Kallie recognized the dozens of dark blue tins even in the dim light. She looked around to see if there was a cute, non-murderous kitty nearby, as Tess had suggested, but she was disappointed.

Finally situated with their backs to the door, unable to be waylaid from behind, Tess took a deep breath for bravery, and turned around to open the door into the stairwell.

"No, no, no, no, no," she whispered.

"What? *What no?*"

"It's locked."

"No, it can't be. I checked it when we came in here. It was unlocked." Kallie turned and tried the door handle, futilely, and then slumped back against the wall. "This can't be happening."

Tess took out her phone and grimaced. "I don't have a cell signal in here. Do you?"

Kallie pulled out her phone and shook her head. "This place probably has a hundred years' worth of lead paint in it – enough to block the signal."

"This is bad, Kal. We're trapped and he knows we're here," Tess said simply.

Kallie shook her head again, suddenly feeling a little more hopeful than her best friend. "Then why did he leave? Why would he walk away and leave us alive, if he knew we were here and onto him?"

"Okay, let's not think too much about that, right now," Tess replied, sounding scared for the first time. "We need to find another way out of here, quick."

"No, but—" Kallie began with a smile.

"Kal, I'm afraid he might've boobytrapped the place," Tess explained quickly. She grabbed Kallie's wrist and pulled her back into the huge, cluttered room.

"Oh no," Kallie whispered, hurrying after her best friend.

* * * * *

"Are you sure he came over this way?" Tess asked, climbing over another stack of boxes on her way toward the opposite corner of the room.

"Pretty sure," Kallie answered, looking around nervously. "Are you sure we should be *following* him?"

"Pretty sure we *shouldn't*. But we don't have time to find another exit. And we've come this far."

"True. In for a penny—"

"Are there any lights?" Tess looked up at the ceiling. "I think I can see some fluorescent bulbs up there."

"I'm not sure where the light switch would be." Kallie took a couple steps forward, and promptly knocked a stack of film canisters off a side table with an ear-shattering crash. "And we'd lose the element of surprise!" she shouted over the racket of rolling metal.

Tess stifled a laugh. "Good point!" she shouted back. "Let's leave the lights off!" They continued slowly through the enveloping clutter, but after a moment, she asked, "Do you smell something burning?"

Kallie sniffed deeply and shook her head. "I think it's just the smell of old books and dust. This building is pretty cool, actually. I love those giant windows," Kallie noted, looking out at the full moon.

"Maybe you can move in, if we survive the evening," Tess replied sarcastically.

"We'd have to chase out all of the rats and raccoons, though," Kallie said, listening to a scurrying sound on their left. "I'd hate to leave them homeless."

"Apparently a packrat lives here too. What *is* all of this stuff? It looks like an antique store exploded in here."

In the dim light of the moon, they could see huge tables with a million things stacked on them. Tons of books and at least a thousand boxes, but also glasses and dishes. Piles of long cardboard tubes for rolled-up papers — perhaps maps or posters or blueprints of some kind. Amid the tables were upholstered chairs stacked willy-nilly, and an antique couch with curvy arms piled with stuffed animals. Apparently plush, and not taxidermied, thank goodness.

Something scrambled quietly in the dark, and something else made of glass fell and shattered.

"I'm not sure whether to be fascinated or creeped-out," Kallie whispered.

"I'm going with creeped-out. One hundred

percent," Tess replied with an anxious croak.

"Only because you can hear their little toenails," Kallie whispered. "Scritchy, scritchy."

"I'm going to punch you," Tess warned.

Kallie laughed nervously, but apologized. "My eyes are adjusted now. Let's look around and see if he left anything in here."

"You want to look for clues?" Tess asked incredulously. "I don't know how we'd find any evidence in this disaster, but it's worth a try, I guess. As long as we keep moving toward the other stairwell."

They started weaving their way between the large tables, tiptoeing around lamps and smaller boxes on the floor. Kallie tried shining the light from her phone on the piles of goods, but it didn't help. The extreme contrast of brightness just blinded her temporarily — and she didn't want to waste the battery. It was easier to see in the moonlight.

"There's a knife on this table," Tess whispered.

"I don't know why we're whispering, after all the noise we made," Kallie whispered back.

"I can't help it. Besides, I don't want to attract whatever's making that chewing sound," Tess replied with a shudder.

"Where did you see the knife?" Kallie asked, catching up with Tess.

Her friend pointed at a table, where Kallie could

see a large, artistic knife behind a pile of glass plates. It was sticking out of the table by its point.

"I don't think that's a murdering-type knife. I think that's a decorative knife, like you'd use in a school play."

"You can kill someone with a butter knife," Tess answered stoically. "Besides, it's sharp enough to stab a table."

"Fair enough. Let me see..." Kallie took her phone back out, and shone the built-in flashlight on the knife, squinting. "I don't see any blood."

"I don't see anything except spots, now. Why are those phone flashlights so bright?"

"It's pretty dusty, too," Kallie added. "I think it's been here for a while, untouched."

Tess nodded and kept walking. "He wouldn't just leave evidence out in the open, would he?"

"In this disaster? Why not? It'd be like finding a needle in a... bomb blast. What is this place, some kind of storage building for competitive hoarders?"

"Oh, jeez. There's a whole stack of teddy bears over here," Tess moaned, from her left.

"I like teddy bears," Kallie replied curiously. "What's wrong with a whole stack of..." she trailed off. "Yikes."

They were like a child's nightmare. Plush animals that roughly resembled bears, but some had their heads sewn on backward, some had human doll eyes that opened and closed. Some had sharp, shiny teeth.

"They must be factory rejects," Kallie whispered, sounding traumatized.

"Do they have factories in Hell?"

Tess seemed to be glued to the sight, and Kallie gently pulled her away. "I can see a bunch of pill bottles over there," she whispered, still pulling Tess by the hand.

"What?" Tess mumbled. "Oh, *pills*. Good."

"We'll get out of here soon, I promise. Come look."

Tess picked up the first bottle in the collection with the end of her sleeve, seeming to push the creepy gnawing sounds and horrific toys out of her mind for the moment. "It's too dark to read the tiny label," she whispered, holding it up.

Kallie turned on her phone's light again, this time after they'd both averted their eyes. She took the bottle and noted, "This is from 1994." She picked up another one and read, "1998, we're getting closer."

She shone the light over the table and saw that most of the labels were yellowed with age and peeling, but one stood out in the bright light. "This one's brand new." She leaned awkwardly across the table for a closer look. It seemed to have just been tossed onto the pile. Shining the light, she puzzled out the odd drug name,

"Gamma hydro... hydrox..." she squinted. "Gamma hydroxy-something."

"Does the 'something' start with a 'b'?" Tess asked. "I'll bet that's what GHB stands for."

"There is a 'b' in there. I don't know how to pronounce it."

Tess leaned over and frowned at the label too. "Hydroxybu— Yeah, no guess from me either."

Kallie took a photo of the bottle with her phone, and then checked for cellular reception again, but there was still no signal, even now that they were closer to the windows.

Tess looked around for something to pick up the bottle and settled on an old dusty handkerchief. She wrapped the bottle and carefully tucked it into her jacket pocket.

Across the room, near the stairwell door where they'd heard the killer – as if to confirm Tess's earlier fears – there was a barely-audible pop, and the first crackle of a fire sparked to life in the darkness. The orange light caught Kallie's eye and she gasped.

"Are you *kidding* me?!" Tess growled in frustration, looking where Kallie was pointing. "This crazy junkyard is one huge tinderbox, and I can't believe they'd build this place with more than two stairwells."

"Well, we know that door's locked," Kallie groaned, pointing back the way they'd come, "and *that* side is going to be a blast furnace before we can get over there, through all this mess."

"Then I guess we try the other corners, and hope the builders were smarter than I think." Tess made a snap decision, and they headed for the nearest corner, climbing over furniture and boxes clumsily. The masses of dust and piles of paper were catching fire quickly, and the room was already starting to heat up, despite the chilly night air streaming through the broken windows.

Kallie was faster, and she reached the corner first. Banging on the walls in frustration, she turned around and shook her head – *nothing here.*

And we're running out of options. I don't want to die in here with those creepy teddy bears.

Tess turned around and started for the diagonal corner, their last hope. Kallie caught up with her quickly and ran ahead, hope fading as she jumped over an ugly plaid couch and skirted past a pile of tumbled filing cabinets.

She's right, there would be stairwells on every corner, or just two. No way there's an odd third exit over there.

We should check the windows, maybe there's something we can climb down. It's only the third floor, maybe we could jump without breaking every bone in our bodies.

But the fire had already spread across the room,

starting to block the huge wall of windows that Kallie had previously admired.

Last chance.

Kallie closed her eyes and wished harder than she'd ever wished for anything in her life, as she skidded across the dusty floor to the last corner.

Nothing.

She spun around, looking frantically for anything that could help them. Water? She looked up, hoping that the building had been retrofitted with a sprinkler system – Nothing. Something to hide under? Hide in?

Nothing.

Kallie slumped against the wall, broken, tears streaming down her face, as Tess finally caught up with her. Her best friend took one look at her face and knew they were in real trouble.

"No way," Tess snarled, eyes watering from the smoke. "We're not dying in this rathole. There's a ton of every worthless, crazy thing in here. There are probably at least ten asbestos tablecloths and six fire-retardant hot air balloons. Help me look."

They scraped and scrounged for a few minutes, until they started to get dizzy from the smoke and heat. The high ceiling and handful of broken windows were giving them a little protection, but Kallie knew they needed more.

Grabbing a wire bucket full of mildew-stained old golf balls, she started hurling them at the windows as hard as she could. She had broken six more of the glass panes, when Tess grabbed a pile of small ceramic animal figurines and joined her.

"This isn't going to put out the fire, you know," Tess shouted over the crackle of the flames, as she pitched a porcelain deer with giant eyes at the windows, smashing another pane into tiny shards. "The extra air is just feeding the fire."

"The smoke will kill us first," Kallie panted, throwing another golf ball.

"That's a great point," Tess agreed, pitching her figurines faster.

The smoke was starting to clear, as it was sucked into the cold night air outside, but Tess was right. The fire was still coming, and it loved the fresh oxygen. They ran out of things to throw and backed away as the antique varnish on the scattering of old furniture crackled and bubbled loudly, catching fire.

"What's our next step, Miss Poirot?" Tess shouted over the noise, gamely. Kallie could hear that she was gasping for air.

"Maybe we could—"

There was a sudden, huge crash behind them, and they both screamed and hit the floor in terror.

Crap, the roof caved in. I didn't even think of that, Kallie thought to herself, feeling strangely resigned.

We're done.

Already on the floor, she lowered her head calmly, and tried to pull her shirt up over her face, for a few last breaths. She felt a comforting hand on her back and reached out for Tess's hairy arm.

Hairy?

Kallie lifted her head in shock and found herself face-to-face with Detective Morrison.

He looked just as startled as she was. "You're alive!" he shouted, still looking stunned. He quickly moved toward Tess and grabbed her by the back of the shirt. "Let's go," he shouted, starting to cough violently.

Kallie tried to move, but she was too weak. "I can't—" she moaned. "I'm—"

She felt his hand on her back again, and then she fainted.

* * * * *

Kallie woke up suddenly, freezing cold and terrified, as the night air chilled her still-sweaty shirt and hair. She swung wildly at something stuck to her face.

The paramedic grabbed her hand gently, and shouted, "She's awake!"

Tess and Morrison jumped up from their seats

on the steps of a nearby ambulance and ran to Kallie's side. She tried to sit up, but the paramedic restrained her again, keeping the oxygen mask pressed to her face.

"You inhaled a lot of smoke," Morrison told her, softly. "We both had to stay under the oxygen mask for a while too. Just relax, we're right here." Their eyes both looked shimmery, and Kallie blinked hard to get the smoke out of her eyes.

"Can I have some eyedrops?" she asked the paramedic hoarsely.

He nodded and gestured to a colleague, who carefully washed off her eyes.

"How did you know—?" she croaked.

Morrison nudged Tess's shoulder and replied, "Some people *text me*, before they walk into a deathtrap."

Tess shrugged. "Luckily, I sent it to Cornwallis too," she pointed across the open space, and Kallie's paramedic relented with a sigh, letting her sit up enough for a quick look.

A few yards away, in the open space between the factory and the swanky hotel, Cornwallis was standing over Dakota Abernathy. Kelsey's boyfriend lay face down on the ground, handcuffed. Kallie could see an old-fashioned revolver slightly uncovered on Cornwallis's ankle.

"I missed everything," Kallie coughed, and laid back on the gurney, breathing deeper under the oxygen mask. She closed her eyes and started to doze off, barely even considering the fact that Tess had been right all along about Dakota.

"Are you licensed to carry that thing, Wally?" Kallie heard Tess ask Cornwallis, as she struggled to keep her eyes open.

Their P.I. replied tersely, "Yes, and self-defense extends to protecting others." After a moment, he added, "You're welcome."

Without sounding remotely abashed this time, Tess added, "Did you drive all the way down here in that cute little Ford Falcon?"

"She hasn't gone that fast in years," the investigator answered with a chuckle.

Chapter Twenty-Four

"Are you sure you're okay, kiddo?"

"I'm fine, Dad," Kallie answered from the couch. "They arrested Dakota for arson and attempted murder, so he's no threat now. He still insists he didn't kill Kelsey, but of course he *would* say that." She shrugged, looking annoyed.

"Of course," her father agreed. "Well, Morrison told me that the Pinellas County crime lab is one of the top ten in the country, and they're assisting since Dakota was caught here. So it should all be resolved and proven soon."

Kallie nodded, staring out the window, frowning.

"Are you sure you're okay?" he repeated.

Kallie blushed and laughed. "Sure. And this case is all but sewn up. So where are you going?" she added, when she saw that he'd packed up a lunch basket. It was dismal outside and had been drizzling for most of the day.

"Anna and I are going fishing out at the pier," he proclaimed, "If you're sure you're okay."

"You're kidding. Anna isn't really the fishing type, is she?"

"Why do you say that?" her father asked, sounding genuinely confused.

"Well it's super windy and cold on the pier. It's raining. And she's a vegetarian. Do I need to keep listing reasons?"

"We can be romantic and cuddly when it's cold and windy?" he suggested.

Kallie grinned. "Okay, I'll accept that as a retort to problem number one."

"And I promised her we wouldn't eat them. Catch and release only."

"Wow, she must really love you, Dad."

Benny blushed to the roots of his hair and shut his mouth.

"I'll take that as a yes," Kallie said with a grin. "You don't even need to worry about the fish. You've got the best catch in town already."

"Don't I *know* it?" His eyes crinkled up as he smiled.

"I'm guessing you haven't told her how you feel."

"I've told her," he answered. "I just didn't realize we were so obvious to anyone else."

"Tess is the only one bringing you random cakes and pies now. That should be enough of a sign that *everyone* in town knows. Were you trying to keep it a secret?"

Her dad blushed a little. "Back in our day, it was considered indiscreet to flaunt a romance before you were married."

"*Married?*" Kallie asked, a little surprised. "Dad?"

"Cool your jets, kiddo. I haven't proposed, I was just making a point," he answered. "You'll be married before we are, anyway. We aren't in a rush."

"Me? I don't even have a boyfriend, Dad," Kallie scoffed.

"Oh, sure." Benny set the lunch basket aside and started packing his fishing tackle box. "I just meant— you know, when the perfect guy comes calling."

"Sure, Dad." Kallie shook her head and changed the subject. "Anyway, I'm going to take Sherman for a walk."

"Oh, we were going to take him to the pier with us. He loves it out there."

"Oh, okay," Kallie nodded. "He does have a great time out there. Just be careful, keep him on the leash and don't let him near any fish hooks. And don't let him eat any... anything," she concluded with a shudder. "Heads, guts, anything."

"You got it, kiddo. No fish eyeballs to spoil his dinner."

"Ugh, Dad!" Kallie made a grossed-out face and laughed.

"Hey, Sherm!" her dad called. "Wanna go to the pier?"

Kallie's dog, napping on the couch, opened one eye and looked at his beloved grandpa.

"Pier?" he repeated.

Sherman still didn't get off the couch but tilted his head in curiosity.

Benny finally picked up the smelly tackle box, and that was obviously the key that Sherman needed. He jumped up happily on the couch and hopped down for a sniff. Then he spun around in a circle and went to the door to grab his leash.

"Be sure to put his seatbelt on him," Kallie added. "Both ways. And take a bottle of water so he doesn't get thirsty and try to drink the salt water."

Kallie's dad saluted agreeably and picked up Sherman's seat belt from the rack by the door. The happy pooch stood still while being fitted with the harness-like seat belt, which would then clip into the car's seatbelt receiver. Benny grabbed a collapsible bowl from the same rack while Kallie got him a large bottle of cold water from the refrigerator.

"We'll be back before eight o'clock. You should try to spoil yourself a little, kiddo."

"Sure, Dad. Tess is working on a project for

Winchester. I'll find something to do around here."

"I'd better not come back and find you've spent the whole day doing laundry and dishes. Do something for yourself."

Kallie sighed. "I'll try, Dad. Have fun at the pier."

She watched from the window as her dad hooked up Sherman's seat belt in the back seat of his old Volkswagen, and then stowed away the fishing tackle and lunch containers. He waved as they pulled out of the driveway.

Kallie walked back to the kitchen and put the last of the dinner plates in the dishwasher, but then decided to follow her father's instructions and do something besides chores.

She had the whole house to herself, for the first time in what felt like years, and she did need something to decompress after the past few days. She sighed happily at the opportunity.

"Bubble bath first?" she asked herself out loud with a twirl. "Manicure? Ice cream, pedicure, and a sappy rom-com?"

She started the dishwasher, listening to hear the water start running.

"I have the whole evening, so I'll let the dishwasher finish running before the bubble bath."

Otherwise we won't have any dishes for

breakfast, she thought to herself. *How did I forget to start it this morning?*

She sashayed to the refrigerator and took out a bottle of lime seltzer, and then twirled back to the dining room and grabbed a bottle of robin's egg blue nail polish from the hutch.

Plopping down on the couch, she set the water bottle on the end table and switched on the nearest lamp. She'd need good light for a pedicure, since it wasn't her usual practice.

Bending her knee enough to prop her heel on the edge of the couch, she shook the bottle of polish and opened it, wrinkling her nose at the acrid smell.

I knew there was a reason I don't do this very often.

All of the glasses were in the dishwasher, so she took a sip from the water bottle and considered the current state of her toenails. *Pitiful.*

"Wouldn't you like a glass, Kalliope?"

Kallie froze, and her blood ran cold instantly.

The voice behind her spoke again, mockingly, a little louder over the sound of the dishwasher, "You seem like such a sensible young woman. The type who would use a glass."

Think, Kalliope. Don't look. Think.

"Not the type of woman who minds her own business, though. Good heavens no."

Kallie fought to appear indifferent as her heart pounded loudly in her ears.

Never show fear. Don't look. Don't panic. Don't cry.

I said don't cry.

Find a weapon. Keeping her head tilted down at her toenails, her eyes shifted wildly, looking for something heavy. *No, something sharp. Something dangerous.*

All I have is nail polish and a bottle of lime fizzy water, her brain cried out desperately.

Think.

A lamp. Sherman's squeaky toy. A book.

She cringed at the sound of his footstep behind her, as the intruder came one step closer.

If I'd taken Tess's physics classes in school, I could electrocute him with some kind of fizzy lamp weapon. If I had six months and a wire stripper.

Kallie's phone was at her side, resting against her thigh. Hoping for a few more seconds out of sight, before he got too close, she carefully picked it up. Tapping quickly, cautiously at the screen, she tried to watch for the intruder out of the corner of her eye.

Hit send. Quick.

It's too late...

"You really should mind your own business," the voice hissed from right behind her, getting closer.

"You should've listened to the nice sheriff."

I don't even recognize his voice, she thought angrily. *Did we really spend that whole time chasing the wrong leads? And it's a stranger?*

"I promise to listen to him next time, if you let me go," she replied, voice cracking.

"Oh, I'm going to let you go, Kalliope," he answered, serenely. "Don't be afraid—"

No worries, freak. I'm not afraid. Now I'm just pissed off.

The invader reached over the back of the couch and gently but decisively yanked the phone out of her hand.

She turned around in her seat and was surprised to see Grant Forsythe, their celebrity lookalike, standing in her living room.

What?!

She could only blink in stunned silence for a few seconds, and then her eyes drifted down to his hand.

Great. Of course he carried the world's biggest knife into my house.

Stay calm, Kalliope. If he was going to stab you, he would've already done it. Deep breaths.

Finally, trying to cover her shock and confusion, she managed to continue, analytically, "How did Badger know you? You live in completely different worlds."

He paused, obviously considering whether he should get caught up in a conversation with his next murder victim.

Psycho killers are nothing if not egotistical. He won't be able to resist telling me his whole life story.

"That's a tale for another day, little Kalliope," he breezed.

Dang it.

Stay calm, Kalliope. He's holding a giant knife, and the front curtains are wide open — someone outside will see him eventually. Even in this nasty weather. Just keep him occupied.

But how? A rousing game of Monopoly? Offer him a slice of cake?

"So that was you that grabbed me on the sidewalk? How's the knee?" she asked with a snarl.

"I don't get involved in that kind of hands-on business myself," Forsythe replied with a smirk. "It's bad for my image, you know. But my *valued assistant* is feeling a bit better now. He had to have a broken tooth extracted." He nodded at her, apparently with grudging respect.

Good. I hope it gets infected.

"We were only trying to warn you at that point, of course. Since you didn't listen to the phone message that my colleague left you at The Lazy Gecko."

That was you too? Kallie suddenly felt ill,

knowing how easily this creep had infiltrated her life. *That stops now.*

"We were *sure* we'd identified the killer, when Dakota lied about being at the parade," she continued, forcing herself to talk through her fear. "And then we saw him at the warehouse."

Forsythe smiled serenely, again looking like his former, fictitiously gentle character with the Golden Retriever.

"But I was right from the beginning, he was innocent," she concluded. She could hear the annoyance in her own voice and tried to contain it. But the anger was growing in her stomach, outweighing her initial fear. "How did you drug the girl?" she demanded.

"You really think I'm going to admit to everything right now?" he replied with a patronizing smirk. "Are you recording this conversation?"

Grrr.

He might be completely bonkers, but he's no sucker.

"No, I'm not recording anything," she replied truthfully. "I'm just curious about the details. You're not going to kill me without telling me how you did it, are you? I'll have to spend eternity wondering?"

"I'm not going to kill you, Kalliope."

"No," she growled in frustration and increasing annoyance. "You're just going to drug me and dump me in the bay. No blood on your hands."

He shrugged with a slight smile. "And they say Tess is the smart one."

"Leave her out of this, you psycho. I'm the one that was chasing you, and I'm still the one that's going to get you locked up for good."

"Don't be silly, there's no one here to rescue you, and you can't even arrest me. Do you expect me to believe you have a badge and handcuffs on your little couch?"

I don't need a badge and handcuffs, I just need you to make a mistake.

"So you're not going to tell me how you drugged her?" Kallie changed the subject back, rolled her eyes, and waved her hand dismissively. "That means it was an accident. You meant to grab her – kidnap her, maybe? And you accidentally knocked her out. Did she fall and hit her head?"

She snorted, meaning to sound condescending, but her heart was pounding.

Are you sure this is a guy you want to antagonize?

"An *accident*?" Forsythe hissed. "Don't be ridiculous, it was a precisely timed and executed plan. You'd know that if you had any sense of—" He stopped abruptly and shook his head. "Tsk, tsk. You almost had me there."

Kallie tried not to sneer.

Why didn't we put this guy in jail when we had the chance?

Because you didn't have any evidence, and he'd be back out already, Kalliope. Now can you please focus on staying alive, here?

Kallie forced herself to look calm, even though her heart was beating nearly out of her chest. "So this was all about Dakota?" she took a wild guess, trying to sound certain. "Why didn't you just kill him?"

"Dakota? No, he's on my side," the killer replied, with a chuckle. "And he's not quite as innocent and reformed as he acts." Kallie must've looked surprised, because he continued, "Oh, did he convince you with that *sweet* Christmas shopping story?"

Kallie could feel her upper lip curling in disgust, and looked away.

"He's been a loyal and regular customer for years," Forsythe added. "Quite a prize. And let's just say he helps keep my business running *smoothly*. I told him to get me her phone, but I was having trouble convincing him to do it." He shook his head in annoyance.

Kallie waited silently for him to keep talking, a trick she'd learned from Morrison.

"Young love is so stupid," he sighed, theatrically. "But Dakota was completely clueless about the two murders being connected, until *you* started meddling in

373

it," he added with a sardonic smile, pointing at her with the knife. "But he was much too useful to kill."

So Tess's intuition was right about Dakota being shady, and I was right about him actually caring about Kelsey. Maybe we really should start a detective agency—

If I survive the next twenty minutes, that is.

"He figured it out when you sent Kelsey that note," Kallie theorized, putting the pieces together. She nodded in understanding, and continued, "You wanted to scare her, but you pushed a little too hard, and she told Dakota about it. And when she turned up dead, he realized that you must've been involved."

Forsythe's face grew red, and his jaw tightened.

"So he started tracking *you* instead, and—" Kallie paused. She thought for another second, and the last puzzle piece fell into place. "Wait, Dakota followed *you* into the warehouse!"

The intruder's eyes flashed in anger. "That's enough, you stupid—"

He seems most off balance when he's insulted, so keep insulting him.

Rolling her eyes as obnoxiously as she could, she laughed caustically and added, "Your own stooge almost *caught* you!"

Careful...

"You screwed it all up completely, with your

'precisely executed plan,'" Kallie hissed. "It was all crumbling like a house of cards around you, and you panicked. You tried to frame Dakota, and then *you* started the fire in the old factory. It should've killed him, but it only made the police think *he* was the killer." She considered the details for moment and added, snarkily, "You're not clever. You just got *lucky*."

Forsythe's sinister poise faltered, and he lunged forward, suddenly inches from her face.

Okay, bad idea!

"It wasn't *luck*!" he snarled, "I may have initially misjudged Dakota's intelligence, but I didn't need that stupid letter to get her phone, the plan would've worked without it."

Why does he keep talking about Kelsey's phone? What did we miss?

Keep him talking, Kalliope. Antagonize him, but only a little. If he gets irritated enough, maybe—

"Whatever," she replied, dismissively, sneering and rolling her eyes.

Perfect.

"Tabitha brought her to a party," Forsythe finally snapped, angrily, unable to face her passive-aggressive mockery in silence. "And she was taking pictures like a nosy little granny. 'Everybody smile!'" he added in a high-pitched voice, mimicking Kelsey. "Like she was some cute little tourist from Cleveland, taking pictures of their old friends."

"So you killed her for being too cheerful, is that it?" Kallie asked, sarcastically. "No way, you just botched the whole thing."

He jabbed the knife at her face. "I was in the back yard, making a *sale*." Another jab with the knife. "I turn around and little miss sunshine has a *camera* in my face, taking pictures of the *buyer* while he's got a foil of *heroin* in his hand—"

Kallie tried not to register her shock. "Marty," she whispered.

"I don't remember his name," Forsythe waved the knife in a dismissive gesture. "But one of my *esteemed customers* told me later that the idiot went and OD'ed that night. And then I remembered those pictures."

And that's a capital murder charge in Florida, now, Kallie thought to herself, sensibly refraining from saying it out loud. A new law had been passed to fight the fentanyl crisis, saying that a drug dealer could be charged with first-degree murder if the buyer died. Could even get the death penalty.

And that's the real reason Cornwallis's contact heard him say 'you know I'll find them.' He needed to get those pictures before anyone else saw them, and realized he was the dealer.

It was never about money at all. So why did he tell her to ask Dakota? Just to show her that her true love was dirty, after all? Just to break her heart?

Did Kelsey even know what she'd captured? It sounds like she just thought it was a cute photo of an old, departed friend, so she wanted to show it to Tabitha.

And if he'd kill her over one photograph, then I'm in big trouble.

Be careful, Kalliope. Stay calm. And maybe start by getting away from that knife...

She stood up, reaching for the bottle of lime fizzy water, and Forsythe took a startled, awkward step backward, inexplicably. Apparently catching himself showing fear, he stepped back toward her, then brandished the knife and smirked. "So you're going to fight, after all?"

"No, I just decided to take you up on the offer of a glass," she answered calmly. "I'm parched."

He looked at her strangely, obviously suspecting a ploy, but he was bigger and stronger – and, notably, he was armed with something more dangerous than a bottle of fizzy water. He swept an arm toward the kitchen gracefully, ironically. "Be my guest."

As Kallie passed him and entered the kitchen, she casually glanced to her right, down the hallway – verifying that she *might* have a workable plan. *If he doesn't stab me first. Or drug me. Or worse.*

Focus, girl. Focus.

Kallie entered the kitchen and opened the glasses cabinet, knowing there would be nothing to use

— she had just loaded them all into the dishwasher. But she had already seen what she needed to see.

Taking a deep breath and hoping for a minor miracle, she tried to sound light-hearted, which she certainly didn't feel. "Oh, silly me! They're all in here." She thumped her palm against the dishwasher noisily, and noticed with surprise that he jumped a little.

Maybe he's not as brazen as he's acting.

And maybe that's not a bet you should take, Kalliope.

She carried her bottle of water back to the living room, taking a swig out of it and grimacing as the fizzy water made her nervous stomach spin even harder. She knew from her new daytime work schedule that it would be dark by six-thirty, and she'd need the house to get a little darker before her possible plan could work.

You call that a plan, Kalliope? And, by the way, if you'd gone to work today, none of this would be happening...

Gritting her teeth to shut up her worried mind, Kallie continued trying to make conversation. Buying time now. The fishing pier was well-lit, so she didn't need to worry about her father coming home soon. "So was the other guy just collateral damage, then? The football player?" she asked conspiratorially.

Forsythe tilted his head and looked at her for a moment before deciding to answer, apparently surprised by her seeming coolness. "Not collateral damage; just a decoy."

Kallie took another swig from her water bottle and silently waved her fingers impatiently in the universal '*more*' gesture, pretending to be growing bored.

"I planned to find someone famous who'd make the news so loudly that her death would be ignored," he explained, growing brash. Feeling brilliant. "There were a dozen celebrities at the parade who would've fit the bill."

"That's a bold plan," she answered sarcastically, rolling her eyes.

He raised an eyebrow, which annoyed her instantly, then said something that stunned her, "Did you know Lauren Bacall died on the same day as Robin Williams?"

Kallie stepped back and leaned against the couch. A huge fan of old movies, that caught her for a loop. She *hadn't* heard. Not a peep even in the many years since his death. "No. No, I didn't," she whispered.

"The media picks its *darlings*," he leaned forward, sneering. "Poor little damaged Kelsey might've gotten some coverage on a slow news day, in Tampa at least, but certainly not when there was a millionaire's body in the morgue."

"But the *police* don't choose their cases that way," Kallie retorted, angrily, not sure why that implication made her so mad. "They've been working on it, night and day, ever since her body was found."

He chuckled and pointed the knife at her. "But they thought *she* was the missing killer! Now *that* was just dumb luck. Instead of begging someone for help, she stumbled away and *disappeared*? You can't buy that kind of coincidence."

"Wait, you didn't move her body?" Kallie blurted out in surprise.

He chuckled again, nastily. "I didn't have to. I dosed her with the GHB, when she wasn't watching her drink, but the little freak just kept going and going, like the Energizer bunny. I finally had to stab her, just to make her stop chattering," he jeered. "But she *still* got away from me. I couldn't follow her into the crowd, and I was sure I'd be caught when she started screaming for help."

Kallie glared at him, wishing he'd stop. Wishing someone would drug and stab *him*.

"But she didn't ask *anyone* for help," he continued. "Not even *you*." He pointed at her with the knife again, and Kallie flashed back to the girl's face, looking at her for just a moment in the crowd. "And then she fell into the bay all by herself." He laughed and shook his head at his own horrible, ridiculous luck.

"It's not funny," Kallie whispered, angrily, hating this guy more and more by the minute. Her first thought when Kelsey had stumbled into her that night was to catch her before she fell, to try to help. But she'd let her run away into the night, instead.

It's dark enough now, she told herself, shoving away the last trace of guilt over Kelsey's tragic end – for the moment, at least. She let the building rage fuel her, while still trying to keep it in check.

"I need to use the bathroom," she stated bluntly, and boldly started walking past him.

"No, no, no, Kalliope," he replied in a sing-song voice, stopping her. "Not so fast."

"I've been drinking this water all night," she replied calmly, "When you gotta go, you gotta go. Besides, when you drug me, it's all going to come out anyway."

He flinched again at that thought, convincing her that he wasn't the cold-blooded, methodical maniac he was pretending to be. She took another step forward, but he blocked her path.

"I'll escort you."

"Great," she growled softly, moving into the hallway toward the main bathroom. She didn't turn the hallway light on, instead stepping into the shadows, and holding her breath, hoping that he wouldn't notice the light switch. She reached out and quietly slid her hand along the wall as she walked down the hallway.

Come on, come on...

There. Her fingers touched metal, and she closed her hand around it, silently, hoping Forsythe couldn't see the movement in the shadowy hallway. She turned left into the dark bathroom, lit only by a wedge of light through the small window, and darted forward quickly. *Find some space. Get to the vanity...*

He noticed her quickened steps, and followed her into the bathroom, obviously suspecting some kind of rebellion.

Kallie spun around, choking up on Cornwallis's walking stick like a baseball bat, and swung as hard as she could. Lucky for Forsythe, he sidestepped at the last second, or his head would have burst like a pinata. The swing still hit him hard enough to knock him into the bathtub, and Kallie lurched forward, smashing him three more times as he fell. She didn't notice that she was screaming like a banshee until her voice cracked.

The monster was bloody and out cold, for the moment, but she stood above him with the walking stick gripped in her hands, knuckles white, for another thirty seconds, just to be sure.

She was trying to figure out what to do with him – and remember where her dad might have a roll of duct tape – when blue lights flashed across the white bathroom door.

Was I screaming that loud?

An instant later, she heard the front door crash open, and Morrison yelling for her. "Kallie, are you here? *Kallie?!*"

Without putting down the walking stick, she

backed away from the bathtub and leaned out through the doorway. "Down here."

"Jeez, Kallie, I—" He walked into the bathroom, and put his hand on her shoulder, visibly relieved. "When I got your text, I thought—" He finally noticed the unconscious, bleeding man in the bathtub, and immediately put himself between them, pushing her out the door.

"It's okay, I handled it," she mumbled.

"I can see that," he said simply. He put his hand on her shoulder again, and then pressed his forehead against hers for a moment. She opened her eyes and looked at his face, so close – she thought he might be praying. Then he stepped back and gave her a lopsided smile. "I don't know why I even bother showing up."

"Well, you're the one with the handcuffs," she grinned.

"That's true," he answered with a nod. "But I think this guy needs an ambulance more than handcuffs." He took out his radio and called in for an ambulance to Kallie's address. Forsythe was starting to stir a little, so Morrison urged Kallie back to the kitchen while he kept her attacker immobilized. "Call Tess and have her pick you up, okay?"

More officers were arriving now, a sign that he'd called for police backup while he was on the way. An officer joined Morrison in the bathroom, and another quickly checked the house for any other threats. They didn't want to compromise the scene, presuming Forsythe was related to the other killings, so no one else entered the house right away.

"Yeah, okay," Kallie replied, backing away from the bathroom, starting to feel, awkwardly, like she was in the way – but still watching him. "I'll tell my dad and Anna to go to Tess's house, too, with Sherman. They don't need to see this."

He gave her a thankful look, and she wasn't sure what that other expression was, in his eyes. *Relief? Exhaustion?* The other officer was talking to Morrison, and she knew it would be hard for him to focus on the case while she was there. They were good friends, and he was worried about her. Physically and mentally. She needed to leave and let him work.

"I'll send Maria over to Tess's house to take your statement, later. And I'll come by when she's done." He waved over Officer Cruz, who had finished her walkthrough, and explained the situation quickly.

Kallie knew Morrison couldn't take her statement, even though he was the first one at the scene, because they were friends. It would cause problems at Forsythe's trial, whenever that happened.

Cruz carefully checked Kallie's hands and collected her clothing for possible specimen samples. Since the assailant was still on the scene, in the bathtub, and hadn't physically attacked Kallie, this was mostly cursory but necessary. She brought fresh clothes and then sat with her in the living room while Kallie waited for Tess, kindly reassuring her that she was safe now, and that the evidence would clarify everything. Kallie grabbed her jacket when Tess's car pulled into the driveway and resisted the urge to hug Officer Cruz.

"I'll see you in an hour or two, Miss Brooks, when we finish here. I have the address. Try not to worry," Cruz added, walking Kallie to the door.

Kallie stepped outside her front door, feeling like she'd fallen into another world. Tess jumped out of the car and ran to meet her at the bottom of the stairs, glancing up in surprise at Officer Cruz.

"Are you okay, Kal?! What happened?"

"She wasn't injured, but she's had quite a scare," Officer Cruz told Tess. "I'll come to your house later, Miss Russo, but don't hesitate to call an ambulance if you need one."

Tess looked confused, but nodded, guiding Kallie to her car. The whole trip was a blur after that, until Tess was walking Kallie to her couch and hurrying to the kitchen for ice cream. She pushed a bowl into Kallie's hands and sat down next to her.

"What happened?" her best friend repeated, softly.

"My dad went fishing," Kallie began, and then the tears started again.

Can't you ever stop crying, Kalliope?

She poured out the whole story to Tess – her dad, the fish eyeballs, the pedicure, the voice of evil in her own home, the whole thing – with tears streaming down her face and into the now-melty ice cream.

By the time she got to the part about the bathroom and the walking stick, though, she was calm.

You did the right thing, Kalliope.

"Oh, sweetie. You did exactly the right thing," Tess reassured her, gently.

See?

"I'm so glad you're okay," Tess whispered through her own tears, hugging Kallie. "And so glad our dads made us play softball, when we really wanted to take guitar lessons and form a band."

Kallie sniffled and laughed awkwardly, "The Savage Butterfly. That was such a good band name."

"It's not too late, you know," Tess teased, wiping her eyes with the back of her hand. She took the untouched ice cream bowl and set it on the coffee table. "I play a mean tambourine. We can moonlight as musicians, after we open our own investigative agency."

"I don't ever want to see another mystery again, Tess," Kallie moaned, pulling her knees up to her chin.

"Hey, don't decide that yet. We're so good at it," Tess added with a smile.

"We are, aren't we?" Kallie answered with her own tiny smirk.

"We need Wally to teach us a lot, but look at all we figured out, and how we collaborated. With my intuition and your tenacity—"

"And your brain," Kallie added.

"*Both* of our brains, silly." Tess smacked her best friend on the knee. "You're crazy smart too, just in different ways. But I promise not to tell anyone, if you don't."

"Deal," Kallie sniffled.

"That Dakota, what a piece of work," Tess grumbled.

"He wasn't as good and innocent as he acted, but he loved her," Kallie replied, sadly. "And maybe he wanted to *believe* he could be that good for her. Maybe he would've managed it, one day."

"I'm just still so mad that he lied to us, over and *over*—" Tess continued, angrily. Then she sighed. "But I think you're right. He was trying to catch her killer, at least. He almost did it."

They sat in silence for a while, and then Tess offered, with a gentle smile, "Hey, if that phone call at the bar was from Forsythe, that means the Mai Tai recipe offer is still good, right?"

"I guess," Kallie mumbled.

"Then I'll send you all of the information I found. They don't make that 17-year-old rum anymore, but maybe Marcy can help you find a replacement."

"Thanks, Tess," Kallie replied, quietly, feeling a little better. "Did Cornwallis really say he'd teach us?"

"That's my girl," Tess answered with a grin. "We'll go talk to him in a few days, after you've gotten some rest."

"I can bring him that walking stick, with extra thanks," Kallie added, and then smiled. "I bet he'll like it even better with bloodstains."

Chapter Twenty-Five

"Hey, Kallie, come in here before you start setting up," Marcy called from her office door, as Kallie walked into the bar from the parking lot. "I brought you a present."

It had been two weeks since the arrest, and Kallie was back on the day shift at the Lazy Gecko. "For me?" she asked. "But why?"

"Just open it," Marcy smiled.

Kallie sat down at Marcy's desk and fiddled with the unexpected gift, carefully unwrapping the silvery paper.

"How can you do that? I love *ripping* presents open!" Marcy made a face, mimicking a snarling tiger shredding an invisible object.

"I like the suspense," Kallie answered with a laugh.

"Nothing has *ever* surprised me less," Marcy teased her back. "No wonder you're always solving murders."

Kallie finally reached the inner box and opened

it cautiously, half expecting something to jump out at her. She laughed out loud when she saw the gift inside. "A magnifying glass!"

"It will help you with finding the next clue."

"I'm not really Sherlock Holmes," Kallie replied, picking up the very appropriate, beautiful gift. The handle was made from intricately hand-carved, reddish wood with visible grain — and the lens was wrapped in copper. Kallie used it to look at the papers on Marcy's desk. "This is gorgeous. It's much heavier than it looks."

"I'm sure you'll use it more than any other person in the world, but it's also pretty for a decoration." Marcy shrugged.

"Thank you so much for your faith in me! You really think we can do this?" Kallie asked.

"Of course. Look what you've done so far."

Tess had finally converted Kallie, with her harebrained scheme to start their own private investigator business, after the events of the arrest. The two of them had dropped the bombshell, as a pair, on both Marcy and Winchester at their respective businesses.

"I wish I had that much faith in myself," Kallie answered thankfully. "I still might decide that Tess is crazy."

"Tess is *definitely* crazy," Marcy agreed. "But so are you. Two wacko peas in a pod."

"We must be."

"You stay safe, though. More researching and investigating, and less chasing scary, well-armed murderers, please. Lots of photos taken with really, *really* long telephoto lenses."

Kallie laughed, "We'll try."

"And you'll always have a place here. I'd still prefer that you work the day shift, but we have plenty of staff now, to cover you when you need time off."

"Those local awards for 'best bar scenery' and 'best bar food' are really helping with hiring, huh?"

"Helping with *revenue* too," Marcy added sincerely. "Owhiro is getting to be really popular with the tourists."

"That's not my favorite part," Kallie groaned.

"Yeah, same here. I prefer our quiet little town to be *extra* quiet. But it's also nice to not worry about paying the bills and payroll."

Marcy had never mentioned worrying about the bills before, in the eight years Kallie had worked there. Kallie wondered how many nights her friend and boss had sat awake, herself. *She'll have some good pointers on running a business*, she realized. *Even if it's a very different industry.*

Kallie looked at the clock on Marcy's office wall and was surprised at how long they'd been talking. "I'd better get out there and set up my station. It'll be crowded soon. Can I leave my present in here for now?"

"Of course. I'll remind you to pick it up after work."

* * * * *

Carlos walked up and leaned on the bar while Kallie rolled and chopped limes, trying to relax. She looked up and smiled at her friend, whom she didn't always have time to see at work.

He'll be too famous to bother working here anymore, soon.

She reminded herself that she usually saw them at home anyway. That wouldn't change, even if neither of them worked at the Lazy Gecko anymore.

"Marcy told me you're going pro," he jumped right into the subject, and Kallie could see that he was torn between excitement for her and plain old worry. "What does your dad think about this?"

"We haven't brought it up yet," Kallie cringed. "It was mostly a silly running joke between us, until one day we just announced it publicly, and it wasn't a gag anymore."

"It'll worry your dad," he added simply.

"It worries *me,*" Kallie answered with a smile, dropping the pile of lime cubes into a glass container and starting on a lemon. "But Dad's pretty stoic. And there's no rush. We still have to take a bunch of classes. Then Cornwallis has agreed to mentor us until he's ready to retire."

"Oh, so he's going to teach you how to *not* get yourselves killed?" Carlos grinned.

"Ideally," Kallie replied with a smile. "And then there's a license required, and a state exam. It's not going to start tomorrow."

"It started two years ago, as I recall," Carlos answered, elbows on the bar, trying to make eye contact while she carefully cubed the lemon.

He was there, he remembers it all.

She looked up and nodded, not needing to say anything.

"Izzy and I are always here, if you need us."

"Thanks, Carlos." She smiled crookedly – so lucky to have amazing friends.

"And you'd better tell us the juicy details," he joked. "This whole 'parenting' gig is way less exciting than they make it look on TV."

* * * * *

Early March is the start of the hot season in central Florida, but Morrison's favorite breakfast café was still cool and lovely when they met at eight a.m.

He was already seated and talking on the phone

when Kallie arrived, looking uncommonly serious for a breakfast call. She wondered if it was a work discussion, and he'd have to leave. When he saw her, though, he smiled brightly and told the caller that he had to go. He hung up as she sat down, and the phone's screen registered that he'd been talking to Tess.

Oh.

Kallie stared at the useless menu, and then reached for her coffee cup distractedly, spinning it slowly in its saucer.

None of my business, really. I love them both, so it's fine.

She turned the same page of the menu, one more time.

Is it, Kalliope?

Justine greeted them like old friends, and they ordered breakfast with coffee and orange juice. She'd brought Morrison's orange marmalade, and she set it on the table before she left.

"So it didn't turn out like I expected," Kallie announced, trying to sound cheerful. "How about you?"

"They often don't," Morrison noted, adding with a smirk, "Those criminals can be wily. Practically *criminal*, even."

"I can't believe Dakota chased Forsythe into that building," Kallie mused. "I mean, what was he *thinking*? He almost got us all killed."

No reply, so she looked up and found Morrison staring at her blankly. Finally he smirked and shook his head. "Welcome to *my* world, Kallie."

"Why, I have no idea what you mean, Detective," she responded, sheepishly, blushing.

Morrison rolled his eyes briefly, but continued, "That security camera you noticed on the balcony is really helping the Tampa police. I thought you'd like to know. Kelsey and Forsythe were too close to the building for a clear shot, but the forensics team found a perfect reflection in the restaurant windows across the street. It'll be great in court."

"Oh, good," she smiled. "I'm so glad our sensitive noses could help the case."

"I don't think the stench was quite as bad while the police were collecting their evidence," Morrison explained. "Your perfect nose was there at just the right time," he chuckled. His eyes sparkled handsomely, and she was captivated for a second, breathless.

Stop it, Kalliope.

"I have to pick up dog food for Sherman," she blurted out awkwardly, suddenly longing for any excuse to leave.

The detective blinked in confusion at her outburst, but recovered quickly. "Do you ever have any down time?" he asked, after taking a long, bracing sip from his coffee. "You seem like you're always on the go. Even when you're *not* trying to get yourself killed."

"A little," Kallie replied with an embarrassed laugh. "I usually spend it with Sherman, that's all. But, I mean, you're a cop. You must have even less quiet time than I do."

"I usually spend mine underwater," he answered, blushing. "We're a pair, aren't we? Spending all of our relaxation time with dogs and fish."

"There was a sea turtle in Anclote Key when you took us snorkeling. I'd rather hang out with a sea turtle than with most people I know."

"Me too, actually," Morrison agreed.

Their breakfast was delivered, and Kallie looked down at her plate, studiously poking her blueberry pancakes with a fork. "What were you talking to Tess about?"

"You," Morrison replied quietly.

Kallie looked up with a quizzical expression to find him looking right at her.

"Me?" She felt a sense of alarm creeping up her spine.

Wow, now isn't that a key childhood fear, finding out that people are talking about you?

No, Kalliope, not for everyone. You just don't want to know what they were saying about you.

That I'm weird? That I'm not as pretty or smart as Tess? That I'm a loner who talks to her dog?

"I asked her what I'm doing wrong," Morrison

396

added, jolting her out of her thoughts, and confusing her even more.

"Huh? You're not doing— What do you mean?"

"We come to brunch here all the time," he continued, now looking down at his plate too. "We talk. We laugh. I text with your dad."

"I love all those things, Morrison," she whispered.

"But why not me?"

"I don't underst—"

"That's what I was asking Tess, when you came to the table. Why not me?"

"I'm not sure, Morrison," Kallie answered, shaking her head, trying to sound sympathetic. "Tess isn't very—"

She looked up to find him staring at her intently. He seemed to be inspecting her, searching for a clue.

"Not *Tess*, Kallie. You."

Still feeling like she was falling off of a hundred-foot cliff, Kallie just stared.

He seemed frustrated but not angry, she thought. She'd never seen him look defeated before, but she suspected this might be what it looked like.

"She told me you're just clueless," he added with a sad laugh.

"About *what*?"

Morrison put his fork down and leaned his forearms on the table. He looked straight into her eyes. "I'm crazy about you, Brooks. You're completely insane, with a never-ending death wish, and you're the most amazing woman I've ever met."

Kallie sat in shocked silence for another moment.

Close your mouth, Kalliope, you look like a dying fish.

Say something clever. And fast.

"I'm just clueless."

Great, brilliant retort. Well done.

This time Morrison was the one tilting his head and frowning in confusion.

"Tess was right. I had no idea," she whispered, blushing to the roots of her hair, and suppressing an almost unbearable urge to pinch herself. "You're pretty awesome too."

"Oh. Well okay, then," Morrison replied with a cautious smile. "If that's resolved, should we order pie?"

"That sounds like a perfect idea," Kallie replied calmly, beaming brighter than the Owhiro sun. "How about apple?"

"With ice cream," Morrison replied with a smile, waving to their waitress. "Absolutely."

Thank you so much for purchasing and reading *Mai Tai Malice*. I'm extremely grateful and hope you enjoyed it. Your feedback and support are always appreciated, and they allow me to continue Kallie's journey.

Please consider leaving a review online at your favorite bookseller or on Goodreads.

* * * * *

Also by Tanya Westlake:

Bloody Mary, Bloody Murder
Piña Colada Calamity